The Destruction of Time

By

ARITRA JANA

Dedication:

This book is dedicated to

My Teacher Prof. (Dr.) Dhrubajyoti Chattopadhyay and Dr. Ratna Chattopadhyay, MBBS, Ph.D.

Acknowledgement:

I would like to acknowledge my Parents (Dr. Malabendu Jana & Dr. Arundhati Jana), Dr. Shree Bhagwan Roy, Dr. Sukhamoy Gorai, Dr. Kamalendu De, Satarupa Sanyal, Ritabhari Chakraborty, Prof. Kanchan Kr. Bhowmik and Dr. Susanta khatua.

About the Author

Aritra Jana is the author of "Science Poetry for Dummies" and "Emerging Genius." He started writing poems from an extremely young age and started doing wonders as well. Jana was born in 2007 to academic parents; they are working for breakthroughs in science at Rush University. While understanding the in-depth and the complicated matters of physics, chemistry and biology seems even hard for undergraduate and graduate students, Jana expressed these topics in poems. Besides this, he has already written 4500 poems on history, philosophy, economics and others, as well as two philosophy, two economics and 6 novel books — all at the age of 15.

Table Of Contents

Chapter One:
A Walk in the Park

From one place to another, in each square that there was, it was made from whose smog will have lasted, for it was put to such a test. All that had endured from one place to another would have shown up. The squares had laid down upon Antonin, whose journey from one being small to one being large and to the destruction of time would be known. Let one rejoice when they see what it truly means for a person to have gotten power, only to have forsaken it once they have abused it. Let it be known what it means to dabble within affairs, not with the power of words, but through the power of a sword. And this is the story of Antonin.

Antonin had just finished creating his plebiscite. He was ignited and infuriated by how much he did not have. He had always wished to own a home and not rent one. He had always hoped for a decent standard of living rather than being indigent. Antonin had once imagined how his grandfathers had lived. He always aspired to be something significant, but as of right now, these were all just his dreams.

He woke suddenly as the dense air stuffed his nose; he could no longer breathe. This woke him up steadfast for the new workday. Still exhausted, he wanted to freshen up for the workday. He believed that one day, he would become the next billionaire. After all, it was his firm belief that achieving whatever can be done within the workplace to get a raise is possible.

It was a world of hope; he brushed his rusty teeth on the brink of falling out. He took off his pajamas, his most valuable possession. He realized that his old jeans were starting to wear out, but it was the best he had. His employer, Bill, worked his way up with hard work. After all, this was human nature. It is only the weak that will perish and the strong that will survive. He poured industrial-grade cereal, which was averse to his health, though it was the best he could have. After all, being modest is the only way you can become rich. Right?

It was a world of despair; he looked out the window. All he had done as a clerk was sell off goods he couldn't enjoy himself. All of the services in the modern world never seemed to benefit him; instead, they ended up helping others. "It's going to be a fine day," he said. In reality, he would be swiping down on his phone, going to older stories when he believed he had a good time. The world of despair and the heart of darkness was merging; however, he didn't realize this himself.

It was time for work; he was already ten minutes late, thinking to himself. If he hadn't made it to work within the next 20 minutes, his career would come to a dead end. This meant being able to refill his gas, which was near rock bottom. He drove to the nearest gas station at the highest possible speed to save as much gas and time as possible. When he exited the car to fill his gas, he noticed that the gas cost five dollars per gallon. *"Five dollars per gallon?!?!"* He thought he might be unable to meet the next bill. However, time was running out, and his financial dependence was at stake. The five dollars per gallon would still add up to a lot of money, even though his car can only carry seven gallons at the maximum.

Months earlier, he had voted for a president he believed would represent a change in his first election. He was enthusiastic until he saw what was happening. Not only did he fail to deliver on anything, but he also failed to stay the previous course, even if it would eventually reach a dead end. His anger was growing; however, he had no real friends. He was an exemplar of the many peers his age. They were content with their childhood but found no life after the brief juncture of adolescence. He believed that things would get better without doing anything and that his goal in life was to repeat the process of getting nowhere. Any joy he had in life vanished; all that was left were many thoughts racing through his mind about the past.

The big technological revolution seemed to change everything, only to make life miserable. Antonin was already getting late; two minutes had passed by pondering his many anxieties while embarking on his next venture. Now, he was heading for work, for a new – but old-day as well. Even if there was much to toil upon, he believed he could someday transform into the next Bill. The day was stormy, with the clouds starting to roll over; however, none of this mattered since he would rarely remember most days. He would repeat the cycle of going to work, participating in temporary "entertainment," and sleeping without a clue. He pulled up to the parking lot for his ride in life.

When he reached there, he checked out at the front office, where the time was recorded. "What are you going to do at work?" Sasha asked, keeping her voice down. Antonin replied, "I will sell the merchandise, which consists of two TVs and one car worth 60 thousand dollars." The price of cars was skyrocketing amidst a shortage of semiconductors needed to build the vehicles. "All right," Sasha said. Antonin moved towards the front desk, where the large lines had already piled up. "Payment number one," he said, registering it on the digital manager. His boss, Bill was at home, nowhere to be seen; this was the new normal since the large-scale pandemic ravaged the country's large sections two years earlier. At the time, he had just started his adult life, being in a blend of adolescence. He wanted to go to college, but all that changed soon, with the price of college going up by almost 20 thousand dollars per year.

This had made college unaffordable for him, even if he did well on the exams earlier. This was a stolen opportunity that would never be found again unless there was some form of systematic change that would end up eclipsing the new world order. As of right now, nothing could be found; the remaining residue accompanied the precipitous decline in any form of hope. All that he had was lost, and he believed it would come someday and go away. Any hope was one of the future's seeds that were sown, not of the present. He felt life would move on without knowing how much the character would retain. He thought there was no real point in persevering; all hope would be lost.

The consequence of the advance of the stark contrast in the sky left his day gloomy. When he went to work, nothing memorable happened. The only incident that tripped up his routine was the unexpected occurrence of his co-worker saying "hello" to him. Nothing more could be found, for he unpacked the quarter pound.

One day, late in the evening, he was invited by the League of Fighters, a semi-large organization that had been growing. It promised a new way forward for Antonin; for everyone else, it was a side organization. For Antonin, it was life. He embarked on his next journey without knowing what days would come ahead. He woke up the next day – not motivated to go to work but to the League of Fighters. It represented a way forward for him; he believed he had rediscovered entirely and turned around his life. After all, any companions that he had were primarily concentrated within the league. He stepped out of his car; this time, he was not going to work. He believed that foreign infiltration was causing his previous suffering and that the only way out would be to remove the foreign infiltration. Pity for him, the foreigners were only about three percent of the whole country's population.

At the first meeting, he volunteered to take the stage. "The infiltrators are largely sabotaging any efforts for our people," he exclaimed. "They are rising in status faster than we are," he said. The tirade was long, but it was his only hope. He believed that he had discovered an entirely new community. He thought all his suffering was because of other groups, ironically, among his rank. This attack made his heart race; his tirade continued; it only ended by the next dawn.

"Our people have been displaced; they are the real victims," he boldly professed. The other members started clapping. The applause lasted more than ten minutes. He believed that he had a purpose now; he was quickly advancing ranks, and the other members started to close ranks on him. Even amid this, he felt that he was primarily isolated from everyone else and that others were targeting him within his league. He grew paranoid about the many threats he believed would pervade his League. These threats were not completely dumbfounded; the original wing of the club had defected. This was satirical because it ended up in complete opposition to those who believed a struggle was going on.

The applause ended when Carl said, "We must defend the future of our children." This was met with instant applause, being a Trojan horse for bigots. This escalation ended up permanently radicalizing the league with an echo chamber. This echo chamber was inescapable as the original members largely left. The echo chamber would grow over time as Antonin and his group, while growing bigger, would largely remain isolated.

This got him out of his place of doom, and his goal was to reform the organization as well as expand it. However, he ended up encountering many issues. The next day, there was a large-scale debate. "I want to see the organization centralized," Smith said. Carl, who wanted to see the organization decentralized, counterargued quickly. In no time, a large-scale brawl had broken out. The centralists wished to see a paramilitary form within the organization's ranks.

On the other hand, Antonin was once again losing hope. The organization of his life was threatening to tear itself. However, it had been gaining members.

When he returned to work, he broke his coworkers organizing in favor of a new consciousness. "We need to see a wage increase," exclaimed Matthew, one of Antonin's co-workers. He compared that argument with the potential downside. He posed a new solution that would entail his league growing bigger in favor of centralization. He cast his lot and returned to his car, burning more oil. When there was no more oil after a fifty-mile drive, he assumed the fundraising that the league had done.

He woke up on Wednesday, wanting to see a complete change in his attitude. After all, he commanded a one hundred members strong league. What else could he hope for? Now, it was time to unpack his backpack and take out the documents of the league. He went to the league's headquarters, located in Waukesha, Wisconsin. To his surprise, people did catch on but were confused about what happened to the league's funds.

"I have no idea where the funds went," said Carl. "I do not know either," said Smith. Ironically, two opponents within the league were united for the first time. The funds had seemingly vanished, nowhere to be found. They contacted the police and handed out any information. In the digital age, communications, and money transfers were easy to find, right?

Antonin was panicking; he had squandered the league's funds, an organization he headed. If he was caught, what would happen to him? He said to himself. He needed to find a solution lest he was found at the harmful shelter. He had betrayed many of the members of his league, but he was able to expel them. A thousand thoughts raced through Antonin's mind in a fraction of a second. He came to one stark realization: why would the police go after him if they were de facto enemies with the league? This question startled Antonin, who now believed it was possible to go ahead and embezzle more funds from the organization. This embezzlement, he thought, could go on forever.

His bank app showed that the money was already out of his account; the start of the month meant that the balance was being redone. This calmed him down, though he was now returning to his old phase of believing in doom. Maybe there was always going to be infighting within the league, he thought. He had only joined the company in need of a friend circle, but already, what ended up occurring was that division was propagated. This division foreshadowed what would soon happen and was the only time that kept him in contempt instead of complete anger.

He identified issues caused by others rather than being localized. These issues included how his depressed benefits no longer satisfied what he needed and the foreign presence starting to build up there. This formulation ended up causing a new rebirth of his league. In the following days, he got the interest of significant capital to back him.

During the meeting with the many holders of significant capital, they promised him enough money to build the necessary machines to bring in more members. "We will give you much-needed capital to build up the organization," said Pearl. Ironically, he did not know that Pearl was a *protégé* of Bill; he was merely a decoy sent by Bill and being trained by him. He would encompass all that Antonin would fight against whom. This was evident in the eventual goal of opening, which was clearly in line with any initiative. For now, any dissenting voices have died down as Antonin's dream is being set in motion.

Chapter Two:
A Growing Tumor

Antonin started the next congress with, "My companions, the second congress of the league has convened; what does everyone want to talk about?" Carl responded, "I would like to see an escalation of the activities of the league as well as a thorough investigation into the embezzlement of the funds of the league." Shouting over Carl, Smith replied, "I would like to see an escalation of the activities of the league and an investigation into where the funds of the league went." Ironically, for the first time, what ended up occurring was that they ended up sharing the same agenda. Lucky for Antonin, what ended up happening was that the funding from elsewhere covered the costs of the embezzlement, which he could prove never occurred. This stunned the league, which believed some form of embezzlement had occurred. However, Antonin said, "The money is there; you were merely dreaming." We could shove the issue to the side for the rest of this meeting.

In the second debate, there was a proposal to escalate the league's activity. Antonin got behind it because of the funds given due to the bargain. This bargain would entail that these large bodies of freely associated individuals can continue operating, with their return amplified if they pay tribute. This was nearly unanimously agreed upon, with the proposal being set mainly in action. This proposal would break up any opposition and dissent within the organization. This ended up causing some of the major individuals of a specific wing of the organization to defect entirely to the other side. This defection ended up causing a split, which was not of significant importance because there was no real point in rectifying it. Even if they temporarily lost members, none of this mattered because they would, in the end, support the same institutions as the rest of the league. This fundamental point is what ended up sealing the fate of society. It would transcend into an organization that further escalated towards one leaning with most of the framework revolving upon an "us versus them" without an actual analysis of the proper conditions. For Antonin, the organization was the regulator of why he was alive; it kept his blood flowing throughout his body.

This dialogue fundamentally changed the course of the league, with many of its other members defecting. It railed against the anti-productive forces of nature, believing that all are in the game together if they are productive to the full extent. It was the character of the league and, by extension, the character of Antonin himself. There was no real difference between the company's many branches to him as long as they fought for the same thing: creating a genuinely pride-filled community of people united in some purpose. It sought to find a middle route between the blood and traditional courses, wherein it believed that they were partially fused. This characteristic would define the league for the next couple of months, at least in Antonin's mind.

The league kept rallying more members; by this point, it netted over a hundred-thousand members. Antonin was considered part of the old guard and the new movement. Smith's wing, growing wary of the quick centralization, was starting to create fission within the league. The new league's name was the "league of the people's pride." This accurately captured the attention of Carl's wing, which was primarily focused on lost pride. This ended up causing some of the movement to come together as well as fracture temporarily. All that was left was an increasing centralization presence that caused further antagonism between the two wings. The escalation of the brawls in the street caught the authorities' attention, though, in those regions, it was mainly at the whims of the league as the police were often members. The league members ended up causing a fight over the issues that prevailed within the league. This was further marred by extreme hostility between the wings, though when the dust settled, it was recognized that all were the same except for a few outsiders who would eventually integrate into the main line of the league.

The league was pernicious because it supported pride without supporting any other factor that could push for genuine pride. This pride will ultimately lead to the destruction of the self through the absorption of the self. The absorption of the self would come in the form of its rhetoric shifting due to the previously held beliefs and the new victory of the center wing, which Antonin represented. While being an old guard, Antonin was part of the league that would eventually dismember itself. For now, all eyes were on Antonin, the head of the group and the most influential person who could bring any sense of unity during these turbulent times. Even if it considerably ditched their views, it still instilled a sense of absolute harmony. The many divisions within the many wings of the league somewhat compromised this. This compromise had one goal: to create a new age of the party's organization. The party's organization was only as strong as those that were dedicated to the party. The party needed true centralization, which made it transform from a league. This party that Antonin now revered largely centralized itself, weakening any divisions. This came at the cost of temporary membership, particularly of the advanced sections of the party. However, the purge of Smith's faction did not matter because they had remained mainly weak; Carl's faction was primarily absorbed into the mainstream, while some of the wings had been disbanded and kicked out. The legacy of Antonin as a force would continue to strengthen further within the region.

Back home in Springfield, Illinois, Antonin thought, what joy was there only divesting his resources towards the party? He also needed a mental break, which could only be done through rest. He went to sleep, and within his dreams, the echoes of his past grew larger. He was once again introduced into his phase of doom. One voice in his brain always said, "You have never made it anywhere; you are cared for by no one; the last time you had a social life was when you were fifteen: long, long ago." This defined Antonin's life; it was a constant state of divesting resources towards a movement where only a cult of personality and power could be built. No real connections were made during his tenure. His dreams would further be amplified; now, he believed that his dreams would be exemplified in real life.

The real-life exemplification of his plans would be the next doom awaiting him. He believed that he was constantly battling this state of doom. He believed it could eventually be won over; however, he had no idea how it would take place. Similar to the idealism that pervaded his mind, so was his growing cult of personality. His cult of personality would grow stronger, laying the seeds for a movement that would stand the test of time, at least in his view. For him, it was important not how anything would work but if it would work. He would set targets for himself that were supposed to be achieved without material reality. He woke up the following day, drowned by believing that all of these dreams and formulations were real and could be put into practice. As always, he was surrounded by no one but himself this time. His small one-bedroom apartment was better than living with a roommate, but it still went nowhere. He felt so drained; it was just about time for work! He had to dress up in his wet jeans, the culture he railed against elsewhere, and left for work. He still had to work regular hours because trying to dedicate himself to the party entirely would cause more people to know about it. Bill himself, in his view, did not realize that the party existed – or did he? He headed out the front door, taking the elevator. When he reached the first floor, he went to the checkout desk. Here, he was looking past the officer, but he was stopped. The guard asked him for verification, which he rudely provided. He went to the parking lot and took out his car. After taking out his car, he noticed the gas was empty after a long drive. He needed to refuel; suddenly, he no longer cared about the expenses as they would be made up by the financial donation he found from "patriotic"-oriented businesses. These businesses would soon turn their back on him, for he did not know.

Even though the party garnered a hundred-thousand member, it was still at the mercy of luck. The members were not wholly devoted, most of whom had been beefsteaks that were turned over by the rhetoric and the false solutions that the party presented. They were beefsteaks that found no place after a failed struggle many years earlier. This struggle died out by 2022 when the federal government crushed it. Earlier, while beefsteaks had existed, they had primarily switched over to the new movement that was extra-governmental and was gaining traction.

This traction was based solely on transforming the decadent state and leading it toward a brighter future. By being able to show the current heavy state towards a brighter future, Antonin's league largely revolved around the idea of rebirth through palingenesis. This rebirth would come as a much-needed appropriation of the past rhetoric. They would end up courting many other groups that could be the opposition through the adaptation of opposing "finance capital," though, through the donors, especially Paul. It was sidelined mainly at the same time. This practically meant fighting certain forms of oligarchic ownership while, at the same time, supporting the institution of further maximizing the support of the "patriotic" corporations. Soon, they would stoop even lower, promising cheap labor found through the immigrants and using that labor as one the corporations could work with. This was the irony that the party ended up facing. They would support the creation of jobs, that is, low-paying jobs for the immigrants who were then given low wages. This process aimed to maximize the profit made while effectively dealing with the question of immigrants in the eyes of their supporters. This two-faced reality was the defining part of Antonin's party. The two-faced fact would end up making their way through all branches of the party, and by extension, what would end up occurring is that the party would devolve into something else. It would soon degenerate; this followed the footsteps of Antonin's life. No new theory was practiced; however, it kept the old order intact. It supported the vestiges of neoliberalism while making the theoretical claim of opposing it.

It was a two-faced reality that no one except the old guard within the party could know about. Due to the lack of transparency that there was, to begin with, none of this would ever be put in the hands of the masses. The party was formed around a myth; it was the myth of the eventual decline of the nation and what caused it. Antonin, being at the top, primarily benefited from this myth. This myth would soon transform into something else resembling a labyrinth. The intensification of the tale came in the form of a cult of personality that would quickly be created around Antonin. Those mainly at risk of falling for this rhetoric already had their time passed. Antonin's story of spiritual rebirth inspired them all. This spiritual rebirth had not taken place had they known. Instead, it was all based on false assumptions that would eventually snowball into a shared myth and the formation of a cult of personality within the party.

Naturally, as time passed, various factions emerged within the party's old guard. Among them was Paul, who had joined the party intending to create a business-oriented group that would advocate for the farmers and small people in business while maintaining ties to the established community of prominent businessmen. That was the contradiction that would arise out of the party. It would have multiple faces with only part of the face being shown. This face would then be obscured by the darkness that prevailed around the sullen touch of the eye. This would signal the beginning of factions within the party, all around the cult of personality of Antonin. This cult of personality was nothing short of a complete hijacking of any rhetoric there was in the past. This was further aggravated by the expulsion of the league's wing that favored a rebirth through real progress. This palingenesis and the party's true face were nowhere to be found. This inherent contradiction within the organization was never resolved because the two sides were too far away. This contradiction could not be theoretically resolved because of different reasons concerning where the funding comes from for each faction. This is because of those that were deceived; they formed their clique. This is still in stark contrast to the breakaway faction that no longer exists within the party; however, this signaled that any opposition would be contained and any significant dissent from the line would not be tolerated. This rebirth principle needed to go further with the more populist-oriented wing that Nick advocated for.

So far, five significant factions formed, with many sections within. Even if there was more to come, much more would not be known until the cult of personality was dissolved. These five factions were found in the form of populists, conservatives, reformists, militarists, and authoritarians. These five factions were only coalescing under the same banner as a result of the cult of personality of Antonin as well as the perceived threat of the other parties. This would shake up the establishment, especially after some old guard had won victories in Illinois and Indiana.

Election day in Ohio was coming up; the election day seemed promising to Antonin, who had his loyalist run and hopefully take charge within the state. Ohio was a largely deindustrialized zone that had fallen from its ashes. A failed revolution in 2022 caused the working class only to find refuge within the fledgling reactionary nationalist movement. This failed revolution caused the dominoes, particularly Antonin, to stack on each other. This seemed very promising, especially when being bribed with Paul's money, essentially causing the defection of the old guard that supported true revanchism and change. This defection was further compounded by the never-ending struggle to acquire more land for the "people" of the country.

The never-ending struggle for liberation intersected the traditional vestiges of right-wing nationalism. For all the right-wing nationalism there was, it never seemed to make a difference in how it was implemented. At times, it would end up causing a deal in the back with the jobs being exported anyhow for profit, while at other times, there would be large-scale negotiations with the business people to retain their businesses and expand their profit. This is the actual state of what would occur, and this fundamental reality is what would later shape the movement as a whole. All of the disparate factions of the party would be united through some form of economic nationalism as well as securing de facto sovereignty on top of that. Was the election truly of this that they see? Was the election that which mattered? Was it of politics only that he built his life?

Furthermore, their goal was to oppress the other nations constituting the country. This is what ended up causing the eventual nadir between the party and the others that had defected from it. Their visions had been torn apart; all that mattered was the Indiana election. This could only be found through unity between these factions. These factions were not different; instead, they were mirrors of each other, with different policies. Some were more leaning towards opening up while others were leaning towards locking down. This difference was negligible when the proper funding of the party was audited. Paul, in reality, was the puppet master of these factions. There is no difference between these factions; they all presented the last legs upon which the neoliberal order was built. The liberation struggle was meant to be never-ending – it was never liberation that was the end goal. This fundamental premise is what defines the party and its merits. The party's merits were solely based on the reformist or expansionist approach. They all followed the same path, corporatism. This common shared attribute ended up causing all of the factions to remain like and on amicable terms with each other – at least for now. The corporatist alignment is what ended up uniting these factions together, and this is what ended up uniting the movement together.

Ahead of the Ohio election, Antonin sought to siphon votes from the two establishment parties at any cost. "The two parties have betrayed the opinions of the true Americans," he went on a tirade. This attracted much applause from specific sectors that have been mainly lost. This especially hit the former revolutionaries, who had become the most fervent reactionaries by now. This was a transformation that had only existed due to the failure of the revolution as a whole. The 2022 revolution was gone. What hope was there? The 2022 revolution embodied the masses of the working class, but with all of the remaining might, there was no strength to be found. The 2022 revolution was their only ticket to liberation, just after the coronavirus pandemic had ended. The pandemic, which had brought large-scale turmoil, was taking another turn. This turn resulted in new effects that would be felt mainly throughout many countries. This would further exacerbate many of the problems in the Rust Belt, further pushing it to the brink of unrest. In a last stand of solidarity, the working class of the Rust Belt had organized though they would be backstabbed by the progressives in Congress, who would leverage their right-wing reactionary allies to crush the revolution.

Thus, the revolution and the people's dreams were lost. The barren land stood sullen at the dryness that had once been non-existent. Before, the many acres of farms owned by the family farmers had accumulated into a few proprietors' hands. These proprietors had no reason but to keep on using the land, which would destroy much of the grass. The soul of the land and the blood that encompassed the land's spirit was gone. The dream was gone; it ran away. The dream that once defined the land, the reason why many generations settled here, had largely vanished. It was already declining, rapidly accelerated by the pandemic and the lockdown.

Deserted towns and cities marred the brazen creature that had pervaded the large expanse of land. The once vibrant music that could be heard was replaced by crime-stricken neighborhoods. Poverty had escalated to levels that were never seen before. We once vanquished Afghanistan – only to turn to Afghanistan's economic policies as the last best hope. Parents would be forced to sell their children away; food was scarce, and poverty was rampant. At the top, there were a few corrupt individuals that would end up siphoning any relief there was from this slump. This is what caused the revolution – and the counterrevolution. The counterrevolution had effectively recreated the conditions needed to herald the beacon of disorder again. Any order there was had seemingly vanished. The letters within the word order were nowhere to be found.

In place, there was destitution, with the indigent masses yearning to be free. They were stricken by the lost times and the good old days. This ended up sparking the counter-revolution. All of this was fine for the futurist Antonin, who saw all these conditions needed to transform society backward. This defined Antonin's life – the constant state of eternal doom and a false sense of rebirth. The rebirth had never taken place – it was all just an illusion. Even outside of his life as the false liberator of the indigent, he always looked back at the good old days – long lost days from when he was a child. His childhood only created scars for his adulthood – which never seemed to end.

Even if they promised a liberating alternative, the liberating alternative is not that liberating when it comes to actual practice. They faltered on specific key points that characterized their movement collectively. These key points primarily revolved around the weakness throughout the movement and a weak sense of the national character. Both of these ended up combining to make the movement more revisionist as well as becoming weaker. This deviant position, which was merely confused while claiming to be different, would be at the movement's core. This position was not the first or second position but a third position. Even being the so-called "Third Position," it almost always leaned towards a confused version of the original core of the false national-liberation movements. Even if there was any foreign interference, it was not the primary force that would end up driving the country's economic status. This decline in the socioeconomic status of the nation would further spark more aggression towards the status quo, which led to the rise of Antonin following the failure of the revolution. When the revolution was lost, the working class only found the option of turning toward the league. This league would come in the form of Trojan horses that would pervade much of society.

The Trojan horse would soon get more robust; it would start to resemble the many movements born out of the new state. The Trojan horse would consume voters' minds and push the league over the edge in Ohio. This would be against a split vote system, where a plurality of votes is needed. As a plurality of votes is needed, splitting the other movements and coming out on top is possible. This is what exactly happened with their relationship with the establishment. They were able to push themselves over the edge and get a plurality.

Antonin's victory speech was prosaic. "We will defend the working class of our nation. The great replacement has only started to occur with the goal of the elites consisting of replacing the forgotten heroes of our nation with cheap immigrant labor that can be harnessed. We must defend our nation from foreign threats and withdraw from the many multinational organizations that never benefit us. This must be further amplified by cracking down on anything that is anti-American. This crackdown is needed to prevent decadent culture from taking over the nation. The decadent culture is what will make us weak. The decadent culture will destroy our nation to its very core. The decadent culture is what will get rid of our unity and our pride. The decadent culture is the basis of our movement that seeks to emancipate. For our children, rise against the prevailing degeneracy and fight to make our nation proud again. Fight to make our nation great again!"

His victory speech was no different from the victory speech of other nations. It was no more than the free among the freed. All it expressed was the promotion of the counterculture there. It portrayed a fake enemy, "the cultural destitution," and the fact that it would take over. It offered no real solutions other than the solution than the fake threat. The solution failed to address socioeconomic concerns and hijacked the significant resistance movement. This resistance manifested in a new turn to the third position. The third position meant nothing; it was life to Antonin, however. The third position was as good as it is played; however, it does not change the pitch. All it does is change how the pitch is played, not with what it is played by. This is fundamental to the eventual change in the current system that develops. The fundamental change in the pitch of the revolution compelled the eventual destruction of the revolution itself. The change in pitch of the revolution coincided with a significant decline in the eventual disbandment of the old movement. The "Movement for National Sovereignty" would later be the name of Antonin's league. It had grown out of the days of the old guard; now, it was predominantly fresh, with many elections being won. These elections would be won in the heart of the Rust Belt once the former hub of the revolution though fallen from its status. The revolution would be lost forever, and counter-reaction forces would consume it. The forces of the counterrevolution would end up transfiguring and obscuring the old movement, now buried in the ashes.

All that mattered was if you were part of the common folk, a different kind of folk. It would appeal to only a specific subset of the people, not to all of the people. This was combined with including a "folkish" appeal that somehow went straight to the masses. This "folkish" appeal would be radicalized from the original third positions as it would go even further than that. It would define the nation with kindred, often obscuring the actual ties. The blood relations, long considered outdated and feudal, would be returned to life. This is what the "folkish" movement would fail to see. The blood relations have grown mainly out of the many sections of the previous wing of the party. This is why the party split in half: it radicalized towards one side rather than the other. The other side, while advocating for similar policies, questioned the eugenics policy's necessity. The eugenics was discarded mainly by much of the old guard that ended up storming out; however, they would remain close regardless of the stances. This was the position of the populist working-class ideology of the fools.

The rebirth of the nation could only come through the complete embrace of "folkish" tradition and the amplification of this national struggle. This national struggle would come at the cost of abandoning the class struggle, for they would be regarded as the same. They would be regarded as the same in the way that the foreign groups represented the elite and the people that would take over the nation. This was how the recruitment into the movement was able to garner support. It solely relied on the actual exploitation of popular belief. The popular belief would come through a new revival in the nation. The revival in the nation would be absolute, at least in rhetoric. In reality, Antonin's goal was to play realpolitik and stay out of any discourse that would end up causing the downfall of his new empire, his party. The party would need to strengthen itself and find unity while being able to kick out those that left the party earlier. This would mean being able to conduct thorough kicks within the party as well as oust any opposition leaders. While there was still dissent within the party, none was directed toward Antonin. Instead, it was directed at each other.

This controlled opposition played somewhat miraculously into Antonin's hands. It would be played with the gentle stroke of the bow. It would be what would later transcend into a significant song. The song would be played beautifully, and the glove that would be used to make the instrument was all built by Antonin. This internal division did not matter, for they were loyal to Antonin. For them, the real question was, "Are you loyal to Antonin and the fatherland?" This is what would soon come to be their slogan, even after the many speeches that would be made and the many provocateurs that would start to instill themselves within the party. The provocateurs were to be integrated thoroughly, with each step being an advance forward. This advance almost always came at one cost: the cost of an actual opposition within the party. This would strengthen the party, allowing itself to reorganize for the remaining elections in the Rust Belt. The Rust Belt had essentially transformed into the New South, barren and lifeless. There was only conflict; nothing more than conflict would have a say in any affair. The conflict would soon escalate; however, what kept the party together was the cult of personality of Antonin.

Antonin, in the midst of this, was still a childish figure. Despite being twenty-three by now, he had still not grown out of his adolescence. This would be a characteristic of his life – his prolonged adolescence, which always seemed to be at his command. This command was known to him as it would constitute the cornerstone of his beliefs. The childish characteristic made him never grow out of his childish fantasies. Even if he were pursuing them, he would do whatever it takes – whether irrational or not, to reach them.

These fantasies would soon build up with the eventual boiling point, causing the dream to come true. He would soon start to organize paramilitaries, with the federal government weakened in the former Rust Belt. This would end up coinciding with the party of Long: his party would be a revolutionary party that would organize in the South. It would organize in the former regions of the reactionary bastion. Long's party was built around many, not few. Long's party, unlike Antonin's, would fight for the typical person, not for some visionary "folkish" movement. The "folkish" movement would be completely thrown into the dust. The "folkish" movement was nothing compared to Long, a person of wisdom and intellect. It was a form of populism organized on ethnic rather than economic lines. Long still believed in the form of national liberation; however, his vision was completely different in that it wanted anti-imperialism and the independence of the minorities of the country. Its goal was to foster a culture of national sovereignty and unity simultaneously. It organized large proletariats, except for the failed revolutionaries. It would soon be apparent that any future election would be a proper standoff between the league and Long's party. This election is predicted to be tense and full of emotions. It would not be banal, for it would be surrounded by avarice. The avarice that would prevail would only help a few, not the masses. Long's party still somewhat put part of the revolutionary struggle to the side; however, it did so with different means. The means, for them, would justify the ends. This would be further aggravated by further polarization, which would follow in the coming times. The intensification of polarization is what would drive the next conflict onward. For now, all that existed was Antonin's clique and Long's mass line. These two parties were entirely against each other, with the only thing that they shared being their disdain for the current establishment. They had completely different views on approaching nationalist fervor and economic hardship. Their strategies were utterly different from their inception. This fervor must have continued onward for Antonin's party, or else; it would end up dying out. It was solely based on this nationalist perception, with no accurate reference to class struggle. What has been put forth was a new dawn between the forces of reaction and the forces of the revolution. The most reactionary bastion had transformed mainly into the most revolutionary bastion of all, spanning from the many states and nations inhabited it. This would form the new revolutionary republic that would develop alongside the original republic with a dual power structure.

The folkish movement differed from one that believed the nation's language was essential and one that tolerated the other nations. This is what set Antonin's movement apart from Long's movement. Long believed in the form of national delimitation, which would mean that all nations within are on equal footing and that all of the cultures native to the region would end up having their institutions funded and republics set up within the country. This combination of linguistic primacy, economic status, territory, and psychological makeup under the same roof for anti-imperialist purposes would soon extend to economics. This contrasted with Antonin's folkish movement, which wanted to see one nation's supremacy over all other nations. Because there is primacy of one nation over the other, Antonin's movement ended up transcending into something else. The primacy of one nation meant that national oppression would be conducted with cultural superiority being found at one end. The folkish movement is one that differed considerably from the collective working-class nationalist movement of Long. The folkish movement prioritized one nation overall, primarily being exclusionary to the rest.

The folkish movement was an outgrowth of the previous schema that was taking place. It was an outgrowth of the nationalism that was there for the few, not for the many. This defined this variant of nationalism starkly contrasting with the others that would prevail. This variant of nationalism was largely reactionary, only built for reactionary purposes. The ancestors of the movement, while having influenced the collective working-class nationalism, also had their way embedded into the exclusionary folkish movement. This was what Antonin's movement oversaw, the destruction of all other nations within the country's borders.

The election of Ohio was a resounding victory that further helped bolster Antonin's party. Antonin's party primarily looked forward to the many victories that could be achieved in the future. These victories would come at no cost as long as the party's donors could keep faith in the party. The faith in the party would only be through fundamental policy changes while being able to satisfy the working class of the Rust Belt. Combined, These two parts will ultimately push the party to victory. The complete victory of the national revolution would only be through the party's unity. It is only through this unity that strength within the party is found. It was a co-option of the old rhetoric that largely surrounded the old working-class nationalist ideals, now replaced by nationalist ideals created for the few, deceptive to the masses and benefiting a few. This was now the factual state of the reactionary order, which would have its tentacles reach out. The tentacles of the national revolution were those of reaction, and its express purpose was to secure power for the cult of personality of Antonin.

Chapter Three:
A False Dawn

Now divorced from his previous work on paper, he could focus elsewhere. His attention to the party only kept on growing day by day. His attention to the party was ascending, as contrary to being diminutive. This was the primary characteristic of Antonin's cult of personality within the party. It was full of the wit that Antonin brought with it. It was one of despair and hope; it was one of returning to the old times. It was one of embracing the future; all of these traits would eventually give rise to palingenesis. It was all of these traits that would give rise to the next rebirth. At least now, it would be the last time the doom phase would strike. This moment of doom was encapsulated within the other emotions surrounding the lost body. The lost body would itself be there as well as not be there. This was the end, the doom of the energetic past. This was the eventual downfall of any real progress toward civilization. All that was lost was not brought back. All that was lost was permanently foreseen, with the extended family also being lost. The extended family came to be through the imagery that Antonin evoked and the "new" ideas he brought to the table. For him, his brand of demagoguery is unpopular in name, though in practice, it is prevalent. This is what marked his tenure within the party: the excess demagoguery. This demagoguery is what largely defined him. To once again serve the country was the platform of Antonin.

The services that the country gets will, in turn, help all of the people of the country. In this case, it was similar to paternalism while also radically departing from paternalism. Corporatism essentially put a strain on class collaborationist relations partly. The class collaborationist relations were made through the many intersections between the many factions in the majority of the population. While the country was put above all, Antonin's goal was to reconcile the forces within the nation (not the country) and have these forces synthetically work together. This defined much of his party, the promises of a new future and to rewrite what had already been done. This corporatist example was in stark contrast to the complete seizure of the tools needed in construction, as advocated by Long. This ended up setting both of these movements together and where the class collaborationism and the corporatism within Antonin's party came from. The collaboration within the party paid close attention to the donors while framing some of the benefits of going to the meek. This synthesis would end up driving the force of humanity and the force of the nation, which must be transformed into the state itself.

The many contradictions within its downfall marred the true solstice taking shape. The contradictions would end up building up, causing a two-sided conflict. The two-sided conflict was thinly veiled, with multiple sides; however, this contradiction was not antagonistic. For this reason, it would soon follow the line of uniting into one and the struggle being rewritten. This would define the movement for folkish culture, which largely defined the nation in terms of certain bloodlines rather than on the integration of all of the country's peoples within. This practically meant that the lifeblood of the country was cut off from this hypothetical nation and that the nation would only serve those with the same bloodline. This bloodline defined the nation throughout its course, being at the core of many of the integrated solutions and problems faced. This two-faced nature of the contradiction further led to partial splits within the party. The party was nowhere to be found if the splits were completely successful. The splits would end up causing many attributes that could lead to its downfall. These attributes, for Antonin, must be restyled. For Antonin, the battle was always on, and there was always some form of paranoia within the party. There could always be backstabbing; at the same time, it was found that the potential betrayals were largely cut off from any source of Oxygen. By cutting off the source of oxygen, these cancer cells would end up dying and the organism would end up reviving itself. The organism, in this case, is the party. The party would be on amiable terms with big capital, largely promising to keep most of the environment status quo while being able to clamp down on the revolutionary movement in the South. The Southern revolutionary movement posed a large threat to big capital because it would mean the eventual expropriation of the tools needed to produce anything. This expropriation would be disastrous for big capital, which is why it pushed back on it with all its might. The expropriation must be overcome for the interests of big capital, and this change is what ended up causing the big capital to support the party of Antonin. This ended up causing the militarization of the party and the further radicalization of the party. The party largely relied on the institution of practically locking out the rest. This was the common characteristic of this largely populist movement while, at the same time, being largely linked to the establishment parties. The party of Antonin only foresaw complete doom and gloom rather than hope. No person wants to be accused of hating someone solely based on some random attribute. The lack of hope in any material improvement of the socioeconomic conditions drove up Antonin's support. Long never faced the problem of defectors to Antonin as a result of being able to have an actual concentration of support. This was what ended up completely shaping the two starkly different parties. The two different parties could not be reconciled through any process other than to change the based funding for the party of Antonin fundamentally. The ideas have always existed, though what caused the party to bloom was the abundance of funding and how superfluous it was. These two factors changed how the funding and the eventual movement came about. These two factors completely caused the difference and the eventual departure of the two populist movements. They were both populist though the difference is that one would end up embracing the frame of reaction, while the other would embrace the frame of revolution. While the old revolution that failed was somewhat dead right now, it would never be lit out. The dead revolution will always be remembered in the people's hearts; thus, Antonin had to make concessions to the revolution. Corporatism is largely the same as the complete, with only one main difference: corporatism has involvement, and the involvement of individuals is truer to its name. At the same time, it largely obscured the true nature of itself, casting as a revolutionary force that could largely save the people. This would be one of the fundamental instruments for framing the die. The framing of the die would be based on how it was rolled, not what it was rolled to. How it was rolled would show that it is different from the primary force that would act on it. The essential difference would constitute the large separation of the two movements and the hostilities. One was a working-class nationalist movement, while the other was an exclusionary nationalist and imperialist movement. These differences could not be reconciled, though they would eventually play their course, especially when the certain forces that would act would end up causing the working class to win largely. These forces would be present within the party of Antonin, which largely relied on the support of the Rust Belt but could not garner support elsewhere. This support from the Rust Belt was shaking, and its collapse would be turbulent for the party. This support was delicately being held up, and the revolution was imminent if it collapsed.

Antonin got a call from the two parties of the establishment, which offered a coalition to contain the threat of Long. This threat for them was much more significant than Antonin's threat because Long's party was the only party offering change. The party of Long was not split when it came to the tallies. It rallied much support equally from the South except for the powerful. This is what caused the establishment's animosity towards Long and his associates.

The party of Long was no more a feeble force; it was now a formidable force that could easily challenge the party of Antonin. By being able to challenge the party of Antonin, it could do anything within its bounds. The established grounds could allow for the eventual defense of any potential revolution. This would start to gradually build up with the force of the revolution being cherished by the people of the South as well as a minority elsewhere. However, the force in which the revolution was brought was starting to rise within the enclaves of the North, which meant that in any imminent revolution, there would always be a substantial possibility of securing the countryside of the North early on. This fundamental shift would start to worry the party of Antonin, which traditionally relied on baiting – which only really attracted support from the same people of the urban cosmopolitan regions. These urban cosmopolitan regions would gather immense support, in which the party of Long tried to fight it with whatever it had. This was the core basis of the new revolution that was brought forth. Its goal was to see the absolute destruction of the reactionary bases of Antonin.

While exiting the phase of doom, Antonin himself largely struggled with an addiction to dopamine itself. The dopamine addiction came at the expense of his physical and mental health in the long run. These expenses ended up causing the many problems that would be seen in Antonin following the relapses he found. He would still rely on social media, and while it would gain him more followers in person by the younger generation, it would end up causing his mental health to decline further. This was to be somewhat expected, as the goal of the donors of Antonin was to maximize as much profit as possible while preventing any chance at a revolution. This was not only the way of a social reaction but also an individual reaction, which would run contrary to the interests of Antonin and his followers in the long run. These interests would end up piling up with the intensification of existing exploitation, which led to alienation. This was compounded by commodity production, which primarily relied on psychological manipulation, especially regarding dopamine. Commodity production would end up mainly causing the same depression in the economy – and in the individual. There was no way to defend the current system from any objective perspective other than the perspective of the already powerful. This meant the system was rotten and mainly relied on the veil of ignorance. This veil of ignorance kept generating more steam, with the actual components of the steam building up to a breaking point. This could not be avoided through simple words; it could only be avoided through actions. These actions would soon intensify, with the enormous rebirth being at the helm of the next turn that was going to be made. These turns would end up collectively weakening the individual's mind through commodity production and alienation while also weakening the mind of the collective through exploitation. This exploitation could no longer go unnoticed, for it already had a significant presence in wealth inequality. This wealth inequality was the cause of the revolution in 2022, and it is the cause of the revolution that is piling up on the side of Long. These two factors make it so that the alienated of the world can now rise, under a collective banner, to finally find the liberation of the individual through the social ownership of the means of production. These concepts for the revolutionaries were not any different; on the contrary, they were directly linked to one another.

The sum of all these movements is what ended up causing the rebirth of consciousness, both when it comes to the physical reality and the metaphysical reality. These two realities, when combined, caused the new rebirth, which was a new, unique position between two other ways. These two ways would end up colliding with each other, teaching the fundamentals of the world back to the disciples. They found no difference between the fields portrayed as different – they found that there is only one solution to every problem in the world. This solution would come in the horse that would gallop faster than the bullet-speed train.

Erik asked, "How may I help you?" Antonin replied, "I need you to gather more funds from our donors; we need much more money to carry on any real struggle." Erik replied, "But we don't have enough support among the establishment businessmen." Frustrated, Antonin replied, "Gather support from the businessmen, now!" After realizing the imminent need for more funds, Antonin used the fear of a seizure of the means of production to woo the business people to his side. This point essentially weakened the establishment; it had primarily morphed itself into a ball and a creature incapable of writing what an insect would typically write. Antonin believed that the party was once again growing weak, requiring an extensive purge of the party. He believed that this would eliminate corruption – which, ironically, he was a part of. This purge would take place soon enough for those who will be purged to be caught off guard. This purge would not affect any actual party members as a result of the fact that they have nowhere else to flee to. Reconciling with Long would mean shoving aside their ideals while, at the same time, there was no establishment party. This double-edged sword would haunt many of the loyalist party members – loyalists to the donors, maybe not to Antonin himself.

The corruption that plagued the party was finally purged, with the members that committed the crimes against the party being put to justice in front of the party. This justice is no different from vigilante justice, for it was not warranted by anything else. This purge would end up being thorough, with many of the associates of the party members also being questioned. Some of these trials would be sham trials, wherein there would be executions, but none of this mattered because the local police were on the side of Antonin. This clear-cut loyalty distinction was starting to spill over past the lines of the factions. Suddenly, certain opposing factions with uniquely distinct members started to work together. The wing that would advocate for reconciliation with the workers was already largely disbanded, with its members being flung outwards. Other members of the party asked, "What was next?" The only people that would be left over were the staunch loyalists – not to the party, but to Antonin himself. These loyalists largely bore the fruit of the forces of reaction as they died as a compatriot for the party of Antonin. These members were no different from the others in that they were largely loyal to the capital that backed them, except for capital that came from international sources other than those approved. This would mean taking a bribe from the "financiers of international capital," which the members of the hardline wing were a part of. Even the reformist wing was affected, with much of its revenue coming from certain other sections of the powerful. These donors often overlap, largely sharing common interests and keeping the party together. These contradictions would only partially build-up, but they were largely collaborationist. These collaborators would put their own civil administration in place, adding a new dimension to the peripheral vision field. Those that were visionaries had already left though some of their sympathizers found themselves among the proponents of centralization. This would end up further escalating the conflict and incite the tension that there already was in the party. Even if they practically shared the same beliefs, they largely fought against each other to hold up some idealistic "universally ideal" line without any basis as an argument. This would destroy the same force that caused all of these factions to coalesce under the same banner, the unity of the shared sentiment of disunity. This chaos and anarchy that would pervade the party were antithetical to anarchy, for it believed in permanent statism and no way to eventually transform into something new, as opposed to the party of Long. This is what ended up causing these parties to be completely set apart from each other, despite being both populists. One would be paranoid, conducting thorough purges with almost no real reason, while the other was a party to educate and fight for the revolution. This fundamental, stark difference contrasted the vanguard of the revolution with the disorganized forces of reaction. These two forces, while being both populists on paper, were completely different in reality. One would be a pseudopopulist, largely using populist slogans for victory and then burying any progress and promises made. These differences were so great that the remaining revolutionary spirit within the older generation was once again awoken. However, it would not mean much because in the case of an imminent conflict, what would end up occurring is that the reactionaries would overrun the previously revolutionary Rust Belt due to the large lead that the reactionaries had within the young population of the Rust Belt. This difference contrasts the Rust Belt with the South to the point that they almost became complete opposites. The latter was once one of the most reactionary regions of the country, almost completely flipping to support the revolution. This was in contrast with the Rust Belt, a former revolutionary region, with the last remnants of the revolution being largely contained to the older population, whose fond memories of the revolution have largely faded over time, with the difference being 20 years. The 20 years have been eventful, with large changes in socioeconomic conditions occurring. This would be accompanied by the rapid intensification of the demographic change that the Rust Belt would incur. Both of these rapid changes combined, revolutions in their aspect would intensify the contradictions that would play out soon. These contradictions stood off against each other, with one supplementing the other and the other supplanting the other simultaneously. This contradiction caused large tears within the revolutionary spirit of the blue-collar of country. By this point, the main nations had solidified, with the first peoples, as well as those imported in the shackles, largely forming their own culture, though those that would be imported in the shackles and boats in inhospitable conditions largely have their nation based around the idea of oppression over anything else. Long capitalized on this and sought to free the burden of oppression, which would, in turn, practically destroy any difference between those peoples while being able to liberate the first peoples. Antonin partially followed this, especially regarding the First People, though the former proposal was easily criticized for being anti-folkish. This could be easily seen in the process of radicalization that would take place within the party itself. The radicalization process ended up causing some of the remnants to largely break away and form their party, with their respective faction leaving as well. Some factions were concerned with national rebirth, especially after the years of humiliation, by a pseudo-workers regime of the rising East. This humiliation would be undone at all costs, no matter the price.

This pseudo-workers regime has grown in strength since the 2020s, when it started accumulating more power quickly. This power accumulation of the pseudo-workers regime was funded by the development of American capital and its might. The might of American capital largely came through the eventual institution of the intensification of the process of capital accumulation. The intensification of capital accumulation is what would end up causing a complete bog-down in the process of the industrialization of the East. This would end up causing the capital to be seized and distributed to the local bourgeoisie, which would mirror the same policies. Both of them wanted to maximize whatever gain was possible, and industrialization took place because of excess surplus labor, in other words, the reserve army of labor.

The reserve army of Labor decreases wages, with the reserve army of Labor mainly being confined to unemployment. The reserve army of labor would pervade, with some of them siding with Long while the others were employed, yet they were largely antagonistic. This antagonistic relationship with the other party members was primarily set off by the fact that all of them were funded by different formations of capital, all of which took up different stances relative to each other. The antagonistic contradiction that took place was one that greatly varied. It had gone past any of the former borders and had now sought itself differently. Long's party largely combined past, present and future ethics. This completely stood contrary to Antonin, who believed his position was completely different from any other position.

Antonin's party echoed the trappings of the ideology of Third Position. This Third Position sought to find a middle ground between the two sides of the contradiction. This contradiction is found within the Third Position rhetoric, which frames itself as part of one side of the contradiction for one and the other side for the other. Antonin never realized that these contradictions go against each other because the rhetoric completely blinded him, and he was largely subsumed by it. The flame of the Third Position was always alive and well; it had never died off. This revolutionary-reactionary position had decidedly placed itself on the opposite side of the contradiction. This revolutionary-reactionary position had transformed itself and morphed itself out of existence. It had no true identity, for it would be situated in the middle of two opposing contradictions. These largely opposing contradictions could never reconcile themselves, causing some open conflict. The first central contradiction was found through the difference in the sum of the economic contradiction, where it firmly situated itself on one side.

This contradiction ended up causing open conflict among the ranks, causing one faction to collapse on one side firmly. This faction would end up leaving the party soon after that. This contradiction could never really resolve itself as a result. The contradiction found no solstice and warmth within the dark sheds where holistic training would run. This contradiction was one whose sight was warm, with each sight largely being a touch. It was a contradiction whose bonds had grown weak, and only one common interest was left. It was for entirely different reasons than the social contradiction, which saw itself firmly on one side of the aisle. These two contradictions ran against each other, mainly at each other's guts. These contradictions had no real chance of reconciliation, only elimination. The reactionary position on social issues sawed reconciliation as long as those issues never boiled down to economic values. This would mean that only some wings could be won over, and these victories would come at the expense of alienating some part of the party. These victories were solely based on the premise that victory was near and possible rather than far out and impossible. This antagonism had reached new lengths, never readily seen by the naked eye. The contradiction pitted the bull against the ox, causing the horse's muscles to gallop, yet leaving the horse. This was the true nature of the party that Antonin had cultivated over his tenure – it was weak, yet it remained strong. These were largely oxymorons that had cultivated themselves, holding each other up and providing comfort. These oxymorons had no real significance when it came to who the party truly represented. This stark contrast was a direct result of the battle that has going on – one that had gone on and one that will. This battle for the reactionaries has never ended – it has only begun. This reactionary backlash would only be in terms of the contradiction, where the contradiction represents the symbolic importance of the constant push and pull there is between the two points. This pull would counteract the effect of the push, with each side making their play widely known. These plays for the reactionaries must not ever end. For them, it was always politics first, everything else second. Any defense of the reactionary order would come through keeping the political sphere first because otherwise, the ground would be given to the revolutionaries or the current status quo (which has the chance of backing the reactionaries if ever the parties are shaken up). If the parties are lost, so will the character be of the insipid creature that seeks to crawl within the doors and the pavement. Even if it cannot talk, it can certainly sing. Even if it cannot purposely respirate, it can still breathe. This was the true nature of the large storm that was coming the way of the soil. The large storm was only gathering, and it was not present yet.

The large storm had seen the dawn of light; it had seen all of the might of the height. It could not see anything else but itself. It only saw whatever was coming, not whatever was going. The light was only going in another direction, isolated and trapped. The light was what ended up causing the storm to gather, with many more years to come. The gathering storm was dusty and windy, with its speed largely slow at first but rapidly intensifying over time. This speed must not be part of the same velocity; rather, it must decelerate or accelerate over time, or it will fail. The gathering storm was always on the horizon; it was always watching. The gathering storm had not wept away; on the other hand, it was motivated by the smiling clouds looking down at the sad Earth that was weeping. The weeping sorrow encapsulating the large atmosphere had transcended out of its stratosphere. The stratosphere had largely descended from its former glory, seeing its doom and destruction. The gathering storm was always awakening; it was always here, no matter any objections there were. The gathering storm would engulf all those that stood out of the way. It was much closer to a hurricane, avoiding any objections to its real power. This power was not a dual power; it was a singular power. The singular power could easily dominate every other people that were there. This power had not seen the end of its fate, nor had it seen its rate. While there was another plate, it still had not seen its light of day. Even through dangerous times, it could not find any place for the many segues made. The many conservative factions of the party had completely loathed the inroads within the movement. The more reformist sections only saw it as a means to an end. The end is the same, for the reform only affects the people of the main country by opening everything up and slashing down on the excess bureaucracy that may pervade the current society. This feeling of angst only started to build up within the movement as it sought no expansion other than to see the peoples of its nation brought back together. Of course, the nation was defined in terms of genetic lineage, not of merit or the reason why many of the immigrants had largely come here. The dream was passing by, for the proud children of the nation had not seen their turn. For them, the greatest law was loyalty, which was unwavering and transcended all other forms of loyalty. They saw these forms of loyalty intersecting while simultaneously seeing these forms of loyalty being separate from each other at times. This two-faced nature had largely replaced much of the old establishment leagues, for they had successfully promoted a message of no retreat from the eventual end goal of reestablishing and reasserting the old reactionary positions. They had seen nothing more than the means to the end; they didn't know what would come. They only saw temporary gains that meant nothing in the long run. However, these short-term gains were the lifeblood of their actual spirit to them. These gains that were completely made by the magnificent advances that were played on the field were only faux. These faux advances were to stir up a public sentiment from the Rust Belt and some minority sections from other parts of the North, largely to build enclaves in many formerly dead cities. Their goal was to revive these cities, ironically with many of the same policies that brought them to the brink of collapse earlier. This contradiction was no different from before, for it only saw the never-ending final struggle. The final struggle could go beyond the maximum they believe they can push. Out of order, none of the party's actions would have any real significance; they only had the strength within the bundle of sticks that couldn't be broken. This bundle of sticks was more important than each stick, which could easily end up snapping. Each stick did not matter, for only the collective bundle couldn't snap. This illustration motivated Antonin, especially when the sticks were ordered in terms of race and the identity behind it. The nation's race was largely what had preceded any other form of reaction, for the nation's race could only be seen through the purposeful manipulation of the current order. The decadent order was no longer decadent, for it would allow for the eventual establishment of the reactionary society they clamored for. This was what largely satisfied the rest of the demands of the reactionaries. The demands of the reactionaries had meant nothing when put in the bigger picture because its goal was to shift to one side on purpose. This ended up causing the eventual break within the ultra-visionaries within the party, who were largely divorced from the other organs of the party. The party's other organs would have no significance, for they could only hold up to certain standards. These ultra-visionaries had found nothing other than the eventual acceleration toward their dystopia, which they saw as their utopia. These ultra-visionaries were only somewhat close to Antonin, for Antonin rejected some of their doctrines due to pragmatism. This is because the ultra-visionaries only had a basis in the vanguard, not within the reactionary branches of the masses or even within the donors. These donors had largely subjected the party to ruthless criticism.

One step at a time meant nothing if the whole image couldn't be completed. No one cares about the individual steps that need to be taken, only the whole image in the end. If not finished, The whole image would wreak havoc within the already fractured and divisive party. The ultra-visionaries needed to be brought back in, with some concessions to complete idealism, not even pragmatic idealism being made. These concessions would keep the party afloat as they are the lifeline of the party. It was dusk's dawn, and the storm hadn't settled. This was because the storm was still coming, though in a direction that was not specified. This storm would take time for it to be dealt with. Being able to deal with the storm would mean completely reconfiguring the basis of the party. The basis of the party was largely in the many echelons of the reactionary sections of the masses, which largely unthinkingly supported the party of Antonin. The Party of National Rebirth was a force to be reckoned with. The party had not seen such a turnout before, for it had grown from a small party largely rooted within a couple niche circles into a large national political machine, which could easily draw in any voters it needed. This change is what largely prompted the eventual transformation of their whole system, with complete reorganization and instrumentalization of the process that would eventually bring about the eventual overthrow of the current establishment – while bypassing the need to gain an alliance with the establishment parties. This would mean being able to appeal to the many establishment groups that wanted to see their agendas being enacted. This appeal would end up spanning the circumference of the Earth twice over. This difference couldn't see the light of day, but it could largely make a complete revolution, with the turn being three hundred and sixty degrees. This turn may not have lasted without the aid of the other parties' voter bloc, with the many blocs that consisted being the instrumental tools of the party. It was a quintessential party based on the fear of immigration and wage losses. The wage losses, while real, were largely seen by the party as being a result of immigration rather than being a systemic problem. This was further combined with a rejection of both empiricisms and positivism, finding itself with a new method. This method was largely questioned, for there was no real solution. This method was thoroughly criticized, sometimes providing wrong solutions, though the party had been largely wrangled with all of it going into the hands of Antonin. This transformation within the party would end up meaning the end of internal party democracy, which would be the end of its last democratic, populist character in favor of a character that was largely based around the few. This was further amplified by the fact that the old order, while still intact, had largely made inroads into the party of Antonin, specifically through the donors' requests. The populist character was never meant to last, for it was solely based on dogma rather than actual practice and reason. This dogma found no limits, being applied to all fields, thus being able to deflect the true solution. The true solution was largely obscured by the foliage which covered the ground. The only gain in the ground there could be would be to completely reorder the society based on corporatism, which was largely built out of the character of councils being comprised of all. This corporatist system had seen nothing but the end of the day when the sun had completely set. The needed experience was not found either, with the large abandonment and the resentment of the old ideals. Corporatism was literal, with many corporations largely taking power within the system of the corporatocracy. This opposed a system of councils comprising the masses and experts, though not the parasitic class prior, which would coordinate the whole system. This form of corporatism is different from the rest as it largely finds no place for the few, largely seeing them as the reason for a downfall. This form of corporatism is much closer to Syndicalism, just with a reorganized motive and structure. This reorganized structure had found no bounds other than those no one else had recognized. These bounds had only found themselves breached, with steps being made to break through the barrier and, eventually, project many of the ideas of the very few on top. This essential change ended up causing a large decline in support of the masses, though, by this point, it had largely gerrymandered its way into much of the Rust Belt, whose support would remain the same due to no real alternative. There was no real alternative to the system, for it largely never represented the masses. The closest there was couldn't etch the surface, with much of the power still being concentrated in the industrialists' hands. The industrialists were largely the financial backers of the party, for they didn't want to see any real change that would be made. The main difference between the two systems relied on the power of the industrialists, most of whom were not specialists; rather, they just held the needed capital. The capital would then be transferred to the masses with the improvement of the means of production being in the hands of the masses rather than relying on the industrialists. This was the main difference, with the Syndicalist faction largely being on the side of Long while the Corporatist faction largely being on the side of Antonin. This clear-cut division couldn't be rectified in any way, for the industrialists meant everything. The current system was largely corporatist, with much of the power being concentrated in the hands of the industrialists rather than everyone else. This power couldn't be easily legislated away, for it was the movement's core. The industrialists' power was greater than the hand of the other factions, for the power of the industrialists ended up moving the party completely. The two main populist factions were backed by industrialists, with some wanting an intensification of free trade (largely concentrated among the larger industrialists), while others favoring a more protectionist system (largely concentrated among the smaller industrialists). This fundamental difference tore up part of the populists, with the rest of the conservatives following the middle course of partial economic liberalism combined with aggressive protectionism. This aggressive protectionism would protect the resources of the state while being able to give out bribes. The corporatocracy in the middle complimented the two corporatist systems. The sum was that one would be a largely protectionist corporatist system, one would be straight-up corruption, with rewards given to the industrialists while the other would be a free-trade corporation system. These factions were unified by the industrialists' support, who had largely reined much of the party. All these factions meant nothing on paper, for the two populist factions were the largest. Much of the power was concentrated in the hands of the conservatives. This tense standoff within the party Antonin would only further exacerbate any current divisions. These divisions would end up continuing down the line, with the only real two factions being the populists, who were largely united temporarily, as well as the conservatives.

This tense standoff couldn't be resolved, for it would drift towards one of the populist factions, which believed that they could solve the problems of division. A plan was carried forth by Antonin himself, which entailed that the protectionist side of corporatism would win while largely carrying the mark of free trade with the many de-facto colonies that had been created. This precise combination would end up drifting the party towards a more faux populist direction, towards the horizon, with the falcon flying up and wide. This corporatist stance would have some free trade, though largely with the many expansionist ambitions. This was combined with redoing how much of the economy was structured, moving towards a true corporatist system and being completely economically unified. The doom and gloom of Antonin had largely destroyed itself, becoming a much more corporatist party.

The nation would largely be dominant within the state, which practically prevented any real deviations. Though one major deviation was made, it was towards an orthodox stance towards corporatism and the issue of national identity. This would still favor one side, with the new perspective largely mirroring the old. This new stance of corporatism, social reaction, and a complete reorganization of the former government was the primary stance of the party, for it promised an end to establishment corruption. Little did their voters know that Antonin represented another side of corruption, one that had not revealed its face yet. This was the primary characteristic of the defining transition between the two systems, with the primary and secondary systems largely competing against each other. For the party of Antonin, liberalism was always a corporatist phenomenon economically, with much of the social phenomena drifting towards the other side and the rest of the political phenomena. This ended up causing true unity within the party, for it was able to capitalize on the many moderates that were largely fleeing the establishment due to an economic crash. This allocation would end up causing a complete revolution, wherein the old and the new would end up meeting together. While nothing was unique, for it largely adopted positions that were slightly more moderate than before, it would still have the pernicious habit of hosting many bigots. This would end up causing the complete collapse of the party later on. The contrast with the other movement, largely seeking comprehensive reform through a practical revolution, was out of bounds for national rebirth. National rebirth through palingenesis could only come through a total movement emphasizing unity. This unity was an alliance that couldn't be broken under any circumstance, for if it was broken, the whole party would end up falling apart. This unity must have lasted one thousand years, for the nation would last for eternity. The party's leader, Antonin, was largely the party's main old guard, with all the factions being dissolved. The sections' dissolution largely helped Antonin get rid of his opponents, Carl and Smith. These two opponents had largely seen their fate with a new night of the purges coming. This rebirth from before had seen nothing more than a complete revolution, a counter-revolution. This counter-revolution had only gained steam due to encouragement by the many factions that would quickly turn against the party while being largely submissive to the party itself. These factions had no real power; even though they were once basically parties themselves, most of this unity had fractured, and nothing could be found. This was the true state of the transformation, with the dissolution of factions strengthening unity, though leading to large purges that were never seen before. These purges were vigilante activity, with many members being thoroughly checked and then purged. This was to prevent any traitors within the party, even though most of the party consisted of traitors themselves.

Even though the flag was flown at half-staff, it still hadn't lost its special significance. The special significance was still there, even if it was altered. This significance couldn't be seen with anything else but through a complete analysis of empiricism and positivism. This flag would never solemnly retreat, for it was revered. The flag was always moving forward, with the party always being brought forward. For one second, it seemed like Antonin had the upper hand compared to Long, only if he didn't know the mass desertions he may incur later. The party was never stable due to the large presence of the masses, who wanted to see the power of the corporations completely stripped down. In this case, it was the rational party of Long that was a complete continuation of the integral nationalism, liberalism, and scientific socialism of the past as opposed to the poorly written party of Antonin, which found refuge in the dark fringes of society while being able to have a cursor that tagged along. This cursor was extremely dependent on the movement, for if it had moved one direction over the other, it had an imminent chance of collapsing on itself, like many dominoes stacked up against each other. The colorful picture the many reactionaries would paint to disguise their party would reveal its true intent of bringing about fascism. The word "fascism" had largely been obscured and rarely talked about other than weak definitions that would not fit most of the movement. This led to the surge of popularity for the party Antonin. The words of fascism may not be popular, but the idea itself was prevalent. The true squad of national rebirth only came through establishing a reactionary corporatist system. This corporatist system would practically be guided by big capital's interests, rather than by any rationality. The same thing was being warned against earlier, though the warnings were not heeded. What largely ended up happening as a result was that Long had largely taken control of the

South, Catholic regions of New England, the West Coast, the Plains, the Mountains, as well as Appalachia, with a minority presence within the Rust Belt. The party of Antonin had connections within the Rust Belt, New England, California, and the rest of the territories outside of the mainland. This difference is what would end up causing a large split between these once two formerly populist movements, with many defections coming from the party of Antonin, specifically within the sections of the working class that were much closer to integral nationalism than they were to fascism. Fascism was material without substance, while integral nationalism largely opposed fascism from a new perspective. This defection towards integral nationalism only bolstered support for Long, who largely capitalized on this social nationalism being combined with social equality and liberty, thus bringing together all of his factions that, while being diverse demographically, were largely united in the end goal. The fraternity had been built up with the abolition of the peculiar institution of bondage, while the First had built up the liberty; now, it was time for a new round for the true establishment of equality. This trio would be perfected through new words and actions that would largely reshape the old struggle into a new one. These struggles were completely different for Long, for he saw the proper implementation of fraternity, liberty, and equality, which were all related together. These principles would guide the party of Long, while the party of Antonin was largely guided by restricted liberty to certain bounds, corporatism, and national chauvinism. This combination largely differed from the mainstream, but it continued to garner support due to the many advertisements that could be put out. These advertisements came in the form of direct appeals, largely backed with much-needed capital to run the advertisements. This would end up causing a complete realignment of certain groups, with the large presence of illegal immigrants ironically crossing into the camp of Antonin as opposed to the camp of Long. Antonin largely changed the appeals, making it much closer to classical fascism, dropping many of the connotations of illegal immigration. This would come in the form of restructuring of the system. This system for the fascists was largely broken, with multiple directions pulling at it. This could only be rectified by establishing a true fascist dictatorship, which would put the needs of their constituents first. The constituents were largely homogeneous, though they had attracted much of the socially reactionary constituents, which completely changed the demographics, causing a complete lockdown and a stranglehold of certain regions. Even though the old replacement theory had been largely abandoned, shifting its ideological base, it still carried much of its former commitments, with the many factions being spurred on by conflict. This conflict was never-ending, with the party's members always shifting, with large surges and crashes. This two-faced nature of the party continued going forward, with the wheel chair only incrementally going forward.

"You have been accused of treason against the party," Antonin told Carl. "But I was the party's director itself," Carl replied. "According to the reports of witnesses within the party, you have been charged with embezzlement of the party's funds," Antonin said. This left Carl in shock; the party of Antonin might not have lasted with the old guard being purged. Over time, the old guard was largely replaced with complete loyalists to Antonin himself. These loyalists were nothing but yes-men, for they never questioned one of Antonin's actions. They had no real purpose but to follow through on what Antonin said and secure his power. By this point, the bid for the presidential election was starting to flare up. While Antonin, being largely part of the youth, couldn't run, he had appointed his loyalist as the candidate for the party. In this case, the loyalist was Oswald, whose poverty-stricken background was used to appeal to lower-income groups without actually giving any real concessions. Oswald largely shifted the party's base towards a certain direction of the masses rather than a few. Oswald was a complete loyalist, largely supporting the struggle against Carl and his almost-dead faction. Carl was put in "prison," which the party ran. The party's paramilitary had quickly grown, swelling to over one and a half million in strength. Long's paramilitary was smaller, though very trained, standing at one million. Long's paramilitary had more of the population's support, for it could draw upon the workforce if needed in case of a deficit if fighting ever broke out. The old two establishment parties were no longer served, with internal divisions always causing the party to completely fragment. The fragmentation of the party had largely overseen the quick dismemberment of the positions that were taken outside of the mainstream. The old establishment parties were no longer entrenched; they were practically forced to step down. The wave of retirement further exacerbated the radicalization, either to the side of Long or Antonin. It was not a two-faced question; on the other hand, it was one of the positions being taken in advance or at the moment. These positions would mean the further entrenchment of the current society and the battle that was taking place. Nothing but destruction was realistically seen, with the party only serving as the instrument that could carry out a counter-revolution. It was the counter-revolution above all, and nothing would stand in the way of the counter-revolution. The despair was replaced by complete gloom, with the sun setting on the former country once the center of immigration. It was marked by rampant poverty combined with an acceleration of the economic depression that was taking place. It had created a fascist party and a working-class party, with the fascists largely composed of big capital and the interests of the reactionary masses. These backward masses would later be joined by those venting their anger elsewhere, seeing the problem not in the current system but in its application. The refined application was seen as a good model to launch off of, for it would mean the necessary abolition of the former order. This quick, dramatic change further destroyed any last bastion of liberal democracy. Liberal democracy had run its course; now, it was the belief that the majority was oppressing the minority. Furthermore, this largely fell into the idea that democracy was flawed. This would end up causing the creation of the industrialist faction within the reactionaries. The industrialist faction of the reactionaries had been through no more or no less of the depression, though they had the tools to recover, for the tools had been increasingly concentrated in their hands. A minority of the industrialists had largely seized the opportunity, quickly maximizing their profits during an economic downturn. This opportunist direction was at the expense of the masses for Antonin, though the reactionary masses proved to be a loyal base of support. The base of support that held on had always seen the party of Antonin as the only party of salvation, with no other party being able to fill that gap.

That gap could only be bridged by the party of Antonin himself, with no real opposition to the party of Antonin. Antonin had gone from a mysterious character to becoming a large section of the transition within the political machines that would form. Nothing less and nothing more would suffice any of the other parties. The creation of the true party could only be seen through the lens of a complete rebirth of the nation as well as the vanguard of the nation, the party. The radicalization process had seen the number of fascists quickly swell, sending their rockets into the air with the imminent threat of destruction. The fascists had largely gained ground, creating their form of democracy that had no respect for the true majority, the working class. Instead, it primarily benefited the industrialists, with most other groups being largely left behind. The process of capital accumulation kept on rapidly intensifying, with most of the capital being left in the hands of a slim minority, with no real variation between most parties. The party would comprise the new rank-and-file of the industrialist class, who was over all others with their needs being placed first. The needs of the industrialists had transcended all other interests, being the core of the party and the new dictatorship that would take place. Everything was in the state, while nothing was outside of the state. The state was now synonymous with the party, the party being the complete dictate of society. The alliance with the big backers of capital ended up causing a complete transformation towards one new side of the aisle, calling themselves the Third Position, while in reality, they are much closer to the first position that would give rise to the second position of Long. It was merely a rewrite of the first position, with the malicious effects being glorified within the cadres of the party. The party's cadres were largely the industrialists, with the old principles of capital accumulation being again reappropriated. The principles of capital accumulation had not changed despite the years that had passed by. They could only really cry, for they haven't fried.

The process of capital accumulation would rapidly intensify through the ages. It was starkly in contrast to the doctrines of scientific socialism and integral nationalism; it was largely pivotal on division rather than unity. This was by exploiting existing divisions to allow the elite to usurp the remaining power that the majority of people largely had. This was largely compounded by the large divisions that would cause the movement's collapse. The new fascist state marred the new division; the new fascist state was not direct yet, but it ended up commanding much support. This new fascist state was a dual power structure, with most of its principles being based on the complete division between a nativist group and a foreign population. This was further compounded by de facto division within the movement. This division was expressed in the gratitude of the majority within the party. This had largely called for the brevity of capital accumulation and nothing to be rectified. The rectification of the new force was completely different from the other forces before. It was a wave in that it had multiple characteristics, being a large chain that spanned numerous aisles. This chain was completely averse to the current state of reality – yet followed it simultaneously. It was a solely anti-populist alliance that was wrapped in populism itself. It was an elitist alliance wrapped in the people's rhetoric. It was no real different than the many deviations of fascism.

Fascism was a system where the totality mattered overall. The individual means nothing, and the nation is the party. There is no difference between the party and the chain that links all of them. This chain completely differs from the antagonism and hostility that would bombard the citadel, known as the great struggle. The great battle wasn't a proper noun because it was undefined, though soon, it would be the largest warped conflict throughout the Earth, twice over. This conflict was fought through propaganda, not through words or weapons. The most important thing, above all, in this war was loyalty. Loyalty alone would determine the fate of nations and the struggle that would continue to intensify. The commitment shown by certain groups of people would cause adversity, among others. This would affect every village and town; nothing would be untouched by it; it was the great struggle that had only started. The battle has only begun, and it is still going on. It lived; it lives, and it will live. There was no greater calling than to draw the line across the field further. In some places, it was completely uncontested. In others, there was fierce competition. The competition had largely superseded cooperation, with both now being antithetical. Despite being a despot, Antonin was viewed by the majority of his party after some members walked about as the party's majority leader. He would envelop the will of the people, at least certain people. It would be evident that it does not die in darkness; on the other hand, it only lives through the past. It would be apparent that there was no real difference between the establishment and the faux populists found within the populists. The fascists would constantly try to remove any progress made in favor of the masses. The goal of the fascists was to allow for the eventual dissolution of any popular power there was. This would contradict any real progress towards a truly populist nation and country. The elitist division would further intensify, with the party of Antonin acting as the vanguard of the party itself.

The truly intensifying struggle would come in the form of a further expulsion of any deviation there was with populist sentiments being rooted out. The only populism there came through psychological manipulation. Psychological manipulation was only a means to an end rather than the end itself. This was found in the form of the eventual dissemination of propaganda, with most of the activities ceasing once most of the population of that region had largely subdued itself to the party. This was on the part of Antonin, who had largely delved himself into the party. The party was ever-growing, largely appealing to the young population that had been an outgrowth of the new generation. This was combined with the last generation going into the middle ages, while the previous generation was largely elderly. By this point, the generations had completely shuffled, with most of the party's support coming from the few from certain sections of the order. Society had not completely approved of the party, with large holdouts; however, by in large, it was the de facto party of the reactionary masses as well as the holders of large capital. This essential characteristic compelled the party to push itself in many directions. The only problem arising from this is that the party always had the imminent threat of tearing itself apart. If it had torn itself apart, the vigilance of the past would largely fade away, with much of the party's principles being based on a couple of sole premises. These premises were completely antithetical to any real change within them. The assumptions were all based on vesting the power of the holders of big capital and masking that through a new form of populism. This new form of populism would be based on division as well as being able to reconfigure the whole landscape so that the party wouldn't decline. It was largely prevalent among the few groups that there were, being the vanguard of the owners of big capital. The industrialists, who were not the people who were going to maximize efficiency, were interested in maximizing how much money came from the plan.

The maximal efficiency only came through proper planning independent of the interests of capital. It would completely bypass the institution of money, being a society in the interests of all but the parasites. This would be formulated by the coalition that would coalesce under Long. The interests of all but the parasites would be put first, with the interests of all taking precedence over those of the parasites that do nothing useful in society other than roll the ball of capital. The ball of money would quickly keep growing without any real barrier to stunt its growth. It would put itself over everything else, not subordinate to anything else. The rejuvenation of the nation couldn't find itself anywhere else. This was combined with the fascist belief that capital would work because it would not betray the country. The capital would end up flipping sides when it was needed. Anyone who resisted within the party was largely purged with the handful that was part of the old guard loyalists. The loyalists couldn't be purged due to being largely under the subordinate domination of the Antonin. Antonin held the party together, combined with the force of capital. These two forces were the most powerful forces within the party; they were essentially the party in itself. The party had only known these two forces for much of its life. The loyalty to the leader was most important above all. If dedication ended up fading, there would end up being a purge in which all were questioned. This would lead to many being turned in by the other members, fearful of any purge. This would end up causing the purges to be quicker through some psychological manipulation.

Carl had largely been lost and, with it, their largest propagandist. Their largest propagandist would quickly end up encapsulating the remainder of the party. The faction of Smith would largely unite with the leftovers of the section of Carl in a bid to oppose the main centralization process that had been taking place. This would mean being able to root out any of the loyalists as a pushback. This pushback caused some trouble for Antonin, where a significant minority could block many of the reforms of the party, which would cause the party to be more fragmented. The minority would sometimes storm out of the convention, largely preventing any reform from being passed. The decrees meant nothing, as the large minority would never obey them. The regulations would have no substance other than many characters stringed together to form words. This would further coincide with the many dubious merits of the process of complete unity by forcing opinions on others. This would further lead to agitation within the party. Smith was next on the list to be purged, but the fact that the remnants of Carl's faction had aligned themselves with Smith's faction had started to raise alarm bells for the party of Antonin. It would sense the signal of a potential end of the domination of the current order, with much of the establishment within the party being toppled by the little resistance left within the party. It would rely on large-scale fearmongering, for it was the only thing known above all else. The fearmongering had superseded every other order that there could be. The fearmongering was the new order; nothing was more important than following that fear-mongering. Fearmongering was part of the daily habit of transformation, wherein the party would keep adjusting itself to align with the interests of the few over the many. The party itself was a flexible jelly that could be easily torn apart if it wanted to, with loose bonds within the party itself. The party was no different from the intensification of the establishment parties. It would only serve as the cornerstone of the eventual sight of the reformation of the complete system. The reformation had only been united in the sense of establishment support and backing by the institution of capital. When acting together, these two forces would end up wreaking havoc on any real opposition party there was. The only opposition party there consisted of the party of Long.

"We make payments to schools, which illegal immigrants are then using," Brandon chanted. This was further intensified by the cheers that were quickly disseminated. The joys would be met with quick applause until when it came to the next point. "I do not know if there is a new story within the new adventure, but I know one thing for certain, I do not want people that are ignorant of our proud heritage to spoil it," this was a clear dog whistle that was largely able to bypass any criticism. This would only refer to a certain type of people, with the words "illegal immigrants" having meaning when it comes to certain sections of the masses. The goal was to divide much of the society and the nation itself. The division within the country could then allow for further intensification, for it would be an eventual goal to split the organization. The society was only cohesive to an extent, for it had many branches within. These branches within would be at the core of division, for the branches would be exploited to completely divide the many sections of the population, all of whom come from diverse walks of life, into different areas rather than being one as a whole. This would mirror the strategy of the ultra-reactionaries, for the ultra-visionaries were merely clones of that themselves. This new strategy being pursued would end up causing a complete turn.

The new strategy was marred and halted by the national rebirth policy that Long had pursued. Long's goal was to see all of the regional cultures be developed to expand the national culture as part of the social policy. This is what made the integral nationalists within the party important – as well as made the integral nationalists within the party dissolve. It was solely based on the premise of establishing a popular society ruled by everyone except parasites. This goal would end up compelling Long to integrate into the former platform, where they shared common goals economically and politically. The society by all was practically compounded by rational order, for it would satisfy all, not some majority. This was further combined with the economic system, which furthered much of these points to propel them. It was once made clear that there would be no real difference with the change of the economic and political plans. The only difference remaining would be the social perspective, which gave birth to the movement. The campaign would become stronger because of the nation's decline and, more specifically, the country. In the past, they were relegated to the minority opinion, where scientific socialism was largely at the helm of the party; however, over time, the new statement of national rebirth through the process of decentralization itself started to take place. The nation was an organic unit built on top of the existing structures. It would be through decentralization and the encouragement of local cultures – which practically includes minority cultures that a true national identity would be established. The nation had no more real meaning besides these two points, where it was united together. It was created due to the reaction towards the country tearing itself apart and being weak.

When put in practice, its goal is to largely decentralize the individual cultures as well as eventually achieve a nationalist intellectual rebirth, to have all of the nations of the country develop. These factors combined to aid in the national revival that took place for Long's party. Long's party had its nationalism resembling a form of integrals. Its nationalism intersected everything else. This was in stark contrast to the nationalism that would develop alongside the party of Antonin.

The party of Antonin found its nationalism within the entrapping of an exclusionary cultural identity. At times, this was further combined with centralization and ethnicism. These policies combined would drive away certain groups, with other groups not having a stance as a result. The result of the collective sum of these ideologies was the reimbursement of the former fallen. These policies combined would end up setting apart the nationalism of Antonin's party from the nationalism of Long's party.

"I've seen the many letters you have wrote," the man of honor said. "I don't know what you're referencing," the other person replied. "You have literally been writing this stream of letters," the man of honor replied. "To be frank, I do not see the scene changing even with the new dust taking effect," the other person replied. "Go get the money that Paul has, we need it for purposes that I cannot disclose right now," the man of honor said. "Doing so may or may not be a worthy endeavor," the other person said. "Paul is in dire financial circumstances right now," the man of honor replied. "What the hell do you mean," the other person replied. "You won't understand until you get an actual brain," the man of honor said. This drove Rover furious; he planned to manipulate the money that Paul was holding to make money off the transaction. This manipulation would take the form of sending the money toward the stock market and being able to bet on it. If it succeeds, he could make up the delay and return the money to Paul while profiting from it. If it failed, Paul's business, a large lifeline for him, would fall apart. He set out by going to the stock exchange, which was nearby as he drove to Chicago. He bet on one hundred million dollars with the hope of having the stocks he would invest in rise by at least half of the original price. These expectations were not known to be fail-safe yet, but for all that was done, this was the only decent thing that has been done yet.

The next day, shocking news came in; the stock market had crashed. The same couple words were repeated over TV: "The stock market is in a dive." The man of honor quickly dialed up Rover and scolded him, saying, "Where did the money go?" This was a question that Rover couldn't easily reply to. Rover said there was a transitional delay and that the bank was withholding the money. The man of honor immediately contacted the bank, saying no deposit had been made. This drove Paul furious, being in a dire financial situation. Ironically, the stocks had soared as soon as that money was put into the stock market, but now, it went in the opposite direction. This complete turn was further combined with mass withdrawal from the stock market, which would quickly decrease the prices of the stocks in the market. This would dramatically alter the value of the stocks to the point that they had no real value left within them. This new reality was faced by the brutal heat wave that had sunk much of the country. The value of the stocks was further plummeting after electricity largely went out. The only way the stocks could be bought or sold is by physically going to the market. All of the capital was liquidated in the risky investment to increase capital. This would carry its ramifications, all ending up feeding into each other. These ramifications would send shockwaves throughout the whole country. This was something that couldn't easily be rectified; it was the devilish imprint upon it that it had collapsed under its weight. All of the liquid capital started to drain and freeze quickly, causing the space between the molecules to end up lessening as it turned into a solid. The space between the molecules was all the excess capital that would build up within the market. The quick fall would be accompanied by a temporary rise, where the ailing government bought back some stocks. This forecast ended up exemplifying many of the predictions that were already made in the past. The forecast was completely separate from the other predictions of the eventual downfall and upbringing of the stock market. The forecast sought imminent doom, for it only saw the stock market completely collapsing though no one would know what the future would hold for them. It would soon be seen that much of the money put in the stock market would end up liquidating, causing a large shock. That capital had collapsed one stock market, with more to come. From now on, the stock market had little relative significance, for it ended up causing Paul to go bankrupt and the cessation of all funding that went to her party of, Antonin. This rapidly intensifying contact and collapse of party of Antonin was not temporary as long as the stocks wouldn't bounce back. The stocks of the country were causing the collapse of the country itself. The government itself couldn't hold on for much longer, and the rapid intensification of these processes would end up causing the collapse of the contradictions barely held together by a thread. These contradictions were largely a result of the current system, not the outside effects or being a temporary problem. This would set apart the integral nationalists, for they would believe it was inherent and the only remedy was a form of populist nationalism. This form of populist nationalism would be found in Long, for it would be embedded deep into his trenches. His gun was that of theory and practice, which would eventually glide him toward experience. Since much of the fundamental theory remained the same regarding politics and economics, his main trigger was the nationalist principle, which would set itself apart. This core principle would change the whole movement in favor of one side. The largely subdued movement of the other reactionaries would end up causing a stockpile and backlog of reactionaries towards Antonin, while the other nationalists would end up joining the camp of Long, despite Antonin being more radical in this sense. The only thing that really set any of these movements apart was the character embodied within the new order's raw establishment. The new order had only one real opposition, with the goal of representing all of the citizens. The only difference was that the citizens were much more restricted for Antonin. It was a form of true populism built on top of rationalism. This populism was based on rationality and practicality, with the practice leading to the benefit of the general population. This is what would make integral nationalism viable, with their goal of establishing a true national identity being made true. This fusion would end up causing the increase in theory, with the nationalist perspective of an increased cultural presence being directly coincided with the decentralized perspective. These two sides would meet each other, for the only real goal was embodied within the populist nationalism that would develop. This populist nationalism was set apart by its lack of fascist epistemology, which would make it develop the character it would grow into within the party of Long. The fascist character found itself in opposition to the character of populist nationalism, wherein the character of populist nationalism largely believed in cultural unity through decentralization. Fascism believed that no individual culture mattered and that all cultures should be hamstrung from above, combined with complete national chauvinism. In some other cases, it wasn't even including those that would largely adopt and assimilate. This would mean they would take a cultural nationalist stance and a stance of ethnic nationalism, which would set them apart from any form of integral nationalism. Integral nationalism, largely a subset of populist nationalism, favored a transition while also seeing a rational-based perspective on populism and nationalism. Populism largely resembled the next mode of production, while nationalism was the true end goal in itself, with populism being the means to the end to develop the organic state. This would mean that the vanguard of the counter-revolution, a revolution in its own right, would end up being the state itself later on, filled up by the masses. The main goal was complete cultural rebirth, for nothing else other than the local cultural rebirth and nationalist intellectual rebirth mattered. Outside of these two goals, nationalism had no real meaning; it was based on these two goals as a result of the fallen glory. Coincidentally, as a result of the stock market crash, much of the nation's prestige would largely die off with all methods being combined and coalescing into one itself. This methodological process would end up being rife with experience.

It was the process of combination as well as dissolution that would make the party stronger in general. The party needed true unity, which it believed it could only find through appealing to certain movements. The nationalists were quickly integrated into the party of Long – the liberation movement. This would end up meaning that the party would end up taking up an integral nationalist character, for the other principles when it came to arranging the economy and the political sphere was already solved. This would mean being able to take up a stance that resembled integral nationalism, for it would mean that the nationalist position would be able to overrule all. A new line would be drawn as Puerto Rico would largely flip to the side of Antonin due to the idea of independence. The only main group that would remain consistent would be the support of a small Puerto Rican minority, who saw the true path in staying with the rest of the country and eventual integration into the nation while being able to have the local institutions nurtured. The line was clear with the die being cast. They tried to rattle their saber, and the lines were already drawn. The only thing that was left was the lines being hardened.

Campaigning would intensify, with most of the South flipping towards Long completely while most of the Rust Belt would flip towards Antonin, with a couple of holdouts who would cast their lot with Long. The new position would come in the form of complete decentralization as well as a nationalist intellectual rebirth that would come in the form of development of the intelligentsia that would support the nation as well as develop the culture behind it. This is combined with the development of the individual local cultures, which would all contribute to strengthening the true national identity. It would mean getting rid of bureaucracy and having the populace rule over their region. This would be the form of nationalism the nation could get behind. This would mean being able to forge a new national identity out of the many decentralized regions. The development of this national identity is what would keep the new revolution together. It was the intersection between integral nationalism as well scientific socialism. It was the intersection between right-wing and left-wing populism. This fusion was what would make the party of Long so powerful. It would be able to gather a decent minority of constituents from Southern Indiana, the industrial centers of Michigan, Southern Ohio, and the iron mines of Pennsylvania and use them to its benefit. The constituencies were largely loyal to the party, with Antonin's constituencies also solidifying.

Disaster struck; the economic conditions of most Americans started to go to the ditch quickly. This would provoke a general strike in the hotbed of Antonin's region. This general strike couldn't be condemned by the party of Antonin, for it included many of his members, but condoning it would make the party collapse on itself. Partial aid was given when the federal police were dispatched. The general strike would be followed by the South as well as Nevada. Antonin announced, "The great war has begun." The militias of Antonin were raised with Chicago surrounded within five days. A little while later, New York City also fell. New York City's stocks had tumbled, sending all the news toward the air. It had largely caused a complete change in generational support; much of the older population was either loyalists or supporters of Long. The federal government still held onto land, though the land was largely sparsely populated. The federal government's authority collapsed, with most of the South seceding. The minorities in the North had largely backed the revolution that occurred in the South, seeing that there was a chance of improvement, not degradation of their lives. The revolution in the previously most reactionary region of the whole country came to light. This revolution was based on popular support, for it didn't have as much military experience, except for a handful of defectors within the military. The nuclear arsenal was largely seized and deactivated, with the nuclear arsenal meaning nothing as a result. This would cause the civil war to become fought on land and bloody. Each state would secede, with the South completely under Long's control, while Kansas, Southern Illinois, Southern Indiana, Southern Ohio, Western Pennsylvania, iron mines around Buffalo, and Southern Michigan would all secede to form the revolution. The revolution largely considered itself American, overriding much of the previously Confederate sentiment. This was partially a result of decentralization and the encouragement of local culture, which would make it so that a large movement for national unity would occur. This would effectively dissolve the boundaries of race between all groups, all contributing to the new national identity. The main exception was the Puerto Rican secessionist movement, which was only temporarily successful. The borders hadn't hardened yet, for the federal government ordered these militias to stand down. The only problem was that most of them were ignored, which would further aggravate the support for the revolution and the counter-revolution. This would end up hardening the border, with an all-out civil war. The three-way civil war would see the quick, rapid advance of the South into the territory that Antonin possessed. A counterattack further repelled this; all maneuvers were made to make the civil war ended quickly. A quick spearhead towards the land of the Rust Belt would cause many of the factories to shut down and some to collapse. This was causing alarm bells for Antonin, who needed to reclaim this land at any cost. This land was rife with industry and his financial backers, who kept the war going. The only way that the counter-revolution would suffice would be through a combination of corporatism and a new political order, representing the opinions of the reaction. This would mean that the fascist party would end up quickly gaining ground. Fearful of a revolution taking over the country south of them, Canada seized New England and Alaska. This would be a key point that Long would rally around, while Antonin would do nothing due to some of his rhetoric being based on race. Long would end up pressing the New England issue and the Alaska issue and waving it in front of the audience to the point that the audience was dedicated to recovering American land. This would end up being a nationalist ambition that would quickly flame support for the civil war, while for

Antonin, it was the will to fight for some mythical race. This national policy would end up inflaming all emotions subsequent to the civil war. The idea was that America had grown weak due to backstabbing from the bourgeois intellectuals, who were against the country as well as against the revolution. The national policy was extremely similar to the national policy of proletarian nationalism. The nation's decentralization would mean that many local cultures would form independent of race. Much of the racial antagonism would fade, as it would be known that the elites were using it to stir up support for liberalism. The solidarity shown would make only one true nation, eventually abolishing the classes. The abolition of classes could only be done through a revolution. The policy that would be adopted would end up causing true national unity. It was a form of social nationalism united through revolutionary instead of reactionary principles. This would mean true national unity as well as true national liberation. National unity would mean that the nation will be united, with the national units within being part of the nation as a whole. It would be a federation of nations united through the complete unity of all nations within a federation. Regionalism would be combined with national unity. The national unity would be a form of proletarian nationalism, where patriotism would take place with the individual nations having their cultures enriched and all cultural institutions being funded, with all the peoples having their cultures enhanced. The drastic improvement of cultural capital would create a new nation that would be the primary orchestrator of the revolution. The orchestration of the revolution could only be through swift actions that would be made through gradualism and direct action. The liberation of all nations would be combined with enriching all nations. This combination largely ended up killing off any nationalist movement within the revolution. The nationalist movement and the nationalist threat to the unity of the proletariat would be easily killed off through a combination of tactics. These tactics would end up causing the primary of one true country – one that could stand any foreign threat. These tactics would be able to crush any nationalist movement that could ever arise from the ranks by being able to reclaim all of the nation as well as the individual nations within the nation itself that are tightly knitted together. This strategy would end up creating a new revolution in itself. The national revolution stressed the concept of Americanism, wherein the revolution would quickly take over much of the revolution itself in conjunction with the revolution orchestrated by the people. This would mean synthesizing a form of nationalism whose believers had only branched off due to disunity with the previous populist doctrine. This form of nationalism would end up causing a large drive, causing a population boom among the border regions to defend them from reactionary attacks. This would end up causing the strengthening of the unity of the revolutionaries, with the nationalists being once again put in place. The nationalists were former revolutionaries who had now reconciled along a new position; they were brought back with the idea of reintegrating the lost land as well as being able to largely decentralize the rest of the nation to allow the individual nations within to bond and become closer to the mother nation while at the same time, being able to find their own identity. This would end up turning out to be different by the extra position is taken, for it would represent a return to the true position of nationalism that is heralded by the general population. This nationalism that was heralded by the general population would end up being different from the nationalism that would be espoused to divide much of the population. This form of nationalism would end up bringing all of the minority groups closer to the true nation while, at the same time, being able to strengthen the true nation in the prospect of the acquisition of the lost land that would later fall into the hands of the bulwarks of reaction. This would form a new nationalism which would be part of the true doctrine, wherein the nationalism would end up crushing any dissenting factions, including the former integral nationalists there were. This would mean that the previous movement would be once again crushed by practicing the principle of making the vanguard of the revolution much closer to the general population. This healthy organism was cleansed of all the foul deeds that would be done against the force of the revolution. The revolution had only begun, even after the civil war started, and the lines hardened. The shift of focus from the force of reaction would be largely a result of no true identity of the reactionaries.

The shift of focus would be made evident with the new embrace of nationalism by Long. This form of national liberation and socialist patriotism would form the basis of the party. The party of Long had largely seen these principles as intrinsically linked to one another. This would end up taking anti-imperialist overtones, with the anti-imperialism being leveraged in the name of socialist patriotism, particularly by other countries' elites exploiting the resources of the nation. Long would use this to gather support from the Rust Belt loyalists. This form of patriotism would be an anti-imperialist form of patriotism, with national liberation being the other key to the puzzle that would make up social nationalism and dissolve much of the integral nationalist faction. This necessarily meant a return to the old method sought. This was further combined with the practical abolition of any reactionary positions.

Regarding the core, since integral nationalism was based on positivism, it reached the same conclusions. This would end up causing much of Long's party to fuse, with the left-wing nationalists being brought into the party with no real effort. This would allow for more support in the Rust Belt, the heart of Antonin's armed struggle. This was combined with a strong anti-imperialist rhetoric which would predominate all of the other sessions there would be regarding a further advancement of the anti-imperialist struggle. The anti-imperialist struggle would overthrow any nationalist power organizations, with nationalism largely being swept away by a new form that would transcend nationalism in the end. For Long, it was a necessary step in truly securing his constituents' rights. Long's militias were born as a partisan, fought bravely, and died as a partisan. The partisans fought for true liberation, fighting hard against the oppressors who were going against the partisans in all directions. The partisans fought for true freedom in all forms with transcendent nationalism. This would mean that the partisan struggle would be for the general population. This was much more prevalent in the South, with any sympathizers of Antonin being eliminated once they made a move.

One morning, the generals of the federal military received a phone call about a rebellion. This was largely dismissed until General Fiore knocked on the door and assassinated the head of the army. This was combined with storming the rest of the building with all of the federal government's workers being put under lockdown. A swift advance was made, "take their communications and hold the supreme commander by the head," Fiore said. One of his soldiers followed this who got the interim president to surrender his little power. The rest of the country had fallen, with much of the country now under Antonin's control. The next day, Antonin woke up with a gun towards his head. This was further combined with fighting between the militias of his as well as the defectors within his army. A mutiny by the sailors and a seizure of power by General Fiore would further connect this. Fiore had become the country's de facto leader, with much of the country spiraling out of control. Fiore was a puppet to his donors, which would make up the military-industrial complex.

The ousting of Antonin broke apart much of the old league, with five new factions forming. Soon enough, the supporters of Antonin in the South would ally with the supporters of Antonin near the capital, able to seize much of Longist territory quickly. Long had no real authority to react; he was now going against all fronts. The partisans were his only last hope, for they would be concentrated throughout the country, though mainly in the Rust Belt. The Black Hand would end up sabotaging much of the federal effort, with General Fiore having to deal with it all the time.

Antonin brushed up and found himself outside of his party. The "loyalty" within his party had been gone, largely being transferred to the deep state. This would end up causing the intensification of the already existing divisions within the movement. It was no longer Antonin's party, for it had completely collapsed on himself. Antonin, once the most prominent figure in reaction, had been thrown completely in the dust. His opportunism would end up causing his career, for all his efforts had gone to the dust. There was no job he could resort to; he had nothing but himself. He was suddenly destitute, with no one recognizing him but a failed leader. The coup would end up causing his militias to fight in the streets with the martial wing that was left. This would end up causing an intensification of the struggle between the army and the militias. These militias were now loyal to the new head of the militias and the previously de facto head of them, Flagenfurt. This would end up causing another split within the civil war, which had already tangled itself. Suddenly, day by day, Long's base was becoming the Black Hand that was present in the North. Some former Confederacy would start flipping towards the militias, who promised another way. The Black Hand and the legions of the minorities that had still remained, ever loyal to their cause, and looking after their families,would end up fighting them in the South, though the former Southern support was starting to fade away except for the states west of the Mississippi River and Mississippi. These states were firmly under control, with Mississippi being part of the new machine that could dominate certain Southern states. These regions were largely fighting for the same cause of liberation, with these states being strongholds of proletarian identity over all else. The class consciousness of these regions would end up being stronger than the rest of the South, which would end up causing the rest of the South to fall apart. The strongholds would be used as a base against the federal government and well's militias of Klagenfurt. This was further combined with an incursion against the Christian revolt of Texas and the surrounding states. The revolution effectively moved North, with Antonin's last hope largely flipping toward Long. This would end up causing multiple civil wars, with the federal government, Flagenfurt's militias, the Christian (distributism) revolt, and the revolution all fighting against each other. The revolts would end up fighting against each other, with Flagenfurt's militias in the South being only as strong as how much the population was willing to support them. The alliance of the Longist regionals and the foreign volunteers would effectively fight against all of the enemies within the region – against the new commonwealth and the militias. The federal government would move into much of Flagenfurt's controlled land, but almost all of them would be quickly refuted, sending their militias back to square one. This repulsion would continue with the rest of Long's militias, seeking the eventual deception and repulsion of the reactionary forces advancing upon the last remaining bed of the revolution. The stances taken were all based on rationality, with the commonwealth and the militias being nearly the same except for how far the corporatist system would go and how far the socially reactionary positions would go. Since they were all part of the same alliance of faux populism, they would collaborate at times to drive back the revolution in the South. The stronghold of the South for Long was no longer his stronghold. Much of the revolution had shifted North, with the Rust Belt being incentivized to produce more. Ironically, this civil war ameliorated much of the unemployment that would pervade the South. The Rust Belt had a large expansion in industry, with much of the industry being built on what resources were left on the land. Agricultural production was ramped up, and cultural institutions were reinvigorated. This plan would end up causing an economic boom during the war, making the region ludicrous and more susceptible to attacks, for it wasn't defended. This strategy would end up having a protracted war, with the militias of Klagenfurt advancing towards the now-reinvigorated Steel Belt, only to be turned back. This constant struggle would be further amplified by the aggravation of the revolution, which would demand all the resources there. New England, which the Canadian government seized, helped further nationalist sentiments. Their anti-imperialism was combined with a whole slew of anti-discriminatory laws, which would make any of the minorities much closer to the national identity. This was rectified with the indigenous populations being granted self-determination, creating a true nationalist nation. This would end up causing much of the revolution to advance, with the reactionary position on race being firmly defeated while the national liberation of all remaining nations being put into practice. This would end up causing a revival in the nationalist spirit, just with another dimension. The indigenous were also embraced by Flagenfurt's militias, though for completely different reasons. His militias found an alliance between them similar to one made during the First Civil War. This contrasts with Long, who believed it would help the final revolution. The exodus of immigrant populations would end up causing a large wave towards Latin America, with much of their population declaring themselves completely neutral. The exodus would end up replacing the previous lost generation, which had never grown due to globalization and decreasing fertility. This replacement would reinvigorate the economies of Latin America but at the cost of a large demographic shift back home. Antonin witnessed all of this, for which he had started but had nothing to gain from. His vision of the party died as he was expelled from his party. The demographic shifts would end up causing large shifts in the Civil War itself. Certain sections of the minorities would end up allying themselves with either the commonwealth or with Flagenfurt. Flagenfurt's militias were nothing more than a charade, aiming to establish a democracy based on reactionary nationalism. It would be largely backed by the military-industrial complex, with the fighting intensifying around the stronghold of the revolution. The difference was one between complete reactionaries, small industrialists as well as the revolution; the difference couldn't be reconciled through any means. This revolution would end up having to bypass and garner support from much of the South and the Commonwealth. The support could be easily done through policy, for it was the collective sum. The only problem was that each side indoctrinated the country during the Civil War. The four-way civil war was a charade and a scheme to weaken the revolution. It was something that hadn't been seen before. In other cases, proletarian forces would end up coalescing under one banner, but in this case, certain sections of the proletariat didn't support the revolution, instead supporting the commonwealth or the militias. This large variation would end up causing much of the revolution's support to be gutted, with the fighting becoming longer and costing more American lives above all. The botched civil war was largely a result of miscalculations. The miscalculations would end up causing the civil war to end up extending further. The civil war never seemed to end, with intervention from the neighbors down North and South growing more likely by the day. A steady stream of refugees, largely from the previous immigrants, swarmed Mexico's previously sparse rural land. This would end up causing a surge in the overall nationalist sentiment within the nation, which some parties would capitalize on over others. Generally, the use of nationalism in the form of anti-imperialism and national liberation was largely stressed by Long, with other factions seeing nationalism as a tool to divide rather than unite. It would end up meaning the eventual integration of the minorities loyal to the nation while many immigrants would flee. The natives would end up siding with Long though they would sometimes side with the commonwealth and the militias of Klagenfurt over promises to extend their boundaries. The immigrants were largely fleeing due to the desperate conditions of civil war. This would end up causing an effective demographic shift wherein much of the population was suddenly predominated by the majority racial group while the next was back to where it was. This would end up effectively creating a nation of three peoples, not of three nations. This nation would end up being prioritized overall. This nation would end up causing a complete reversal of the situation, with much of the resources of the South being once again depleted. A lack of manpower severely hampered the material effort of the South, for many immigrant families started to flee. This was further combined with a large migration of the second largest group towards the new belt, with the further depletion of any manpower that the South had. The commonwealth wasn't hit as hard by the latter, though it was hit especially hard by the former. The federal government had the crisis escalate out of control, with much of the population of the Southwest being completely depleted within a couple of months. This rapid demographic shift ended up causing many bankrupt landowners, who largely relied on cheap immigrant labor, which would lead to open land that could be harvested. The complete shift in the population's demographics would end up causing many of the recent high-skill immigrant laborers to turn away and head back home. This would effectively lead to a country of three peoples largely united in common objectives.

Liberia, the new land of the free, would start to be swarmed with migrants. These migrants came from the remainder of the South, effectively knocking down the demographics of this minority group to only about a twelfth of the population. All groups had promised them autonomy, though some wanted to curtail some of their rights.

This would end up causing multiple factions, with the neutral faction heading to Liberia winning out in the end. The Liberia plan would end up causing insane demographic shifts, with the only real minority population regarding the second largest group only remaining within the belt from which the rest of the civil war in the South was conducted. The lion of Liberia that truly was, because Liberia became the great sanctuary for all those that were oppressed, and in process, it was the will of the lord, who had given his torch to Liberia as that which would come in the end. Nowhere would this first be seen through the will that Sirach and Lazarus would soon bring onto this world. Sirach and Lazarus would become determined to put an end to chaos, at all costs, and it was amongst the last days that they would see all those would become resurrected, no longer in the form that they had brought as of right now, but in the form that they will ultimately find, maybe not even on this planet! It was of Lazarus and Sirach that the actions that would take place would all stem from united Africa first, and from united Africa they would see, they would give to the world all that they had. It was from united Africa, once upon a time, a dream, but now one, that is a reality. This was because most of the other sides had their ideas regarding running the system incorporated. Nationalism and the revisionist line would be refuted, with only certain parts winning. The defections that this would cause would ultimately lead to a new reconstruction. What only kept the South and the Commonwealth together was not their ideals but their character in the sense that they represented the side of no real change. The demographic change would further harden their stances, forming a potential alliance between the South and the federal government. This would end up causing further stratification of the already broken population; the war never seemed to end. Advance after advance, all that was there were dead compatriots – some weren't even old enough to serve under normal circumstances. This would end up causing a deep penetration of the front line into the rest of the Steel Belt to secure it. The Black Hand was completely dissolved, and the professionalization of the military of Long would take place. This would both reinvigorate the economy and create employment – though this would come at a steep cost. The cost would be in the form of inflation, which, while being lower than the other factions in the civil war, was still something undeniable.

The revolution only seemed to get stronger; there were talks of a complete alliance between the federal government, the South, and the Commonwealth. "Maybe we should put aside our minimal differences and fight our true enemy," General Fiore said. "Of course, it would end up meaning that the possibility of a victory by Long would be averted," General Flagenfurt said. Baptist John Parlor said, "I will if there is a compromise." General Fiore responded with, "What kind of compromise?" John said, "A compromise that will include some form of corporatism while minimizing the rhetoric of certain parts of nationalism would do fine." This was met with unanimous approval, with the draft of all three sides going through. This would end up causing all of these forces to coalesce under one banner, though with the looming threat of a general strike. The federal government was democratized to a certain extent, with Fiore and Flagenfurt agreeing to a new popular basis for a new representative system. All embraced The corporatist approach, with the nationalist rhetoric being shifted so that some of it would remain in good shape. The nationalist rhetoric would end up causing a complete reversal in the direction that the wind blew, with the system being completely redone. The compromise would effectively cause a new era with only two opposing sides. The opposition would be met with harsh punishments, leading to an effective partisan movement underground regarding the Second American Republic—a new contradiction formed between the two sides. A Peoples's America rose, and the Second American Republic rose. These two sides would end up clashing at the border for the whole time, looking to break the stalemate. However, one threat was imminent – Long's belt could fall in any second by now.

Who is Antonin? Antonin would practically be removed from any position he had. He was completely unrecognizable, largely falling into the addiction to drugs. The Second American Republic would partially carry on his legacy in his view, but it didn't go far enough. The Second American Republic would end up betraying his interests– for they have already betrayed. The power was no longer concentrated within Antonin, for he was a complete alien. The only people that had previously known him only existed within the old guard – whom he had purged. This would end up causing any companions to be nonexistent in reality and only in his dreams. He would go to sleep and never wake up again.

The Second American Republic started to rapidly enact policies that would practically make it so that a corporatist system would be established. This would allow capital to flow in, for the civil war was much more stable now. The foreign capital would help rebuild the South in total and the Southern Plains. California would be attractive to foreign capital, despite its population hitting the rock. The demographic shifts would end up meaning nothing to the investors, for their main goal was to avert a victory in which the revolution would win. The purge earlier had found no meaning, with large amounts of foreign capital being quickly put into the country. This would end up causing the partisan movement to gain in strength promptly. The professionalization of the partisans would end up causing a permanent struggle that would not easily be rectified. The civil war would rage on, with the slow advance of the partisans being the main method that they would quickly encircle the cities and get them to surrender using the countryside. The countryside was their primary weapon, while their opponents didn't. The country would end up allowing for a true revolution, with the countryside being a source wherein manpower could be quickly reserved with the grain being harvested. This would allow for grain production with the rescue of all of the casualties that have not yet perished. It is better to rescue all of the losses than to end up leaving them on the ground, where the enemy would kill and torture them. This would end up causing many field hospitals to quickly sprout up, with the countryside being a great tool for the revolution. The country was practically impenetrable by any real force, with the countryside standing like grit. The countryside was a wall that couldn't be jumped over, with the countryside's fighting largely leading to many victories for the partisans. The partisans would achieve many wins because of their hiding place. Their hiding place was of extreme benefit, for it allowed for solidifying the defense of the revolutionary state. The revolutionary state would end up seeing the proper implementation of popular policies. Implementing these policies would end up overseeing the transformation of the economy into one completely controlled by the general population. A rebirth in the idea of the nation would end up coming with the partisan movement fighting for the true nation.

Antonin railed against foreign capital in the past, only to see that institution emerge into power. This contradiction would see the complete reformation of the system with much of the foreign money causing the nation to be a slave to other imperialist countries. This imperialism would cause the intensification of the exploitation of resources of the government. All of the resources, including those in raw manpower, would be depleted. This would be evident when the Second American Republic ended up having much of the population of minorities fleeing as a result of the worsening conditions. It was hard to get by within the new republic, which was rocky. The democracy only turned out to be a sham, with the military largely taking power. The only real force of democracy there came in the form of Flagenfurt's faction and the commonwealth faction. These two factions would end up having their leaders eventually replaced, with the democratic system of corporatism being used with compromises being drawn. These compromises would eventually cause all of the parties in Congress to abolish themselves, similar to the parties within the revolutionary republic. The new revolution would cause the parties to practically vanish, with the only group remaining as an effective direct political force being the vanguard. The vanguard of the revolution and the vanguard of the counter-revolution both shared common aspects, which would end up causing the forefront to lean towards one side over the other. The vanguard of the new revolution was nothing more than a force that would bind the process together. The vanguard of the counter-revolution was much weaker, with the many corporate groups fighting against each other. Effectively, two groups had formed, with each group not having much opposition on paper, though when it came to practice, corporatism was on a completely different road than the popular economy.

Corporatism would end up maximizing the profit of the industrialists, who were the primary backers of this new system. The industrialists would provide everything that the counter-revolution would need to succeed. The grain shipments were effectively hoarded by the aristocrats, who allied with the industrialists. The major reversal of many original reforms proposed would further combine this. This would end up causing one party to represent the industrialists and the aristocrats while the other party to represent popular sovereignty. These parties were irreconcilable, which would lead to the outbreak of the civil war itself. These differences would cause much of the antagonism between the parties and the civil war participants.

The new line that Long would adapt would crush any of the dissenters. It would be the only force of rationality for the proletariat. The other troops would be firmly integrated through any method within the system. The new line could crush any additional power that would stand in the way. This would mean that the line of nationalism and other lumpen-proletariat distractions would be eliminated. This would end up causing a complete turn in the new revolution. The new revolution would allow for a true line to be adapted. The true line can combine the forces of national liberation and true liberation. This would build on the old idea, with nationalism aiding the proletarian struggle rather than being one of national chauvinism. National chauvinism would be completely displaced, with a true proletarian revolution. National chauvinism would be crushed through any means possible, with national chauvinism linking up to collaboration. This collaboration would end up destroying the common movement which Long killed. National chauvinism would end up abolishing itself by abolishing the old line. The new idea of emancipation was coming through the complete liberation of all forces. This would be combined with the abolition of false freedom, similar to liberalism and nationalism. This would end up causing a complete revolution which would end up causing a permanent change within the vanguard. The vanguard of the revolution would end up upholding the new line. Any revisionist struggles would end up being thrown out. The supremacy of Marxism-Vanguardism would end up abolishing all of the faux positions within the party. The party line and discipline would end up being greatly strengthened. This strengthening would end up causing Long to solidify his movement completely. The campaign would become stronger than before and stronger than the Second American Republic. The new revolution would carry on the legacy of the first revolution. The revolution was merely a continuation, with each constituent part working for the whole. This revolution would transcend the divisions within the proletariat and achieve true freedom. Marxism-Vanguardism would guide the whole party to victory, with all regional sections secured. The party needed expansion, meaning the regional divisions would be expanded. This could raise funding, with the partisans becoming stronger as a result. The disunity that plagued prior would end up being erased. The force of faux liberation of the Second American Republic would end up faltering when it came to the final moments of the revolution. The troops would collapse on themselves, with each constituent completely altering at their base. The components of the base would end up causing shifts within the superstructure. This would ultimately cause Long's party to shift towards where the people would go.

Marxism-Vanguardism was the core principle behind the party in total. Marxism-Vanguardism would be the science that would be upheld, with all of the party's organization being based around Marxism-Vanguardism. Marxism-Vanguardism would be the strongest force within the party, with all other forces being completely discarded. Marxism-Vanguardism was part of continuing the theory that would coalesce under the populist banner. Marxism-Vanguardism would be the line that would be upheld, with all other revisionist lines being completely discarded. Maoism would be denounced for the reason that it would end up leading to collaboration with the reactionary parts of the masses as well as what the party would vow to fight against. Maoism would further have the problem of departing from the original vanguardist conception. These forces would end up completely discarding Maoism, with the theory running against Maoism in the sum. This would further strengthen the Marxist-Leninist line, further expounded through new knowledge.

The party would see the transfiguration of Marxism-Vanguardism as a formidable force. It would advocate for carrying out the revolution permanently while strengthening the connections with the masses. The rewrite of the original Leninist and Marxist theory would be similar to reordering the equation. Long would use this to his benefit against the Second American Republic. The Second American Republic would reform into a corporatist system, with certain sections of the masses being appealed to through the land redistribution program, which was now possible due to many farmers fleeing and causing the landlords to go bankrupt. The bankruptcy of these farms would end up causing those farms to be seized by the republic. This land would be redistributed to loyalists, which would be able to secure that land as well as repopulate the rural countryside. While depleted of a large population, the cities would still benefit from the much-needed capital flow. The international capital would benefit the large owners of capital within those depleted cities. This would cause a large population to shift, wherein the population of the South would start to go out west. This would shift the mentality of the region, with more people identifying with the South rather than the nation as a whole. This would cause a complete redistribution of the population which would be used to the advantage of the Second American Republic. The corporatist agenda would be enacted with the many corporations forming that is made of the combination of workers and owners. These corporations would work for the common good rather than working for the benefit of themselves. This would be done with a focus on destroying materialism. This new spin would cause corporatism to take up a new face. The national identity would precede all other identities. All other identities would be identified as a distraction and materialist. The owners of the corporations could keep them as long they were patriotic. This would be further combined with ensuring that the workers would have a decent standard of living. The goal was to maximize profit for the exploiters while also satisfying the needs of the working class. This nature would end up allowing for increased support among religious groups and the reactionary masses. These two forces would push the party over the top and establish complete unity. The new system was de facto segregated. This segregation would end up carrying over into all spheres, which would cause the nation to be completely divided using race. This division wouldn't apply to the Steel Belt yet, though the advances towards the Steel Belt made that more likely by the day. The military-industrial complex would be completely restarted, with each component dignifying the situation. The military-industrial complex would have to be destroyed for true progress in the eyes of the revolution. The military-industrial complex could only be successfully destroyed through a general strike, though the problem was that much of the proletarian population of the South would start to move west. The new settlers gaining land would make them part of the petite-bourgeoisie. The new republic would redistribute this land to gain complete sufficiency. The corporatist system would be followed by national chauvinism as well as religious chauvinism. These two forces would cause the collision of all of the national forces of the right. These forces would end up taking precedence over any other force there would be, with any other struggle completely discarded. The de facto segregation would end up pervading much of the nation. The de facto segregation would cause a strain on the labor supply of the country. The country's labor supply could only be made up by forcing people to work. This could only work through surveillance and expanding the prison system to punish minor crimes. This would end up causing an abundance of cheap labor, generally from minority populations. The minority populations would be used as cheap labor to win the war. This would lead to a surge of minority support for the revolution, which would start to organize a slave revolt. The true revolution was always near, with all of the workers united. The racial system would be completely abolished with the end of the power of the elites. This is what Long would strive for. Antonin, on the other hand, had become a drug addict. The police of the Second American Republic would at any time capture him. This would end up meaning going to the prison system. This would mean the end of his life, with those in the prison system starved to death while constantly working off. They were completely expendable, being ready one by one to be completely starved to death while being worked off. Their labor was completely expendable, with the profits going to the military-industrial complex. Every one of the laborers would see their fate at the gate of heaven, only to remember that their oppressors have not died yet. The revolution was their only hope for liberation, with their families being torn apart. Nothing was normal about this new system, yet it seemed to be the natural order to many elites. The corporatist system would be extended into the political sphere, with segregation being adopted regarding social policies. Corporatism was both political and economic, largely going over the same problems. Ultimately, the industrialists and the landowners would win out every time against everyone else that was a representative. The industrialists could greatly expand their power to provide more funds for the complex. The complete rearmament would cause more deaths and overexploitation, whose surplus would get to the elite. This new rearmament would allow for the bloody civil war to rage on. It would be behind the shadows and in front of the trees. It would be unknown yet being noticed all the time. The civil war would escalate between the revolution and the counter-revolution. The important turn would come in the intensification of the revolution, with the remaining revisionists being kicked out. The remaining revisionists would consist of the gradualist social democrats, who were just puppets of the elites. The social democrats would end up being completely kicked out of the coalition, with their social fascism completely discarded. Social fascism was nearly identical to true fascism, with corporatism being a large element that would be shared. This would be combined with social policies regarding national chauvinism that would be nearly the same. The bones of the working class of the Second American Republic would end up sticking out. The only people that benefited from it were the industrialists and the landlords. These two forces were the primary group that would fund the new republic. This is most of where the support came from; all forces were united together in the destruction of the revolution. For them, the nation was, above all, transcending all other identities. A primary class perspective would be ignored, with the class being completely tossed out as being anti-nationalist. For them, class consciousness would be the worst thing that could happen. Class consciousness would mean the end of their power in all terms possible. Their power was based on weak class consciousness, which would be able to push against the revolutionary forces. The revolutionary forces drew their support from the class-conscious proletariat. If they increased in number, what would end up happening is that the revolution would only get stronger. The founders of the counter-revolution were completely opposed to such a dangerous suggestion, which would mean that they wouldn't be in power anymore.

The Marxist-Leninist vanguard of Long would end up causing the decline in the revisionists. The permanent revolution would be thrown away, while at the same time, the idea of collaboration would be thrown out. This would be further combined with the destruction of all other positions. This would effectively mean that the liberals and the nationalists would be merged and the different places completely broken. This would end up causing only one part, created by Marxism-Vanguardism. The idea of socialism in one country would be adopted with a unitary government while the individual nations inside have their cultures brought closer to the nation as a whole. The individual nations would be quickly dissolved as they would be brought closer to the primary government. Socialism in one country would mean that all arms would be used in the revolution instead of being deflected off. The Second American Republic would follow the idea of corporatism and a stance that would remain the same regarding social policy. Their social policy would be excessively reactionary, with the force of reaction being an integral part of the counter-revolution. Their social policy would be one of national chauvinism, with their corporatist policy aiding this unity that would end up transcending all other forms of agreement. This would displace class consciousness, in large contrast to Marxism-Vanguardism. The Marxist-Leninist line would end up causing new scientific socialism to develop and take over the party.

There was nothing in the party but this scientific socialism, which had largely become synonymous with Marxism-Vanguardism. This theory would use the material conditions, aiming to adapt the systems to where they were brought forth. This line would end up displacing any other cord that would be there in the past. The revolutionary force would cause a large shake of the base, with the superstructure largely following when it came to the changes that would be made. The base and the superstructure would directly change with each other, which is where the positions of Long came from.

Chapter Four:
Many Bills

Many bills would be passed during the party's time in office. The Longists and the Second American Republic would see transformations in their society. The Second American Republic would bar any revolutionaries from being in Congress, and the Longists would do the same in the opposite direction. The counter-revolution would pass bills to reform towards a corporatist system. The Longists would improve towards a syndicalist system, with the workers owning the means of production through institutions backed and built by the workers. The workers and the consumers are the same units and serve themselves. This is further combined with the end of the national bourgeoisie and the end of the flow of international capital, which would mean that the proletariat's power would be completely secured. The bills would all come in a row, passed one after another. They would all complement each other, being able to raise and support the military that was being raised as well.

When it was discovered that there was corruption within the revolutionary navy, measures were taken to root it out and reform how the production process was being done. This would streamline production, which would increase production as well as completely root out any corruption. This restoration of faith back into the Navy would allow for better equipment that not even the military-industrial complex could produce. This benefit would translate over to other fields of the military. The military-industrial complex would be outmatched by the enormous production capacity that the revolutionary army would bring. This was further combined with a large increase in morale, with the powerful military being dedicated to the revolution as well as the defense of the motherland. These concepts combined would put scientific socialism at the helm of the new system. The scientific socialist system would raise the partisans needed to fight for the motherland. The reinvigoration of the Steel Belt would cause a large migration wave from the Smoldering Belt, which would cause the country's demographics to shift once again.

The previous migration out of the Smoldering Belt would knock down the population of their hated to a mere four percent, a threefold decrease in percentage compared to before the civil war. The four percent would largely be split among the Smoldering Belt as well as the Steel Belt. The complete integration of this key minority group would end up causing the identification as a separate nation to fade quickly over time. This fade would leave a permanent mark, with the American national identity shifting again. All but the Black and Steel Belt would see their populations emigrate en masse. This would be accompanied by a large resettlement in Liberia, which would become the new home of the free. Liberia would once again assume the position of being another America that would consist of the previous federal government, which had largely recently died off. The resettlement of these demographics would completely shift the American demographics, with the new composition being 94, 4, and 1 for the three constituent peoples, respectively. This would mean that the minority population, besides these main ethnic groups, would drop beyond recognition. This would mean that the depopulation of the second-largest ethnic group would cause many old cultural bonds to loosen completely. The refugees in Liberia were becoming more permanent by the day, with only the deep, agricultural Smoldering Belt being part of the majority of regions where the diaspora would persist. This was further combined with the complete integration of the population in the North that was left. This reorganization would cause the Southern force to weaken as well as establish new ties elsewhere. The remainder would end up allying with whatever forces of Southern aristocrats there would be against the Second American Republic. This would cause a slightly stronger South at the expense of the prospects elsewhere.

This practical genocide would cause a complete restructuring of the nation's population. The nation would no longer remain polyculture, for it would start to be concentrated among a couple of key groups. By this point, the Hispanics had only made up a third of a percent of the population, being completely driven out during the civil war. This would be further accompanied by the rapid decline in the Asian population, which would start to see prospects back home. This combination would devastate much of the current order, for the ethnic group balance was tottering. The complete reversal of positions would cause a complete change in what would make up the nation, with each group contributing in its own way. The genocide couldn't be reversed, for the expulsions were permanent. Liberia had now developed a pan-nationalism that would remain throughout the years while the nationalism of the minority within the states would quickly decline, with most of the existing bonds being significantly weakened from every dimension. To be part of the pan-nationalist league, what would end up happening is that there would need to be a certification of refugee status. This third position would go against the two main positions of the counter-revolution and the revolution. The counter-revolution would work hard to implement the corporatist system.

The minimum wage would be increased, hours would be shortened, and conditions would be drastically improved. However, this improvement would only prove useful to a certain extent, as there would be a large push against modernization. The corporatist system could only be held up by increasing the profit the industrialists and the landlords would make. Doing so meant the rapid expansion of the military-industrial complex, for it was where most of the gain would remain. Everywhere else, the profit that would be made was much weaker. Only the military-industrial complex had enough to compensate for the system's deficits. The military-industrial complex would oversee the construction of agriculture as well as the construction of heavy industry. This rapid industrialization would only be temporary, for capital would run out soon, and the motive would return to seeking profit. This was merely a means to rejuvenate the former industry and increase profit in the short term. Now, it was needed to increase yield over a longer period. Of course, none of this could go on forever, but economic planning with the industrialists and aristocrats would be adopted. Agriculture was rapidly improved, albeit this would be at the cost of the consumers and the producers themselves. Agriculture was the basis of the new economy, representing the nation's core. The cause of the new economy would be corporatism and the organic interaction between many groups. The nationalist stance would be compounded by intellectual expansion, wherein the funding for these groups would rapidly explode. The complete change in how the budget would be acquired would end up causing the corporatist system to strengthen itself.

The corporatist system would see heavy industry construction as a means to improve the light industry later. The goal was to bring in as much profit for the industrialists as possible. The industrialists' eventual replacement of the aristocrats would be instrumental in bringing back the new agrarian-industrial system. The aristocracy would be toppled from any real power it had. The concessions were given as a bid to increase productivity overall. The increase in sales and profit would further compound the increase in productivity. This was monopoly capitalism at its finest. A form of central planning had been introduced to bring in as much profit as possible. This centrally planned system would see no competition; instead, there was cooperation between the country's major forces.

The revolutionary wave would end up sweeping much of the nation's proletariat. The intellectual rebirth of the counter-revolutionary system would see a national identity forming due to a hamstrung national myth. This hamstrung national myth would transcend all other myths, taking primary over everything else. The national myth would directly coincide with the benefit of the industrialists, for their goal was to avoid the discussion of class struggle. This method would seem to work with increasingly concentrated capital among the financiers. The financiers and the industrialists would be merged, all part of the new product class. This was even though the industrialists would only carry the capital and do nothing else. The financiers and the industrialists would ally together to overthrow any government. The order would be completely corporatist with these corporate structures at the new society's helm. The corporate structures would form a complete system wherein all forces within the society are organized from the top down. The corporatist system would be built as a centrally planned system while also being decentralized and representing the will of these guilds. These guilds would be comprised of the industrialists as well as their employees. This structure would run into many problems as it would not represent the interests of the workers. This would lead to nationalism in the end, with the national unity from this system being prioritized. The prioritization of the new wave would end up meaning that the Longists would ultimately win a complete victory over the Reactionaries. The national cornerstone would be largely altered, with pride surpassing all other forms of identity. This national pride would be further synthesized with other forms of adherence to the social conservative orthodoxy. These forces combined would coalesce under a single banner.

All of these forces would represent the imperialist, fascist, and corporatist systems that the reactionaries would uphold. This system would line up with the popular opinion of the reactionary backers. The imperialist system and the corporatist system were both intertwined with each other. The corporatist system and the imperial standard were both parts of the same goal of being able to expound how much profit would be made. De jure liberties were curtailed, with the only part remaining consisting of nationalism. The imperialist system was the highest stage of the capitalist system, which the party would constantly uphold.

Corporatism represented class collaboration, for it went from an idealist angle. All forces are believed to be inherently productive; thus, they would all exist for a purpose. This would be against the scientific socialist line that would be practiced elsewhere. The Marxist and Leninist line would end up creating the scientific socialist line that would be made. The other lines of liberalism and nationalism would be discarded due to not finding any real justification outside of metaphysics. The Marxist and Vanguardist lines would be held up, with their lines being integral to the understanding of complete liberation in the framework of scientific socialism. Scientific socialism would be placed above all; the revisionist lines would be completely abandoned, for it would be part of irrational logic. The scientific socialist line would find a true reason, which would be vested in the party of Long. The scientific socialist line represented a true scientific analysis of the current situation, for it would be intertwined with the material conditions present.

The true conditions present would replace all of the manifestations of the previous mode of production, including all of the theories of false liberation. This new line based on a scientific analysis would predominate in the party of Long. Long's primary goal was to oversee a complete reorganization with hard reasons to do so. Long's goal of finding a new path would be instrumental to the vanguard. The vanguard would use all the rational reasons to deduce a new plan. This plan would be used in the revolution to crush the counter-revolution.

The revolution was in full swing. It was full of life, and its blood would flow throughout the body. The revolution would establish a new system that would work for most of the population. The new system would have its respiratory system, with all parts being organic to survive. This would be followed by the extension of the line into practical use. It wasn't sufficient to think of progress towards a utopia; rather, it was instrumental that the process could be fulfilled. This is where the situation would come from, with work towards complete internationalism after the reconstruction would work in one nation. This revolution would end at the dawn of the new golden age. The nation's rebuilding would end up causing a new revolution that could transform the nation with the end goal of internationalism. It would be one part of the restructured system. The practical experience brought by one would end up being combined with the hardline theory that would be carried on to the end. The practical experience and hardline theory would be combined with the end goal of completely transforming the system. The hardline theory would be at the core of the scientific analysis, while the practical experience would be instrumental in developing all other positions. The corporatist and fascist system of the Second American Republic would be part of the imperialist stage that the system goes through. This stage would be simply an evolved form from the previous stages that would be part of the same mode of production. It would be part of the end ditch that would be no different from the buried corpse. The Second American Republic would continue the following series of theories which would develop out of the material conditions previously. The liberal and nationalist mix would be part of false liberation against the scientific socialist system, supporting true liberation in all forms. True freedom would be both on an individual and a collective level. The mix would be completely different from any other mix that would form. The line would have liberation in all forms; it would be able to bring forth the new society completely.

The liberation would be part of the eventual plan to root out any other form of reaction completely. The liberation would cause the only vanguard in those regions to consolidate themselves. The Second American Republic would mirror the People's America in this case. They would remain united through the congruent force of the vanguard. The vanguard of the new Republic would be part of the system that would uphold the interests of the elite. The interests of the elite would be masked in a system that would be supposedly for everyone. The interests of the nobility would follow the same vision as the elites before though they had refined how to hold onto their power. This meant that many concessions were given, participation would be de jure increased, and a false consciousness would develop over other forms of consciousness. These would be all the conditions the elites would use to suppress the oppressed peoples. They would use the mask of participation in both the political and the economic processes while developing a system that would end up allowing for false consciousness. False consciousness was at the heart of the villain that would end up creating within. The false consciousness would be combined with concessions that would be given. These two forces would end up diverting all of the true consciousness that could develop. By being able to create a boogeyman as well as being able to give concessions under the name of solidarity, what would end up occurring is that the false consciousness would end up reigning throughout the counter-revolution. The myth of American Exceptionalism and the economic concessions that would be given would end up solidly defining the reactionary positions. The goal was to break false consciousness as well as to be able to disregard any privileges. The concessions are no longer given; they are united into a single movement.

Suddenly, as the nation's status once again started being revived, what ended up happening was that many foreigners that would end up immigrating to Liberia would come back, albeit in significantly smaller numbers comparatively. This would increase the number of foreigners as a percentage to 8% but that would be of theirs. This would end up causing more loyalists to the revolution, which was starting to trap the counter-revolution quickly. Texas would fall with revolutionary militias overrunning the loyalist militias. What ended up happening, as a result, was that the revolutionary militias quickly trapped the counter-revolutionary militias. The Longist militias followed the transition towards the next mode of production by fighting off all fascist forces. The Longist militias could quickly move around, with the state of Massachusetts being completely encircled. This would prompt a reaction by the counter-revolution soon running out of support. The counter-revolution only really had support from certain sections of society. Outside of the industrialists, the support for the counter-revolution was largely muted. The support for the counter-revolution only went as far as the industrialists had willed it. They could move out at any time, for the movement was only based on the military-industrial complex. Large amounts of divisions of volunteers from former army recruits would end up being raised throughout the revolutionary land. This would largely benefit the counter-revolution, though some of the militias that would be raised were revolutionary. This revolution and counter-revolution process was largely followed by the scientific socialist side implementing policies for the masses.

In contrast, the counter-revolution would end up with favorable policies though in many cases, what would end up occurring is that the counter-revolution would end up running out of support. Massachusetts would end up following, while the other states of New England were starting to crumble from within. The foreign fighter population would increase drastically within the South due to the repatriation of refugees. This would bolster the revolutionary war effort, for the new impoverished that would develop in the South had started to see the revolution more favorably than their counterparts who were largely able to run as the aristocracy of labor, wherein concessions were made as well as false consciousness would be instilled. This would end up causing the revolution to swarm further with support. The revolution had just started and still had many ways to go. The idea of regional identity was beginning to fade, causing a larger identification with the label "American" rather than individual states. This would end up facilitating a large-scale immigration wave toward the Smoldering Belt. This would not only consist of foreigners but many of the underclass as well. This would end up causing the further integration of all peoples in society, with all minority groups no longer being called out as minorities but under the common label of American. This would end up soldering racial cohesion, quickly dismantling adversity. The American nation would end up quickly being reconstructed, with its cultural institutions rapidly strengthened. The strengthened nation would end up allowing for more cultural development. Cultural development was at the core of the nation's identity, for it constituted all the major integral parts of the cultural identity. The national identity was at the party's soul, and nothing more would end up eclipsing it.

Chapter Five:
The Rise and Fall of Antonin

"We need to bring the stock market back on its heels," said one congressman. "There is no point in trying to bail out a failed system," a congresswoman said. "But our donors need the bailout," the congressman replied. The congresswoman, frustrated, responded with, "So what?" "To hell with our donors," she said. "Have you forgotten the whole purpose of our counter-revolution? Its whole expressed goal is deeply ingrained into our values. Maybe you should study them," he replied. "We need to support democracy in true terms," she replied. "Of course, democracy in true terms can only be achieved through a program of corporatism," he replied. The implication of this would mean the descent of the counter-revolution into a true counter-revolutionary force with no real support for the counter-revolution. The counter-revolution was a bunch of bones, some of which would support a strong leader, while others would support a weak leader. Above all, the main thing that united them was the fear of the revolution. This would end up causing a large drift toward the industrialists. The industrialists would end up being heralded as the nation's core. The industrialists are those that brought the country prosperity in all terms. Even if they conducted imperialism, so be it if imperialism helps the nation. Imperialism would be a force that would improve the standard of living for the domestic proletariat, which is why it would be essentially preferred. The domestic proletariat's standard of living would be determined by how much imperialism would end up being conducted elsewhere. A true improvement of the standards of the proletariat would not end up occurring; instead, what would end up occurring is that the labor aristocracy would end up forming as a result of some manipulation. This manipulation would end up causing the standard of living to change completely. The standard of living would increase within the true nation due to the imperialist policies, most of which would end up being amplified. Imperialism would reduce the standard of living of some countries while increasing the standard of living of other countries. Such was an example of uneven development. Uneven development would mean that some places would be far more developed than other places. Uneven development would end up being linked to the imperialist standard that would be raised. Imperialism was at the nation's helm, for it brought prosperity – to the detriment of other countries. In the end, the nation itself would end up suffering as the domestic exploitation would start to increase due to increased global competition. This would end up can affect in which many dominoes would end up falling on top of each other. These dominoes were only the beginning of the process – they would start to build up with increasing force. This force would ultimately lead to the nation's collapse in all possible terms.

On all terms, what would end up occurring is that most of the forces would end up cascading. The new position that would be taken would be the scientific socialist position, which would completely entrench itself. This would be fighting against the fascist forces that would pervade the whole nation and the counter-revolution. The counter-revolution was nothing more than the charade of the ruling elite. The ruling elite would hold onto their power through the fascist counter-revolution. Imperialism would be supported while concessions would be given. Most of all, a false consciousness would end up developing. It was not a rigid ideology, though it was based on the method of holding on to class power. This ideology that would form would end up resembling the echoes of fascism above all. The rigid ideology of scientific socialism would completely differ from scientific capitalism, which would be fascism. They would be completely antithetical, largely being present with the outbreak of the civil war. This form of fascism would follow the same line, where the aggravation of any existing phenomena would be undertaken. The base and the superstructure would end up leading the way for fascism to end up taking root.

The base and the superstructure are all part of the same league. The base and the superstructure all end up reinforcing each other. They are all part of the same part of the dialectical method. The base and the superstructure are all part of the same part of the cycle. The rational approach would be intrinsically linked to the process in which the advance would cause the dialectical materialist method to oversee the surpassed material conditions. These material conditions would come in the form of the current phenomena.

The scientific socialist method would be heralded as the strongest method out of all – one that would end up defeating idealism and seeking the truth outside of natural philosophy. Long would concentrate this to free the peoples of the counter-revolution. The counter-revolution relied on subjugation, both foreign and domestic. The counter-revolution was the worst enemy of the revolution. The counter-revolution was all but a revolution in suppressing the working class's rights. The rights of the working class were those that would free the working class.

The only way a person can be free and have their character developed is by ending the process of alienation and the process of shortages. Their goal would be to pursue their interests, which is where complete emancipation and proclamation would come from. The national identity encapsulated in the nation would be a prime example of collective emancipation, while individual emancipation would come from liberal rights and rights that are made real regarding the material circumstances. This true liberation would define the scientific socialist model as abolishing the current state of things. This would end up propelling the struggle for scientific socialism to the forefront. The new man's idea of the fascists would be easily surpassed by a true society where work can eventually be broken down due to the development of super efficiency. All these struggles would collectively culminate in the liberation of all prevailing forces. It was all of these present forces that would be transformed – it was the current force that would be absolute and indefinite in the end. The current forces would end up being overruled. This was the cornerstone of the ideology of the scientific socialists. The scientific socialists wanted to see the abolition of all current phenomena that would lead to no true free people. The only way there could be free people would be through true free expression. This true free expression would end up being interwoven. Thus, the true way forward would be through the acceleration of everything in which the eventual utopia could be achieved. The only goal of politics was to instill a society in which everyone would be happy. This was linked to philosophy and economics, for their goal was to satisfy the population and find explanations. The main goal was to seek reason over everything else, and this is what scientific socialism provided them. It was a framework to analyze all of history, for it would dictate that the next mode of production would include all of the ideas of the previous modes of production. It would mean there is true freedom in every sense of the word. The polemics of the past would be upheld and expounded upon. The only truly free person is one without any obligation. The obligation is when the person receives less than what they put in. This free person can resist any forces that seek to take away his golden freedom. He has space in all spheres, economic, political, or social. Nationalism is integral to this as it promotes the healthy development of national culture. It is part of proletarian nationalism, not bourgeois nationalism, that this culture can be developed. This common nationalism comes in the form of the national right to self-determination, which soon connects to the system of liberating nations as a means to be able to quell imperialism. These policies combined would make up the party of Long. They were the party of the free and the party that would defend these liberties. These liberties would be cherished, for they all brought in the merits integral to the new system.

An overhaul of the cultural institutions would follow the establishment of the Longist Revolution. Soon, much of the language became Romanized, and the lexicon shifted. This would end up firmly breaking off from the standard English language, for it would become a complete dialect in its own right. This Romanization would cause a total shift in how the general population viewed the language. The literary talents would start to bloom at a much faster rate. The decadence of the previous society would begin to fade away in favor of a blossoming culture quickly. The decadence would destroy itself from within, following the vision of the new person while being able to bypass fascism. It had strived for true liberation in all forms. This would end up causing a complete revolution in how the current state of affairs would work. The national culture would end up blossoming as a result of this mix. The dialect would move closer to Latin, representing a break from the past. This break couldn't be rectified in any possible way, for it meant the revolutionary path. This would be done with the extreme goal in mind, not the reactionary goal. The revolutionary plan would be to bring humanity all closer together, and by being able to further Romanize English, what would end up occurring is that English and many of the indigenous languages would be brought all closer to each other. This would effectively establish a new language in its own right, for many of the cultural institutions were flooded with new ideas. The language would completely change with the superstructure allowing for a linguistic revolution that would dominate the whole nation. The nation had largely been transformed, with all previous superstitions being weeded out. The antique that would be essentially created would be at the heart of the new communication system. It would see its path shining as the new dawn had arrived. The new dawn would revolutionize culture, for it would be able to bring mass literacy in all forms to the masses. The illiteracy that would take place would be lifted, and the veil of ignorance would be completely demolished. The priorities would no longer be shifted towards commodity production; instead, they would take a completely new turn independent of any other form. The illiteracy problem would be completely rooted out with every step against the blood-stained wall. True emancipation in all efforts would be undertaken, with individual and collective freedom maximized to the fullest extent. This would require time though the plans were already set in stone. All that was needed was a world revolution, and America was the first country to fall to the revolution.

The standardization of the revolution would deeply ingrain the mindset of the population. The revolution was now in full swing and could be felt in all forms. The vivid imagery that would be created and the cultural process that would be absorbed were all just characters of the revolution. The real power behind the revolution was the acceleration. None of this would be possible if there weren't any acceleration. The scientific socialist method, in this case, would end up benefiting all of Long's party and the revolutionary movement as a whole. The party of Long started to attract more and more members, essentially being able to dissolve itself in the end. The vanguard would end up finishing its purpose of being able to stir up public support for the revolution.

However, disaster struck within the ranks of the revolution – Long himself had been shot and was in critical condition. He would be rushed to the hospital, with his final words being "vox populi." This would end up marking the demarcation of the revolution in short order. The revolution would need new leadership, though this would take much time. The revolution would end up falling apart as the revolution was starting to near the end. New England and the Plains had been liberated while the South was on the verge of collapsing. Hearing this news, a day of prayer would come, and a new leader would be elected. However, the former head of state had largely represented his people. The new head of state must not be partisan. This would end up causing many problems. The will of the consensus would be embodied within the head of the state. However, trying to do so would prove futile as the power struggle now broke out. The revisionists were not completely eradicated, with nationalist and liberal elements sprouting up.

However, as these elements sprouted up, the majority of the party would remain the same following the next election cycle in which the line of the people would be held up. All that was missing was a capable leader that could lead the nation through the revolution. The revolution couldn't be dead because people are dead. Long-lived, Long lives and Long will always live. Long was the father of the revolution and the liberator of the people. Now all that was needed was someone that could end up carrying the work of the revolution. The will of the people had not yet been lost.

The will of the people had only cried out for help – it was never dead. Even though the foliage it would have to carry through, it never thought of itself as a creature without a life. Vanguardism would be adopted a change from Marxism-Vanguardism as a result of the death of Long. This would be combined with being able to crack down on any revisionists. The Leninist line would end up attracting the dissent nationalists and liberals, keeping the revolution together. Vanguardism was Marxism adapted for the modern age, which coincided with the death of any revisionists as a position within the vanguard. These deaths would mean that the core socialist movement would all be unified under the same banner of scientific socialism. It would end up spanning all rational thought, for it sought to establish the first revolutionary republic that would be able to defend itself and industrialize. This revolutionary republic would follow the old revolution's footsteps, coinciding with the many concerns that had risen prior to the old revolution. This would allow all revolutionary forces to coalesce under the republic, which followed Vanguardism and Marxism. The other socialist lines would be completely abandoned in favor of a strong one. This would be further combined by a complete deserting of the nationalists with the banner being rallied around the revolution. Lastly, all of the true liberal forces would coalesce under the revolution, being able to secure rights for the new dictatorship of the proletariat.

One person couldn't fill the leadership gap, leading to collective leadership. The collective leadership would be a council that the revolutionary congress would choose. It would end up mirroring a dictatorship of the proletariat, wherein all power would be vested in the proletariat and liberal rights, and eventually, complete emancipation economically would be given. This would be further combined with advances towards national liberation, which would all end up making up the theory of Vanguardism. Vanguardism as the party line would end up meaning that the party line would be one that could end up holding up against any other foreign forces that sought to destroy the revolution. The party line would effectively dissolve the nationalists and the remaining liberals and revisionists, for it would be able to get rid of the petty squabbles that had broken out after Long's death. Now, a council consisting of Weinhart, Tusk, Bourbon, Arlon, and Frankfurt would all take over. York would later join the council due to the creation of a new part of the executive branch. All of the forces within the executive branch were directly linked to the revolutionary congress and the people through direct elections and recalls with the representatives representing the will of all peoples. This would end up getting rid of corruption, for the candidates were largely a result of the revolutionary struggle that would be brought forward. This would effectively lead to no real opposition, as all opposition would end up folding in. The leadership would end up closing in ranks, with much of the revolution being completely backed by the population. The revolution would end up escalating as much of the unemployment would be relieved, and new methods were constantly being discovered to increase the output and decrease how much is being put in. The increases in efficiency would lead to shorter workdays and larger pay, with most of the benefit going directly to the general population while the rest would end up remaining with the managers who would be now chosen. This would secure support for the revolution, as its strongholds could not be defeated. Even after a temporary fracture that arose from the death of Long, the vanguard of the revolution was never dead, and it had completely recovered from that loss.

Vanguardism

With the core of what Antonin had done, he had looked forward to unite his movement with the others. He had held negotiations with others, while suppressing those that were not willing, and wanted the full way. It was from here that Antonin's group had not only grown, but had been that which had foreseen the acts that would come ahead.

Belief in Antonin's group was all that was needed, yet, if there was a great dissenting line, then what would occur is that they would get fully expelled and their life would be in risk. It was of this that the party of Antonin had consolidated itself, and when there was such consolidation, his opponents felt the weight that was crushing them as one that was breaking them. With such an undertaking that they had seen, they had looked forward to what had ultimately come. With the undertakings that there were, it was clear to all that Antonin's own organization was one that had maintained its power only through the sole will that was ahead of them. Through the sole will that was ahead of them, Antonin's power that they had seen was that which was built on ignorance being knowledge. Yet, for the world would see what was there to come, it was of this that they had looked through each single point that was there.

The counter-revolution would be at the core of the revolutionary struggle, for it would always seek to fight against it in any form that would be taken. The South had capitulated, and the Plains were nearing their end when it came to counter-revolutionary rule. Furthermore, New England was on the brink of falling, for New England would represent the momentous defeat of the current order. New England would end up hosting many landlords who had built their wealth generations ago. The fall of these landlords would end up signifying a new era in agriculture. The landlords would run out largely of time, for they would flee to Canada. The landlords would end up having their wealth expropriated, with the land being completely redistributed for the time being. This would be combined with the industrialists living in New England actively resisting the revolution by fighting tooth and nail to keep their power. These factors combined would cause the complete end of the reactionary forces that would go against the revolution. These factors all had multiple parts to their eventual goal of being able to achieve the revolution. The revolution would end up depending on all of these parts functioning together. From populism, Vanguardism arose, which was the basis for the revolution. The revolution was solely based on defending the principles of Lenin, for the principles of Lenin had the immediate recognition of the revolution. The principles of Lenin would bring emancipation in all forms, not in one form or the other. This would mean that complete liberation could be recognized through the Leninist agenda, which the party would end up supporting. The party had the primary agenda of favoring the people, with Vanguardism being an outgrowth. The party agenda would end up favoring the people in every possible way, with the agenda being used to completely achieve the revolutionary means by which the party could survive and thrive. The revolutionary agenda that would be played forth would be one that would only see the proletariat at the helm of the nation. No other force would end up being in front of the proletariat. By extension, the proletariat and the vanguard were at the forefront of this new struggle. This struggle would transcend all other struggles, for it would be able to reign in the other proletarian factions. This true liberation would be at the heart of Vanguardism, for it would thrive upon the ideas of true orthodoxy. The true orthodoxy would be embraced with a return to the main principles against the corruption of the West. This would end up causing much of the culture from purer times to be borrowed. This would especially have an effect when classical culture is borrowed and refitted for completely different purposes. This would be further combined by the complete modernization of the nation and the establishment of national unity above all. The Second American Revolution was the new Roman Empire, for it brought together all of the peoples of the new country to completely establish unity and prevent it from fracturing. The civilization process was only starting to intensify, for it would end up allowing for the complete overhaul of the system. The revolution was only beginning, and no reactionary would know this. For them, the revolution would be limited to countries themselves with more than enough time to end up outracing the revolution. However, they did not know that the revolution itself was worldwide. The revolution can't be avoided - it was always there but rare. Now the flame has been lit for the revolution to succeed. The darkest hour would pass with the people's flag deepest red. It would be made out of the martyrs of the revolution. The names of those who have passed away will be remembered in the songs. They would end up representing the struggle for soil and the people. The people had not fallen; they had merely been suppressed. The people spoke louder than the elites, which led to the revolution.

The revolution was in full swing, and it could not be halted. Every attempt to do so would end up causing it to go faster. The revolution couldn't be stopped through any method – it was here. The new dawn was gleaning on the bright faces that would appear. The forefront of the revolution would cry tears of joy. The revolution was in full swing, and no one could deny it. Now, it was just the game of time, which would allow for the victory of the final revolution. The revolution would never back down; conversely, it would amplify. The sorrow of the people had lightened up their hearts. The people are above all; no institutions exist but the people. This would end up being proclaimed in different words every time the new citizens would meet each other. The revolution was embedded deep into the culture. It would represent what the nation was truly about. The pride and glory that would develop along with it would only aggravate the revolution. This would incorporate patriotism into internationalism, for the nation would be the bastion of the revolution. It would become the true home of the brave and the true home of the free. These were no longer empty words but words that would be put into action. These words would be raised scarlet high, and the standard would be raised along with it. The revolution was unstoppable – the train of the revolution was moving. All those who had wept previously had become enlightened. The martyrs would be remembered forever. All of their names would be written in. However, it was of this vanguardism that they had seen their own downfall. It was of this vanguardism that they would see what was their right become one that was wrong. All power that was concentrated as such was one that had effectively broken on itself, and through such power that was kept, many of those who passed for freedom had mothers that wept.

Their names would end up being part of the revolution; the dialectical materialist method would end up being part of the primary part of the party of the revolution. The revolution would end up going on with the revolution being part of the eventual goal of purging any decadence within the cadres of the party. The party would be thoroughly democratized with all of the principles said to be followed. The party would end up being the complete vanguard of the revolution. There was more than the social revolution; it would also encompass a scientific revolution. It would be a state that would end up embodying the principles of civilization itself. It would be the absolute solution that would be made, not through deliberation but through direct action. Direct action would be the core embodiment of the party of the revolution.

A new form of regionalism would end up taking shape. This regionalism would end up being in the form of being able to transform the nation completely. The nation would become completely decentralized, with each region developing its cultural heritage. Some parts of cultural heritage would be completely overridden, while others would lead to assimilation. The Steel Belt would develop regionalism, while New England would do the same. All of the regions were united with each other like they were part of a multinational state. The regions would break away from the centralized culture previously due to the eventual decay of the system that would bind them forcibly together. The reinvigoration of new Southern culture, which largely consisted of all of the peoples there, would end up causing a complete revolution in how the culture would be used. The culture would end up changing for the benefit of the masses, not for the few. This new regionalism would transfigure the previously existing social relations, using another wide-open path that could be exploited. This regionalism would be further amplified by creating cultures that would merge into the native cultures of the local region. This blend separated much of the West, with those regions being completely redone when it came to culture. Certain forms of tradition would be abandoned, particularly when it came to the separation between the cultures of the South. However, this merger would be much stronger than before, for it would entail that a new identity could take place. This complete revolution, when it came to the conduction, would end up causing a fundamental shift in the nation's perception. The nation was now regionalized, following the footsteps of the Roman Empire. This did help in one major thing, however. This largely helped the recruitment drive for the revolution, for the counter-revolution was being pushed back on all sides every day. The counter-revolution would only see its foundation to the detriment of the people.

The liability of the people would end up allowing their frustrations to once again vent elsewhere. However, much of this continuum was interrupted as the demographic and cultural shifts completely changed how the nation's makeup would end up being constituted. The South would be reinvigorated with the younger, completely new rule; the South would rise again from the ashes, though with a different purpose. Much of the Southern elite would be thrown away, being replaced by the general Southern population, irrespective of any genetics. This would lead to a large shift in how certain regions' identities and regionalism would be viewed. This would effectively cause much of the frontier of Appalachia to be completely loyalist in the sense that it would end up acquiescing to the primary culture found within the standard Steel Belt. The same would apply to New England and the Corn Belt. These regions would end up being completely locked down. The Pacific Coast would start to present problems, for it would be a partially rebellious region, while the South and the free-flowing states that run East of the Corn Belt would end up being completely localized. The same would apply to Hawaii and Alaska. This would effectively cause a division that had the possibility of secession. This time, the secession was not from a counter-revolutionary perspective but from the standpoint of localism. This was not an old phenomenon but a new phenomenon. The idea of a new Southern identity would end up causing massive deliberation within the halls of the revolutionary congress. It had threatened to tear the country completely apart through any means it had at its disposal. This revolutionary flame could not die out in any way, and this would end up being the strongest indicator of the revolution. The revolution had only started. The revolution would gain a new stronghold in the South, provided that it would have autonomy. The rest of the country would soon lock-in, including the region surrounding Arizona. This would all culminate in a fused identity of all of the peoples. The only obstacle left was the South, adamant about keeping its identity. The South would become part of the larger charade to keep the revolution alive. The revolution would only mean so much, for it would be a part of the broader movement that would be able to root out any reactionary forces completely. The new Southern pride would end up causing an upsurge in agrarianism, for it would be concentrated in the other main part of the Republic. What would essentially happen is that a North-South divide would end up sweeping through the whole country. This divide would completely differ from the previous divide between the counter-revolutionary and the revolutionary movement. The uptick in nationalism would further lead to the collapse of the rump counter-revolutionary state.

The news had struck – Charleston had fallen. This meant a complete victory for the revolution, which now had to rebuild itself. Charleston was at the heart of the counter-revolution, and since it fell, the counter-revolution completely went into a spiral. This would end up exacerbating the North-South divide. However, this would cause another wave of defections. The loyalist population had largely become loyalists, while the Appalachian mountains were starting to flip towards the South partially. This would end up exacerbating the already present divisions. Something new had struck – the idea of a limited South. This would exclude much of the population, with the transplants being completely weeded. Even though all of the peoples are the same for the most part, the belief that they were different would end up causing complete division.

A new counter-revolutionary movement had emerged, with its roots firmly established in the South. Though not open to negotiation, this movement aimed to eradicate certain aspects, such as the entrenched bigotry associated with the Old South, which would no longer prevail. The only problem was that it was warped in rhetoric that largely contributed to that. It would keep the old system for which it had economically, and the same approach would be mirrored politically, but the nationalism would end up stomping over any American belief there was. With the backing of many legislators, the Southern secession movement would end up causing many bills to crash. The executive breakdown of the South would further amplify this. This would cause a purely nationalist South to rise in its place. The nationalist South would go against the rest of the union, for it would try to outmaneuver all of the opponents of secession.

Furthermore, forced unity would be present, with many of the implants being largely excluded, some even returning, as well as the systematic movement of the loyalist population towards Liberia. This time, it would be permanent, unlike the last. The last time, it resulted from wartime situations regarding the counter-revolution posing a threat to their lives. This time, it came with the threat of the destruction of cultural heritage by the Southern nationalists. They were only revolutionaries in name as they were counter-revolutionaries when it came to action. This counter-revolutionary movement caused the large-scale expulsion of the population of the Smoldering Belt. This would end up culminating in a total war, with many of the expelled families not returning. The Smoldering Belt would see its population cut by 25% over many years, with the percentage of foreigners going down to a meager 4%. This would end up seeing the most brutal conflict that the nation would ever know.

Foreign aid would pour in for the remainder of the new civil war. This would especially be concentrated when it came to the South. The South would be the hub of the counter-revolution, just with different actions when it came to certain areas. The counter-revolution would establish Atlanta as its capital, for it would move against the sparsely-populated Smoldering Belt. The Smoldering Belt would be forcibly integrated with a large population of settlers being flooded in. The transplants of the North in the South would be completely expelled, with the other minorities being completely decimated. The North and the South were completely different regarding their attitudes toward the revolution. The South would be part of the new counter-revolutionary movement that would end up sweeping through the whole country. This counter-revolutionary movement would be part of the continuation of all forces that would work against the revolution. There would be many loyalists, for they would be concentrated among certain specific rural regions, while other urban centers would be largely working-class nationalists. The urban centers largely supported this new counter-revolution because their old convictions were not wiped away. The only difference was that their attitude had become far less soft as a result of the concessions that would be given to the working class. This would reduce the idea of nativism and the general trend of bigotry. This, however, didn't halt their support for this counter-revolution, which would end up raging on. Many rural regions would support this counter-revolution with the only regions that wouldn't consist of the extreme agrarian land that would end up being sparse and rich. This land would favor the union due to the investment that would be poured into this land. This would allow the populace of these regions to benefit the most. The crowd of the rural South would be split into two lines, with the urban population largely being completely centralized towards the old rural regions where the population would be pulled from. However, the union did have one major trick up its sleeve, which would end up decimating the support of this new counter-revolution regarding the population. The population would be completely remodeled, aiming to prioritize support and root out the counter-revolutionaries that would lurk in the South. These rebellions would culminate in the large-scale destruction of the union held in the South. It started as strong under Long; however, it would soon start to fade quickly.

Antonin was destitute as he was begging on the street. He had nothing but empty pockets, only being able to live off of the generous patronage of others. Antonin's old guard would be given amnesty by the revolution, only on the condition that they would completely change. This would reinvigorate Antonin's career – who now used new pseudonyms. His new alias was Stykhl, for he would use this where ever he went. Stykhl would once again transform his life, redeeming his past. Stykhl would reorganize the bureaucracy of the South, being able to purge it of nepotism effectively.

The hammer strikes down. The head of state would be chosen with the goal of being impartial. Thus, the purpose of the head of state was to end up having popular support, for it would be selected every couple of years. It would not have much power, for the councils would choose it. This would be done through a unanimous decision, wherein collective leadership of opposing views would take over. This would make the party largely part of the whims of reason and civilization. The party would be further separated from the state, mostly confined to the goal of running agitation. If some other element had been elected, it would mean that the party was doing a horrible job. Since most capitalists and elites had been gone, the petite-bourgeoisie would gain rights following the general process of defending the revolution. This would be followed by other forms of what would normally be considered reactionaries. This amnesty would weaken calls for Southern secession, bringing much of the petite bourgeoisie back into the fold. The last of the brunch would be eliminated as the intelligentsia and the priests would soon support the revolution, though they were not coerced. Their presence in the government would indicate that the party was starting to lose support and that the agitation had gone wrong. This alliance of old conservatives and the petite-bourgeoisie would be completely rehabilitated, effectively ending calls for Southern secession. The only remnant left consisted of the counter-revolutionaries who were part of the ultra-reactionary wing. They were completely detached from the rest of the movement, which would end up causing their identification to be straightforward. The petite-bourgeois elements would be rehabilitated with the religious factions given rights. This would end up causing the proletariat to be at the forefront of the revolution, as all of the subversion was gone. There would be no more conservative or liberal opposition as a result. This would be further combined with the complete devolution of all of the forces of potential reaction. The head of state's impartiality would primarily mean there would be complete unity. The detachment would be through a system in which the power was vested within all of the people – not just the majority, with all the power being concentrated among all the branches of the revolution. Institutional respect would mean that the revolution couldn't collapse on itself no matter what happened. This would be further combined with complete dedication to the people's revolution. All of the nations would end up serving this revolution.

Southern secession would be halted through measures calling upon the idea of decentralization in the form of all nations being liberated together. All programs would be distributed locally, for they would no longer be done with bureaucrats but with machine calculations. This would mean that the whole economy could be managed from the center while catering to local interests through the decentralization and centralization of such a model. Furthermore, everything that would be enacted of main significance would be done at the center, while everything on the side would be given to the local regions. This would be done in the form of complete links to each other while, at the same time, supporting the complete decentralization of the system. This systemic decentralization would further lead to the economic progress of certain regions, for decentralization practically meant the end of corruption. This decentralization would not see the weakening of power; conversely, it would mean that crime was being thoroughly targeted at all levels. This target on corruption and the focus on local regions would mean that the Southern secession movement would switch sides; with the other force that opposed it being gone, it was possible to wrangle the whole vanguard under the people. The only part of populism adopted from the other side would be the anti-bureaucratic elements, their primary focus. Such anti-bureaucratic features would unite all groups, for it could make the vanguard into one effectively.

Furthermore, the anti-bureaucratic stance would be a leaf and a testament to the other wing of the populist movement. The anti-bureaucratic stance that would be taken would be simple, for it would be part of the general stance that would go against the whole system. This anti-bureaucratic stance would be fused with the large economic platform that would prevail. This financial platform would see the creation of an effective rule of the proletariat, though this time, it would be combined with anti-bureaucratic stances, for there would always be a stage of siege. The bureaucrats would be forced to bow down to the people's will, for much of it had already gone away due to artificial intelligence economic planning. This would soon be followed up by measures that would rewrite the laws outside of the constitution on local levels, for local efforts against crime would all be coordinated locally rather than on a large scale. The secret police would be completely curtailed, for many other non-automated efforts would all be done locally except for those that require the constitution to be guarded. Anti-bureaucracy would be the most important part of their platform, for it served as a plank in which it was possible to shore up Southern support. This was deemed a great plan and would go ahead without any obstacles.

Even though culture had been decentralized, it would end up fusing. This fusion would determine the true country, for the cultures would all be in tandem. This would eliminate the reactionary positions that would end up pervading society. The force of reaction would be completely demolished, with the individual cultures being instrumental in the complete end goal of national unification. All of the individual cultures would be brought together towards a national culture. This would also mean the end of Southern nationalism, for the country had become completely unified. The governors stirring the tension were instantly recalled, with new governors being established. The new war had effectively been subverted due to the collapse of support of the counterrevolutionaries. Still, many problems loomed on the horizon. The first question was one of reconstruction and economic recovery. These situations would be diffused by the head of state, Alvin. Alvin would oversee the large recovery, with most of the industrial capacity being rebuilt from the dust. The infrastructure had been destroyed, with many commodities no longer working. This would be rectified by completely rebuilding the workshops. The petite-bourgeoisie largely lost their property as a result of the war. Now, the goal was to rebuild them as proletarians, though being given amnesty. The same would be done with any religious officials that would end up siding with Antonin before the war. Antonin himself was no longer Antonin. He was now Stykhl, with his new alias serving him well. His ultraconservative faction would never reoccur, for it would become part of the new Southern bloc. He would quickly rise through the ranks, being elected as a representative of the council from Tennessee. There, he would serve in the upper echelons of the revolution. He was not a party member, for he had won as an independent. This would further contribute to his new reputation as one of serving the people rather than subverting the interests of the people. The people's interests would end up being put above all, and this would be done especially during the reconstruction.

The complete reorganization would be done, with the agricultural sector being massively expanded in favor of the South. This would be further combined with the reconstruction of the rest of the country. Uneven development would be quickly washed away with any imperialist garb being thrown away. What would effectively end up happening is that the revolution would place itself as the world's superpower, though it would end up running into many enemies that would threaten the revolution. These enemies were no longer internal as many capitalists had fled to Puerto Rico, the core of the last remaining reactionary base. This influx would end up changing the demographics of Puerto Rico as it would be turned on its head. The influx of immigrants would cause most of Puerto Rico to completely change directions, with its population being redone in favor of the capitalists. It would remain the last capitalist holdout, with all of the petite-bourgeoisie and the traditional reactionaries being completely assimilated into the proletariat. This assimilation would be done by leveraging the state's power to represent all of the proletariat. The ultra-reactionary movement would carry no more weight while other movements would collapse on their head. The ultra-reactionaries would end up being completely abolished due to the assimilation of their key constituency into the revolution. The ultra reactionaries and the petite-bourgeoisie would end up supporting the same interests due to the liquidation of their identification. These forces would all interact together to completely displace any reactionary force that would end up looming over the revolution. These forces would be vetted, with any of their power completely liquidated. This would entail that reactionary socialism and petite-bourgeois socialism would be completely rooted out, being in the form of integral nationalism and liberalism, respectively. A collective leadership position would be taken up with complete impartiality, allowing the nation to be decentralized. This would be combined with safeguarding institutions, including all of the principles that would free the people in all aspects. This combination would be completely disastrous for the reactionaries, for it would end their monopoly on power. Their power would end due to the many alliances formed with the nation being liberated. This would end up holding up all of the principles of reason and civilization against the test of time.

This would once again validate the classicism and the new advancements that would be made. This would completely get rid of the presence of reactionaries from all echelons of society, with the party power being completely constrained, with the goal being to root out any power that would be vested within the bureaucracy. The war on the bureaucracy would shake up any entrenchment as there were mass dismissals by the people to completely remove any corruption. The head of state would remain popular due to remaining impartial and being supported by all councils when the recalls were brought in. These principles would be forcibly followed by all levels of society, which would cause distrust in the bureaucracy. However, this would refine the sword which would be used in the final revolution.

The goals had been met with the collectivization of agriculture being complete. This would be further combined with equipment modernization on these new collective farms. This would be further connected with increased industrialization in the South, which had destroyed the wave of nationalist sentiment. The integral nationalist sentiment was largely based on thin air, for it would share most principles except nationalism itself. The nationalist code would be tamed with all the peoples being united against all the struggles awaiting them. This rejuvenation would be part of the final solution of ending any reactionary force from storming the revolution. The rapid industrialization of the South would be combined with a steady process of sub-urbanization, with many of the rural populations entering the city and then defecting into the suburbs. This would end up causing all of the South to follow a new method soon when it came to how the production would be done. New associations would form throughout the South with an effective anti-bureaucratic revolution coming to power. The bureaucracy would be quickly slimmed down, with the rest thoroughly examined. The South was truly a revolutionary society, for it would end up allowing the horse to run in all directions. The horse would soon choose one direction as a result of the complete unity that would form through the process of democratic centralism. The respect for the institutions would greatly increase with the individual institutions being put in the hands of the people. The nationalism in the background would end up being the last part of the revolution, for nationalism would be the unifying force throughout the new vanguard. The vanguard had meant nothing other than being able to agitate. The agitation that the forefront would do is what set it apart from every other party. The party's goal was not to win elections, for it cannot run; instead, the plan would be to agitate. This agitation propaganda was at the forefront of the revolution; however, the party did not mean much besides this. Parties no longer had any real significance due to how the voting system had effectively changed. The parties' importance in the past would be derived from how they could campaign and lie. The only problem was that the representatives would encompass all of the nation's people. The representatives would effectively become the region's consensus that would be elected. The old parties had run their course that they had charted themselves with their only purpose being found in the fact that they were largely useful idiots that ended up serving no other purpose other than being able to safeguard the revolution from scratch. The party would protect the revolution by distributing pro-revolutionary material, for it would legitimize the revolution. Besides this, no other party had effectively existed, for it would represent the general population of the region that they were elected from. The parties would end up being rife with corruption, so that they would be completely avoided. The vanguard would not lead the nation, for it would only show the way forward for the revolution. The fore would use whatever it had to completely secure support for the revolution. The revolution was the most important object; the rebellion could never die. The revolution lived, lives, and will live. The revolutionary spirit has not yet passed away; the revolution has only begun.

The nation would end up being completely lined with the revolution. The revolution would end up meaning that true national unity would be established. True national unity would directly coincide with the revolutionary movement, with all of the revolution being used to harness whatever the proletarian revolution had. The goal of the revolution was to spread it outwards, with nationalism being used as a stepping stone towards internationalism. The internationalist step would be through a nationalist revolution that would end up taking place. This nationalist revolution was at the helm of what would occur. Nationalism would mean that an entire American nation would end up forming. This would be followed by many agreements that would end up allowing for the expansion of the revolution. The revolution would be given precedence over everything else. The revolution was the most important part in which lives would be given. The nation was only a part of it. The instrument of the nation would be used for the end goal of the revolution. The vanguard had the task of the instrumentation of the revolution. The agencies would play with the nation being at the core of everything. The nation would embody the force that would play towards the world revolution. The nation would spread its wings to spread the revolution towards the South and the rest of the Americas. This would mean that alliances would be made in preparation for the revolution in Mexico.

The revolution would end up setting off with stunning success. Baja California had fallen to the revolution, and Northern Mexico was about to fall. The imminent threat ended up causing the end of the rule of the capitalists. This would be combined with an incursion by the new Cuban revolutionary government into the rest of the Caribbean. A coup in Cuba had taken place to depose the liberal dictator to be able to spread the revolution. Many revolutions would end up flaring up in Latin America. These revolutions would all be tied together directly to spread the revolution in every direction. These revolutions all sought their glory in themselves.

Nationalist ambitions would take root, primarily with the goal of anti-imperialism. This would be reflected in the unity of all Americans, no matter where they came from or their DNA. This nationalism would supersede the nationalism of Stykhl. This nationalism would turn the whole goal of nationalism on its head, for the end goal primarily consists of internationalism. This form of nationalism would end up being carried over, with all of the nationalist dreams being part of the eventual end goal of demolishing many of the problems that pervade the world. These problems can only be destroyed using the internationalist revolution that will quickly sweep the world. The revolution will end up saving the nation, for the country is merely one part of the revolution. The complete unification of all peoples would follow the nationalist fervor. This unification would end up defining who is part of the nation or not. The nation would consist of those loyal to the nation, with the only identity that would be followed in this sense being patriots. The patriots would be the primary force that would end up advancing the revolution. Patriots would unite to promote the revolution through any available means. The revolution and the nation were inseparable from each other. This nationalism would end up varying throughout what country it would be practiced, but the essential principle of multiple nations creating one nation holds true. This national sentiment would further allow for the American system to be propelled forward.

The American way would be at the core of the national revolution. The national revolution would eliminate the remainder of the capitalists while cementing nationalism as a part of life. Nationalism was at the core of all of the merits of society. Nationalism would end up binding the proletariat of the nation together. There would be no place for the capitalists within the nation. This would allow regional identities to develop as a means of liberation while keeping the overarching figure uniting all these peoples together. This national self-determination is what ended up making the nation. The national self-determination process meant that cultural institutions would be nourished and a true territory would end up being created. This is combined with the institutions being completely rewritten in favor of the revolutionary fervor. The revolutionary fervor would cause the old institutions to fade away with the new national institutions on the individual level, causing an upsurge in support for the revolution. For the vanguard, the main difference between integral nationalism and social nationalism was the values that the nations were united around. The deals would be different under integral nationalism, which would end up favoring a reactionary approach, wherein religion would be a common factor. This would be contrasted with social nationalism, wherein the revolution would be a common factor. This difference was largely minute, and due to the abolition of the petite-bourgeoisie and the religious hierarchy and their assimilation, the reaction no longer posed a threat. The social nationalist agenda would be put through with large-scale decentralization to a certain point while keeping a form of democratic centralism. This would mean that all of the peoples would be united under the same ideal that would end up encompassing the nation. The endeavor was not based on DNA or culture; on the other hand, it was based on a spiritual drive. This would form the base of the new nationalism, for it would end up liberating the oppressed cultures to bring them together under one flag once again. This would mean that the overarching nation was nothing but the culture of civilization itself. The overarching nation was at the forefront of civilization, for it would end up representing the ideals of progress and modernity. This nation would end up setting itself apart from other countries.

Fiery speeches were given. Flames of a revolution were ignited. Forests would be penetrated with their revolutionary guard being stationed there. This was not in the Americas; it was all over in Croatia. "Our nation died twice over," Antonovic said. He would continue the legacy of social nationalism until its last days within the country. The country would end up seeing the power of the Krajina and Istria being centralized under one. This would be met with opposition by Antonovic, who had become the new Long.

Antonovic would end up advocating for the cultural liberation of the minorities while advocating for the expansion of Croatia into Bosnia. This would end up being a popular position, for it could end up mustering support from the minorities while flaring up the jingoistic elements within the nation. This contradiction would be resolved by the double-edged sword that would be held up. The nationalism that would end up developing was itself a contradiction. It would be a contradiction between national-liberation against the eventual centralization of the nation. This contradiction would be solved through a two-faced approach wherein civic nationalism and social nationalism developed alongside the rights of minorities. All were Americans, but some were given autonomy as well. This would end up redefining what the nation consisted of, for people now rallied around the banner. The same would end up occurring in Croatia. Croatia would end up seeing the process of complete assimilation and the eventual decay of the separatist movements. Istria and Krajina would remain separate though their culture would be brought closer. It was not a process of complete assimilation; rather, it was a process in which the minorities were given rights though detached from the primary nation that they would otherwise have identified with. This would effectively cause the end of neighboring ambitions in Croatia.

A coup had taken place in Croatia with a civil war in Bosnia. The Croatian state would end up aiding Herzeg-Bosna throughout the war, for it would emerge successful in this endeavor. The Herzeg-Bosna government had swept through much of Bosnia, with Herzegovina being completely in the hands of the government. The civil war had effectively ended for the most part, with Herzeg-Bosna being annexed by Croatia. The population transfers earlier had effectively made it so that most of the Croatians within Bosnia were under the banner of Croatia. This did carry the risk of Croatianizing the country due to the influx of Croatians form neighboring countries. This would consolidate the borders of Croatia, with most Croatians being under the banner of greater Croatia. The nationalist agenda had been successful. It was able to rally massive support from the population while, at the same time, garnering support form the minorities in the country.

This success would be repeated within America, for the population influx would allow for further assimilation. Many of the Americans that had moved to Canada during the war would come back in large numbers, causing America to end up having more loyalists that would serve the nation if it needed help. The nation would end up having many paramilitaries raised temporarily to defend the revolution, as the military's professionalization couldn't occur when the industry had been damaged due to the civil war. The industry was being rebuilt one step at a time, with each step being carefully planned. These steps would mean that the nation would end up getting back on track in no time. This was accompanied by the collectivization of agriculture, which would immensely increase the output of agriculture. These agricultural lands would be harvested to benefit the nation and its people. They would also be shipped to other countries with the surplus value through this partial commodification of goods used to industrialize. The Steel Belt remained the Steel Belt after the war, while the South became a beacon of progress. The industrialization of the South did carry one risk. It would be filled with air full of smog. This air was unbearable though it hadn't reached all corners of the globe. For many decades by now, the world had been largely submerged, with many of the individual regions being completely driven underwater. Some countries had completely sunk, with New York City fighting for its life. New York City represented America's old cultural heart from the North; if it had collapsed, the American spirit would end up collapsing as well. The American spirit and the city were inextricably linked in every venture they would go through. The city's industrialization based on harnessing the power of the water had temporarily caused much of the flooding to be drastically reduced, though it would still see itself in imminent danger with the foundations of the city being terribly shaken. The foundations of the city and the other constituent parts of the city would end up being at risk of submersion through many means. The revolution had sought to correct this, though originally, it was under the guidance of Antonin. The recovery effort by Antonin largely meant getting rid of the number of people there would be in that region to reduce the eventual consumption. This plan would end up turning out to be decent on paper, though horrible in reality. This would advocate for ethnic cleansing, which was already being carried out. This was no real solution to the looming crisis and only aggravated it. The situation had been largely knocked down the shelf with the abolition of extreme energy consumption though the sources were eventually altered.

It was through a combination of civic nationalism and ethnic nationalism that a new nationalism formed. This form of social nationalism put the revolution at its helm, giving individual nations complete development privileges. This would end up unifying the rest of the nation as the unique cultures are being constantly strengthened at the same time. This would be further combined with the complete development of a true national identity that would suffice. This national identity would end up overruling any other national identity that would form when it came to the parallel sum. The national identity would consist of each nation serving the nation whose identity was no longer obscured. This would mean that a largely progressive national identity would end up being created with any of the dissenters regarding nationalism being largely absorbed. The end of indigenism would be through this compromise which was a third position contrary to both sides. This position would override all other positions on nationalism in the party, for this nationalism would end up being anti-imperialist. It would mean that the nation's core would be built around the many countries that would make up the nation as a whole. This would allow for de facto assimilation, bringing all individual nations closer to the primary nation.

A sudden turn would end up being taken in the party. The party would see the reversal of the old national policy; this time, national chauvinism would be aggressively attacked on all fronts. National chauvinism would end up being torn apart, with each constituent of national chauvinism being completely destroyed. This would be part of the policy that would uproot Southern nationalism and save the union. The nation would end up being united again. The main base that America itself was a nation resulted from the psychological makeup. This would end up allowing for American unity, which would be further compounded by the liberation of the indigenous and the destruction of any rival nation other than those major nations that would end up being created. However, a separate loyalist nation would be made with complete integration and be able to dissolve it completely. It would end up dying out as an independent nation as much of the culture had been displaced over from the continent. As a diaspora, they would end up being completely integrated through the institution of anti-discriminatory measures. These measures would end up destroying the psychological makeup of the nation, for it was the only factor that set them apart from the rest. As they no longer were different from the rest, what would effectively end up happening is that the nation would end up being completely united once again. They were a nation with their creation by the institution that would end up being one of the harshest in the world. This merger would end up causing the government to be once again integrated into the anti-discriminatory measures, completely getting rid of any division that there would be within the broader nation. These measures would all be part of this nationalistic turn different from true liberation. The true liberation line would be completely abandoned, with the true line being once again relegated to a minor role. Such a liberation line would be detrimental to the true line. The liberation line would be completely abandoned in the years to come, with more of it being stripped away for this permanent revolution theory. This permanent revolution theory would see the end of the liberation line. The permanent revolution theory would end up giving primacy over everything else. The endless revolution line would be utterly defeated through the machinations that would be played through the new bureaucracy that had effectively consolidated itself. This was because the permanent revolution theory would lead to factionalism and the state's degeneracy into the bureaucrats' hands. The permanent revolution theory would be quickly abandoned within some sectors though it would remain the official policy that would go unopposed with the loyal sectors. The loyalists and the dissenters would soon take up fights against each other, though in the name of preserving the vanguard, the dissenters would be kicked out, and the bureaucracy under the system of the permanent revolution would quickly form. This bureaucratic apparatus would quickly oppose any progress that would be made toward holding the reforms of the old era down. The spirit of the revolution had effectively died out.

The reconstructions that would take place would all be in the name of the bureaucracy. The bureaucracy and the vanguard would be infused together, with the forefront no longer remaining in its original role. The vanguard now had been effectively turned into a party that would be rife with corruption. This would lead to the further dismantlement of the structures due to declining stability that would take place through the vast breadth of time. Such dismantlement was taking out the original purpose of the vanguard. The vanguard was becoming completely ossified into a new bureaucratic structure. This bureaucratic structure was starting to kill off any of the progress that was being made. Everything was beginning to be replaced. This is combined with the bureaucratic structures being completely removed from any remaining power.

The world had seen the greatest economic collapse since the pandemic that had swept the world twenty years earlier. This economic collapse would end up being accompanied by the further degeneration of the nation. The economic collapse had completely shaken the nation before the revolution and was still vibrant throughout many other countries in the world. This would end up causing the death of the unity that there would be within many nations. Africa would end up falling into a series of civil wars and genocides with brothers fighting against each other. The repatriation of many foreigners back to Liberia would end up being the result of the counter-revolution. The painfulness that would end up following the subjugation of many nations throughout Europe would be rectified by many protests that would soon erupt. Some demonstrations were revolutionary, while others would end up being counter-revolutionary. The death of certain nations would be the direct consequence of the assimilation process that would take place throughout the national revival of many countries that had fallen. These nations now sought the complete liberation of their nation. One was lucky to document the revolution throughout Brittany, France.

"We want freedom, national self-determination, economic prosperity, and the end of our oppression as a nation," many protesters would chant in Brittany. "Our day is here for the nation to once again rise throughout the world and provide an example for independence,' this would echo throughout the whole country. "Our fellow countrymen, it is an honor to be a Breton (a native of Brittany, France), and you should be proud of it," Arazaih said to the crowd. "To serve the fatherland is our duty," the crowd cheerfully responded. This would pave the way for the revolutionary flame to sweep throughout the country. "The nation of Brittany has risen up," Stykhl would respond. "We have to help the nation of Brittany when they need it the most," Stykhl would further go on. An argument would end up breaking out, eventually being decided to aid the nationalists. This revolution would end up meaning that a free Brittany in all aspects would end up rising against their oppressors.

"We must defend our beautiful motherland," Korthy said. "Our motherland has been stripped of her territory and her resources by the foreign powers that conspire to destroy it from within," Korthy would further go on. The intensification of this rhetoric would be carried on by the call to action to conspire a revolution against Slovakia as well. Hungary would be once again greater concerning the other populations as equals. This Hungarian revolution would mean that greater Hungary would be re-established again. This Hungarian revolution would end up unifying with the Croatian revolution, which would only sweep through Slavonia and Croatia. It would end up not crossing into Dalmatia, with would end up causing the country to be divided in half. The country's division would be the key principle that would end up guiding the shifted geopolitics of the region. Croatia would end up being united with the revolution, while the reactionary holdouts in Dalmatia would end up fighting against the Croatian authority. The last remaining division in Croatia would end up being rectified and completely united. This would end up causing the end of the reactionary forces as a large opposition, for their grip on Dalmatia, would be weakened significantly. Though the revolutionary movement would frequently overrun, Dalmatia would be the core of resistance activity. The trend of Vojvodina toward the revolution would end up causing Vojvodina to join as an integral part of the Hungarian revolution. This would be further accompanied by Transylvania and Carpathian Ruthenia, which not only had large Hungarian populations but also allowed for incursions regarding the revolution down the line. The revolutionary army was rising, with the liberation of the rest of these nations being near. These nations would end up being united when it came to the revolutionary spirit each of them would end up possessing. The rebellious spirit would see all these nations as equals within the same federation. This federation was heralded to be the identity of the revolution. This would be a mirror copy of the revolution that would take place back home in America. Stykhl was a revolutionary agent, providing funding for these revolutions as well as money to reconstruct following these revolutions. This would end up causing many of the bourgeois countries to be divided throughout the Balkans as some of their territories fell to the Hungarian revolution, which was no longer just Hungarian. America would support this federation with massive amounts of aid flowing in with the express goal of being able to reconstruct the industry. Luxembourg and Germany would fall to similarly executed revolutions, with Austria on the brink. This would be further combined by their unification and the uprisings that would take place throughout Latin America and Brazil. Brazil, especially, would be the home for the revolutionary base as it would end up falling with all of the individual people being part of the rule of the proletariat.

This crafted revolutionary scheme had no bounds though it was starting to hit itself in the head. It would be impossible to make France and the UK budge, for they would take many precautionary measures to prevent a revolution. Cuba would join the revolution, with Mexico being trapped in a civil war. Though when it came to Mexico, the unstable revolutionary regime we would prop up was starting to unravel. This would end up causing the remaining loyalists to face off with the counter-revolutionaries. What would end up happening, in the end, is that the counter-revolutionaries would end up pushing back on the revolution. The counter-revolutionaries would see the revolution as the embodiment of imperialist ideals, being backed by America. The lines had been drawn, with each revolutionary nation being united. The mantle of the revolution would end up being placed into the hands of America.

Now, a crash was coming to the forefront. A new cold war would end up brewing during this crash. This cold war would entail that either side would have to progress towards getting rid of any spies the other side would deploy. Germany, Cuba, Hungary, Brazil, and the US would be allied. They would end up facing off against France, Russia, the UK, and their sphere of influence. These spheres of influence would incur the most fallout from whatever these major powers would do. Hungary would end up rapidly industrializing, while Germany would see a recovery in the industrial capacity that it had lost. The main disadvantage that the revolution had was the population size compared to the counter-revolution. The population of the US had been largely reduced by the civil war, where many had perished. The German people stagnated for many years before the revolution, while the Hungarian population incurred a large hit due to the emigres that would form. These emigres would establish a home in France, numbering three hundred thousand. This large emigre population would be dedicated to crushing the revolution in Hungary. This would be further combined with other emigres, particularly those that would end up arising from Croatia and Vojvodina. Many Croats would flee the border towards Bosnia, setting up their state where they would be at the top. The anti-revolutionary Croatian forces would end up invading Bosnia, from which they would evacuate. These evacuation forces meant many people were being pushed out of the land. Bosnia would go through a complete demographic shift as many Bosniaks would be expelled to Sand zak. This would end up redoing the demographics of Bosnia in favor of the Croats, who now made up a thirty percent minority. In Herzegovina, they would make up most of the population. This complete shift in the concentration of the population would cause the counter-revolutionaries to cause a backlog throughout Europe. Many counter-revolutionaries and revolutionaries would travel between borders, irrespective of nationality. This would end up causing a large French minority in France, while many Germans would flee to Austria.

The minorities that would form would end up transcending any previous nationalism. They would end up representing governments in exile. A large-scale migration of Christian Albanians would reach Hungary, for they would represent a revolutionary Albania in exile. Similarly, a large wave of Serbs from Bosnia and Serbia would end up migrating toward the Serbian government in exile, that would be in Vojvodina. These governments in exile would absorb many immigrants who would end up fleeing persecution. This would end up causing extremely large diasporas, with the Albanian diaspora in Hungary largely assimilating. These diasporas would end up meaning that the revolutionary organizations would be strengthened through many ready volunteers. These diaspora populations would end up assimilating partly into where they immigrated towards. This would end up causing the Krajina Serb population to be reduced to almost nothing due to immigration toward Serbia. These population transfers would end up causing a complete demographic shift that would occur throughout Europe. They would form new nations on their own, though many would lack any real territory. This would end up causing large minorities to pile up in Hungary from the rest of the Balkans. Greece would send many refugees toward Hungary, with many Romanians assimilating voluntarily. This would bring Transylvania closer to Hungary without making it start as Hungarian. Ultranationalists would end up defecting towards revolutionary movements, causing a large ultranationalist presence to pile up though many would change their creed. Their creed would be modified due to believing that a revolution was imminent and that the nation would be put first when this revolution occurred. This did come at the cost of practically reworking the demographics of Europe. Many immigrants from the Middle East and Africa had largely immigrated back, with many wars being fought in Africa. Africa would end up being the hotbed for many wars that could determine the future of Africa in any direction. This would end up causing a labor shortage in many reactionary countries while there would be an overflow of labor in the revolutionary countries. The Rhineland had especially garnered French immigration, reaching new highs from Wallonia and the rest of France. It would also garner immigration from Brittany, causing the population to end up supporting a revolution in France and the liberation of the nations that consisted of France. The indigenous populations would be liberated throughout Latin America, with the indigenous populations and the other populations being completely intermingled with complete justice and cultural development. Since other diasporas shared the same culture, they would be given equal rights. The main difference was the particular promotion of indigenous culture, which would complement the cultural development of the primary culture that would roam throughout the land. The rich allotments of land back to the indigenous would end up meaning that the land could be once again grazed on again. The diasporas would end up being integrated into the primary culture, for which they merely had branched off. This would mean that the other previously oppressed nations would no longer remain oppressed by any metric. The revolutionary spirit that would be taken when it came to the question of nations made it so that the complete liberation of nations could be pursued first, with the eventual goal afterward being internationalism. They were inextricably linked to each other, with their bond being eternal forever. The revolutionary spirit would end up meaning that all of the diasporas would end up being dismantled, for the diasporas were merely an extension of the primary culture that would be sought throughout the nation. This extension mentality allowed for the eventual dissolution of boundaries between each diaspora. This would mean that all could be completely unified in every aspect. These diasporas were no longer discriminated against, for they were completely equal. Instead, what would end up happening is that they would all be integrated in, with the first peoples having new nations being created. These nations would end up restarting the continuum of culture that would end up previously developing. These nations would end up being at the helm of the revolution, for they would allow for the dissolution of racial boundaries, with the only real national-liberation being those already there. All immigrants would assimilate, with their presence in the nation being completely integral. The last remaining part would end up being the indigenous, which would end up registering as those already there. These nations would end up recreating themselves, with the complete liberation of these nations being part of the end goal of the first step. These steps would be taken to secure the revolution, wherein nationalism would end up being acknowledged to dissolve nationalism. These nations that would form would allow their own cultures to form – carrying on the legacy that Long had laid out. The discrimination that would be done based on color was no different from the discrimination that would be done against immigrants prior, with both being rectified in every regard. The main difference was expressed through the indigenous, who were largely part of their clique. The indigenous were the first there, for they had their culture completely eroded. The bar lifted to complete racial equality unified the nation, for they had already shared the same culture. All that was left largely consisted of the indigenous, who had their land robbed from them in the most barbaric ways possible.

The liberation of these nations would end up being part of the policy that would end up being practiced throughout the vanguard. The vanguard of the revolution had practiced these policies out of pragmatism, leading to the end goal of completely spreading the revolution towards the world. These policies of lifting the bars when it came to immigration would end up meaning that solidarity would end up being expressed throughout the nation and that there would be no conflict between different groups of people. This would be further compounded by the liberation of the indigenous, who constituted a nation in their own right. The removal of the barrier of immigration would end up paving the way to an integrated society with the individual countries being completely liberated. This would be found in Brittany, now the source of another revolution. Some Bretons fled to Germany, believing the revolution would fail. This was partially justified though there would end up being a complete stalemate, even after the advances that would be made throughout the rest of France. France would see a civil war with Occitanic and Provence seceding in favor of the revolution – allying with Brittany. This would end up overseeing the reconstruction of France though on revolutionary lines.

A large sound of footsteps would be heard. This would end up being the journey of the Roma towards Hungary. These Roma were no longer looked down upon, for they would settle in large numbers. The Roma immigrant population would end up completely integrated, with many losing their previous Roma identity. However, this ended up causing the people of Hungarians, relative to other groups, to swell throughout the new Hungary. Transylvania had been thoroughly Magyar zed though it would be de jure its nation, being able to use Romanian. The forging of a Hungarian national identity would extend towards Slovakia and Vojvodina. They would end up being thoroughly brought closer to the central Hungarian Republic. This Hungarian republic would be transformed with its constituents being brought closer. This would soon include Croatia, for they would develop a brotherhood other than being proletarians. This form of internationalism would end up meaning that the brotherhood of peoples would end up spreading far beyond proletarian identity but also through linguistic similarity. This identity would end up causing the large-scale benefit of self-determination of all peoples, which would see their nations completely unified.

The liberation of nations and the end of chauvinism would mean that nations would all transform into one. They would all carry one identity, which would be the revolution. By being able to recognize nationalism, they ended up transcending nationalism, with a federation of nations being formed in the end. The nationalist dream would be fulfilled with all radical nationalist factions being completely uprooted. These nationalist factions would be completely rooted out with a complete renovation of their bases. The nationalist factions would find themselves in the dustbin, for their ideology would be practically merged with the doctrine of dialectical materialism. Dialectical materialism would end up being at the core of the revolutionary movement, including nationalism. Nationalism would be part of the dialectical method, for it would be an interlude to the testament of the revolution. Nationalism would represent one part of the revolution, for it would be the intermediate stage. The immediate background of the revolution would be linked to the complete turn that would take place throughout the nation. The nation and the revolution were one; they were united. They all sought the revolution as a means to their end. The revolution only represented one step that would be made toward the revival of the nation. It would be the opposite way, with the nation representing one step toward the revolution. Many of these inversions would be part of the many twists and turns that would take place. These twists and turns had seen their day with the revolution becoming superior. The revolution was the primary thing that would end up being protected over everything else. The revolution would end up being concentrated in Germany and Hungary in Europe, for they would end up hosting the primary populations that could end up carrying out the revolution. The immigration of revolutionaries towards these countries would end up meaning that the population flow would be further intensified towards these countries. These large immigration populations would end up bolstering the activity of the revolutionaries, for it would reinvigorate the industry on and on. The sector of revolutionaries of Hungary and Germany would see the rapid intensification of how much would end up being produced. Producing commodities would be a temporary measure necessary in accumulating the means of production that these revolutions would rely upon. The means of production these revolutions would rely upon largely depended on what the other nations would use. The large flow of immigrant populations would end up expanding the reserve army of labor, which would be completely transformed into those equal. These immigrant populations would develop patriotic sympathies, for they were already linked together when it came to the complete demise of the counter-revolutionaries. The total cessation of the counter-revolutionaries would be part of the general process of being able to root out any of the reactionaries. The reactionary nationalists would be completely gone, for their populations would be hit at their core. Many of them would end up defecting to the revolutionary nationalist factions. These extreme nationalist factions would end up unifying together into one, for they would be part of the revolutionary line that would pervade throughout the whole nation and its subjects.

The complete turn in the national question would be marked by anti-discriminatory measures against anyone, with other measures being implemented on top of the socialization of the economy. The liberation of the indigenous nations would be another step that would be undertaken. This would end up giving true independence combined with the institution of the complete solidarity of all peoples. The end of antagonism would be characterized by proletarian internationalism, which would be at the forefront of the revolution. The revolutionary spirit was at an all-time high, for it would be vibrant throughout all sections of society.

A reporter would end up embarking on the journey that would take place in Toronto. Even though many reactionaries had swarmed in earlier, Toronto would see the revolutionary fervor at the maximum that was ever there. Quebecois nationalists and indigenous liberation fighters would attend it. The proletariat of Toronto would be present within the largest crowd that would ever gather throughout history. The group would shout the slogans of liberation and revolution. The revolution, for them, meant a complete fulfillment of the ideals of liberty, equality, and fraternity. They would shout and cheer with a pompous attitude that would prevail throughout the echoes of history.

History, for them, meant the continuation of the revolution. An election for the executive council had taken place, returning Robert as the winner. This would permanently eliminate any antagonism within the nation, for Robert was a proud American, even if the color of his skin was different. In the new country, your skin color no longer mattered as they were now one nation no matter what. This would finally finish the Southern "nationalist" movement once and for all. It would no longer be brought up earlier, for it would end up turning out to be a reactionary proposal that had no merit as the culture would be shared among all. The Canadian Revolution was only starting with the revolution being the core of the new Canadian identity. However, this would only garner support from certain districts of miners and farmers, for it would end up being weak among the factory workers and the other sectors of the proletariat – at least for now. The new dawn of the Canadian republic would be one that would see its ties to imperialism severed for the final time. The class war that would take place would be directly part of the national struggle, for the last nationalist movement that would be separate would end up having its air. The nationalist movements were an interlude to the revolutionary spirit that would develop. The nationalist movements merely represented a step towards complete liberation.

The only effect this would have on the world as a whole is that many movements would end up sprouting up. This would be done with the aid that Stykhl would constantly rave for. This would end up effecting the world by making it so that they would lead towards one side over the other. The flames that would end up being sprouted up would end up showing the advance of the revolution all over the world. The revolution was now a cliché, for it would end up signifying the whole of the movements that would end up taking place. The revolution and its merits would be shown in full force when the revolutions were complete. A stance of internal development would be taken, for a world revolution was not imminent and would take time. The revolution would not happen overnight, even if the progress would end up occurring overnight. Canada would end up signifying this where the revolution would end up stagnating in progress, while in Mexico, the counter-revolution would end up pushing back much harder than before. These movements had failed due to the rush that would be done with the revolution being done over everything else. The new turn that would be taken would signify the development of the countries that would be liberated – and more specifically, the internal nations. The internal nations that would be embodied within the revolution would end up showing a drastic turn towards liberation. Some nations would only be partially developed, like the core American nation, whose development was decaying, and the South would end up much weaker. This uneven development would be bridged, and similar to the immigrants elsewhere, they would be completely integrated. The main difference that would end up arising is that the natives would end up having a liberation perspective similar to the rest of the world in that sense but is different from when the many settlers would end up coming. This difference would make the revolution different in every country it would be implemented. This difference would make the revolutionary fervor go on permanently, with the revolution never ending until it had eclipsed the whole world over. The revolution cannot exist in one country – it must spread.

Theories that would come ahead would be those that were being looked over. Each single step that was ahead of them was that which looked forth towards the collapse that was ahead of them. "Stykhl who," was the common phrase. With Lazarus and Sirach's planning, they had come to once again meet, now this time, at a place nowhere else yet seen. For all that they had put forth, it was of Sirach's and Lazarus' planning that would push both of them ahead. Many countries had taken upon the path of rapidly industrializing. By having taken upon such a path, they had their contradictions that had unfolded within, with that of the workers and the industrialists that fought. Lazarus and Sirach met back up. Lazarus had shown Sirach the tools that he had at his disposal – a Kali set up for sniffing packets, a cyanide pill for if anything went wrong, and a

The opposites that would be in the contradiction would turn out to be against each other. The rejection would end up being resolved in neither side's favor, for the solution would end up being a third position that would end up being undertaken. This adventure would end up dissolving any nationalist sentiment that was left. There would be no separate nationalist movements now, for they would all be part of the same liberation mentality. The mentality of liberation would end up being at the core of the revolutionary movement that would utilize nationalism for its purpose. It would end up being completely transformed towards one side over the other. The new extreme rhetoric would end up eclipsing all different identities that would take place. The revolutionary rhetoric would utilize nationalism for its benefit to defend national interests completely. These national interests would be part of the proletariat's general interests, for they would be linked to the revolutionary program based on dialectical materialism. The proletariat's broad interests would end up being inextricably linked, for they would oversee the same principles. These principles would end up seeing the complete liberation of all world nations, for they would no longer be oppressed.

Pan-nationalism would be dissolved in favor of internationalism, through which they could be reunited with a different purpose. Pan-nationalism and other forms of nationalism that would exist in many of the states that would form within the Latin world would have all of their minority nations being preferred if they had flipped over to the revolution. This national-liberation would fly past chauvinism and the idea of autonomy, for it would end up demanding equal status. This equal status would be integral to the new idea that the nation could only be built through a revolutionary program. This revolutionary program would be heralded as what could bring liberation in all forms to all peoples. The national program would be a simple subset of the eventual revolutionary ideology that would be formed as the superstructure out of the base of class struggle. These two forces would end up changing how the revolution would end up having its conception, for how nations were organized and how demographics shifted largely threw off how the nation would be liberated in this one case. It would be part of the larger program of establishing the rule of the proletariat over the state.

"We must stand up for all proletarians throughout our glorious country," Stykhl had said. "The only way this will work is through internationalism, wherein we cooperate with our revolutionary allies," he added. "Our revolution must last forever, for it is the eternal flame in which the will of the people would end up being carried through," Stykhl will go on. "I am firmly convinced that the revolution can only last by defending our ideals. The defense of our ideals is paramount, and it should come before everything else. Our revolution would last the test if only we could control it. The revolution must be executed with multiple steps, with the people's will being expressed in the state as the people control the state. Popular control of the state and the economy is ensured when the people's will is expressed through the state. Furthermore, the social sphere can transform with further liberation of those oppressed. We must finish enacting complete equality for those considered deviant though not disgraceful by the previous society. It had previously been shunned as being against family values. Now that we have rectified these family values by providing true economic freedom, it makes no sense to go ahead with the liberation of all disparaged.

Furthermore, the last part would be the liberation of nations, which I have traditionally advocated for – even as a reactionary. The sovereignty of all nations would also entail the dismissal of all oppressed nations in our country and worldwide. It would be dishonest only to provide liberation for certain countries over others. We aim to end national chauvinism and bring glory to the American worker. The American worker has broken out of the neoliberal system, which I have also fought throughout my life though the neoliberal system would be rehabilitated under my old proposals. I have never been a politician of the right – I have always been a politician of the people. I have always been past left and right. For me, there is no such thing as a politician. There are only the people. Together, we have lit a path our sacred peoples will walk upon. It will enlighten humanity until its last days. We, the revolutionary guard, must defend the ideals that will forever emancipate humankind from its shackles. Now is the day and the hour – our time is ripe for the revolution. I do not see anything that could end up conflicting with our pride.

America is a rhythm; it must be played in unison. If not all beats are the same, we will all collapse. Only unity saves us," these powerful words would end up transfiguring the hearts of those in the revolutionary congress. "Today, whether we want to defend our nation against the foreign powers conspiring to destroy our liberty is our choice. We decide to uphold the revolution and its ideals. Liberty, equality, and fraternity are our guiding principles, and they guide our nation. I have called upon the people of our country and our nations to stand up for all victims of oppression and fight for the liberation of the human race. The only race that exists is the human race, and nothing goes below that," these calls would be met with support and applause. The old reactionary had turned out to be revolutionary in the end. While he would be forgiven, he would not be forgotten. While his sins were erased by those he had gone after earlier, those sins made a permanent stain on his record. Now, he was doing whatever he could to save the remainder of his reputation. The revolution had completely transformed his life, from which he originally started as a counter-revolutionary to becoming a beggar and then a loyal revolutionary that had been rehabilitated. The rehabilitation of his former party associates would mean that the counter-revolutionary movement, or more precisely, what had been left of it, would coalesce under the new federal government. The old federal government had been put on trial, while the remainder of the rehabilitated reactionaries would end up supporting the new government. They would end up being commemorated, for they would see the harsh realities of the people. Stykhl would go from a bigot to becoming one of the greatest champions of minorities in the country. This would end up causing the world to flip upside down for Antonin.

The birth of the new Lenin had already been found within Leed. Leed would assume the new party secretary, while Robert held on to his position in the executive branch. Leed would end up seeing the intensification of agitprop with all of the agitations now being gathered against the remainder of the reactionaries that would end up being spread over the world. Leed would end up following Long though he would take a new position. Since most of the positive reforms had already been passed, now all he sought was the end of the reactionaries in the world. He understood that this couldn't happen immediately and that the current progress was already being shown. The recent progress was leaning towards one side over the other. Now, the progress needed to be defended at any cost. The improvement would lose its significance if it believed that it failed. The revolution could only exist if it had the oxygen that would keep it burning. The reaction was a direct result of a change in something else, allowing the revolution to rise. These contradictions would spark the proletarian revolution, now sweeping the world. While the revolution slowed down on paper, it was starting to amass firepower in the background. The firepower would not be direct, for it would be held in the environment, but a rapid industrialization process would end up being pursued. This immediate industrialization process would pave the way for the de facto end of any reactionary force seen throughout the country. Rapid industrialization was only a means to an end —not the end itself. The fast industrialization process would be pursued at any cost because, without it, the country would immediately collapse if there was a war tomorrow. If tomorrow brings war, with rapid industrialization, the people will survive. War was imminent; now, it was a question of where it would happen. It was no longer a question of time as time lost its value. Time meant nothing other than the subjective association that would be given to it, and time had no value for the revolution as it was already here. Now, it was just careful planning that would save the revolution.

A million refugees from France would end up coming to the Rhineland, which would have its industry rejuvenated. The rejuvenation of the sector would allow the immigrants to assimilate. This would furthermore invite immigrants from all over the world, for it would end up qualifying for the process of industrialization. This caused one main problem; the industrialization of Africa now seemed impossible as many specialists would end up moving to Germany and Hungary to assist in mechanization. Germany and Hungary had a labor shortage, causing many peoples from Asia and Africa to migrate toward them. This labor shortage would end up causing a lack of technical experts within Africa, leading to famine and many disease outbreaks. This was on top of the current turmoil of many civil wars that were taking place. The revolutionaries believed that not only was original America perpetuating imperialism but also what drove America to defeat. The goal was to abandon the imperialist endeavors abroad and focus on an anti-imperialist stance that would be national-patriotic at its core. This revolutionary formation would capitalize on anti-imperialism and make it so that it was another struggle in itself. All of the state boundaries would effectively be dissolved as a result of the effective anti-imperialist struggle that was the nationalism that was being practiced by the true working-class. This nationalism would be part of the anti-imperialist struggle in the end, being nothing more or less. The realization of such a program would be part of the anti-imperialist means to an end, where all of the oppressed nations – in this case, the end of imperialism, would take place. It was merely a means to an end, for these sentiments had already been growing many years prior due to the current order. These sentiments would all show the contradictions that would be all laced on top of each other. These contradictions would further the cause of anti-imperialism, which was being offered as much of the Rust Belt would be emptied by the elites in favor of moving abroad. This way, imperialism only benefited the elites over everything else, and everyone else would be left completely down. This imperialist act would be completely crushed through the anti-imperialist motive that would reverse the previous imperialist ambitions.

Why was there much to be true? For they had been slaves of their own heart, with what they had exactly seen with their process of breaking down in some regions, and developing in other regions, it was of their action that every day and night, explosives had continued to detonate. When such explosives had continued to detonate, people had evacuated en masse, while those with the expertise would try to disarm. With all war that had went upon the world, there was one that was truly coming. There was one that was truly coming – so as long as all nations in the end foresaw who came, and if they truly saw who was going to come, then the world that they would face ahead of them would be that in which their exact situation would be truly rectified. It was of this that there was nothing else decried. If they had brought forth their world ahead of them, then the world order that was of the old would be replaced by the order of the new. That itself was from which, the basis had ultimately been drawn. If they truly looked ahead to the bright days ahead, then they may have gotten over their dread. And when they will have one day gotten over their dread, it was of their project that was soon ahead of them, that they would truly master what would be there. Sarah, too, was starting to notice Antonin ahead of her. Sarah too, wanted to see that Antonin would eventually stop his endeavors that were out to destroy the world.

The original nationalist project would take place during feudalism's death. This new transition would require all nations to be liberated as an intermediate stage to move to the next mode of production. The nationalist project would be carried through the liberation of all oppressed nations which are defined through certain characteristics. The nationalist project would be determined by the liberation of all nations that would exist worldwide. This is combined with a federation created due to proletarian internationalism, which ends up following national-liberation. This would be put into practice on paper, creating the international. The nation would end up being defined by certain characteristics, determining whether it would be a nation. These characteristics made it so that the migration of certain peoples during the current mode of production or settler colonialism would not fundamentally shift the nation. This would end up seeing the liberation of nations as a means to the end goal. This would encourage nationalism because it would end up binding nationalism to the general proletarian movement. This was exactly what would end up being supported for the sake of liberation and nationalism. Nationalism was viewed as a means to an end rather than being the end itself. This nationalism would transform all other forms of nationalism by large numbers. The nationalism that would form would be able to bypass any reactionary ideology. Foreigners would end up being part of the nationalism if they were sufficiently loyal enough, in other words, not part of the oppressor class. This would end up being the course that the international would take. This path would end up superseding all other forms of nationalism, which would all be denounced as reactionary. The main idea was that the only way these foreigners could achieve liberation would be through unity with others. This would mean that all immigrant populations would be given true freedom. This freedom would end up meaning assimilation, for they would end up serving the nation. This would be achieved through the world revolution, which would take place over time. This world revolution could only happen if individual countries were developed one step at a time. The radicals would further bolster the sense of nationalism, which was being used for an end. The nationalism would be temporary, for it would end up allowing for the future of oppressor nationalism. This nationalism would further redo immigration, for it would end up integrating the immigrants while providing national-liberation to all the oppressed nationalities in the world.

This policy would be the last modification that would be done to the national policy, for it would no longer be brought up again. The previous change would end up being part of the means to an end that would end up taking place. The last international would end up ruling over all of the others. It was the voice of all of the oppressed of the world. The global would be the first and the last international that would spread throughout the whole globe. The world revolution could only come through revolutions that would take place in individual countries. Trying to plant a revolution in every country would end up proving to be disastrous. The revolution that would take place in every respective country would end up allowing for national-liberation. The revolution was the mother of all nations, for it would end up creating them. The goal was to spread the revolution worldwide and have every nation liberated from its oppressors. Immigration never consisted of a nation by itself with this doctrine, but they directly resulted from the current system. Immigration was being used by the elites in multiple ways. The first way was to divide the proletariat. The second way was to allow for the division of proletarians to sow discontent against their fake enemy. The last way would be to import cheap labor, which could more easily allow for exploitation. Immigrants would need to be integrated into the revolution for any revolution to be successful. After all, everyone was once an immigrant, and any form of bigotry would not be tolerated. It would end up carrying significant reprimands, for all people, especially the indigenous, were integral to the country. The indigenous of the world would see liberation in places where settler colonialism had taken place, while all immigrants would end up seeing full equality.

Immigrants had already been developing equality prior, but now, it was in full acceleration. The immigrants would no longer be a question in themselves, for they would end up being completely dealt with. The last question of national liberation had been completely solved, with the solution largely relying on supporting national liberation wherever it is — provided that it is proletarian self-determination and not a part of irredentism. Irredentism and national liberation would prove to be complete opposites of each other. Irredentism would end up being what Stykhl would formerly believe in, while national liberation would be the form of proletarian nationalism that would take place.

There was nothing more proud than being American. Being American meant that there would be the freest country in the world. This free country would build on the past while being able to vet out the reactionaries. Furthermore, every effort would be taken to preserve such freedom. This freedom had no price in the terms of the negotiation. It could never be negotiated away, for this freedom was free-flowing throughout the whole country. This pride would bolster the revolution, for the revolution would adopt a distinctly new character. This pride would be part of the general effort to link the past to the present. This would mean not remaking the whole identity but remaking certain parts of the essence. If the identity had been transformed, what would end up happening is that there would be resentment. This would mean embracing the idea of Americanism, which would keep on spreading throughout the whole country. The effective demographic shifts had made it so that there was no resentment towards other groups. Rather, what would end up happening is that the cohesive country would stick together.

Furthermore, such a plan would mean that the other programs sketched would be thrown away. This pride would be the most important part of the whole equation. The taxes on people with low incomes would all be lifted, continuing to bolster such support further. This was on top of the further reductions that would be made in terms of excess fees. What would effectively happen is that many forms of usury would no longer exist while, at the same time, taxes would be heavily reduced. Such a reduction in taxes would mean that the effective bill that would be footed would be far lower in the end, for the system was based on each according to their ability, to each according to their labor. This was the most important part, for such tax cuts would mean that many bills would be effectively erased. This was on top of the effort to persevere through the times. This perseverance effort would be mounted by this new populist clique that would effectively cling to power with popular support. Not a single inch of American land would be surrendered, while at the same time, the internationalist goal was being worked towards. This would mean that an effective democratic system would form, which would not be tainted by a couple of uncontrollable groups.

Furthermore, this effective democratic system would bolster the support for internationalism that would take place. This effective democratic system meant a free union built out of a former empire. Furthermore, this union was never meant to collapse; this was where its durability came from, for the union was meant to last. This would mean that the borders and the demarcated lines would not matter in the end due to such a prediction.

This contradiction would end up being further intensified with every step that would be made. These steps would end up piling up on the ground, representing what progress would be made toward destroying any revisionism. The story of the revolution could leave off here, but it would have a complete turn. The revolution would grow in every country, but the reactionaries would catch up and show severe repatriations. Canada, for instance, would have a complete crackdown on revolutionary activity. This would be done by making Quebecois nationalism reactionary; thus, they could cooperate. By cooperating with one set of nationalists, they were able to crush the other. This would be further combined with dispersing all of the strikers that would form around Toronto. What would effectively end up happening is that any revolutionary movement would have a complete reprisal. This reprisal would end up including forced labor, which would be given to corporations behind the reprisals.

Furthermore, ethnic repatriations would end up taking place. Any minorities in many bourgeois countries were held with an iron fist. Many would perish in the long journeys that would end up following up. Those journeys were built out of blood. He gave his left hand, and now he couldn't be freed with his right hand. It is painful for someone with so much pride in being someone else's subject. This would end up leading to some national-liberation wars though what would end up happening is that most of them would be hijacked by the reactionaries. They would commit the most horrendous atrocities possible, backed by counter-revolutionaries. The funding for dissidents in Hungary would come from the counter-revolutionary forces. The remainder of the bourgeoisie was able to capture nationalist sentiments, which would end up inspiring some Transylvanians. Those that remained loyal were killed in a massacre with the Transylvanian war starting up. This war would mean that genocide would be committed against the local Magyars. This genocide would be done through the most horrendous methods possible.

Furthermore, the loyalists would see the reactionaries target their Romanian population. This would cause a large exodus of Transylvanians towards Romania, which would completely depopulate the region and cause the majority of Transylvanians to become once again Hungarian. This barren land was inhospitable, for it would be filled with the smoke from the nearby war.

In the end, Hungary and the revolution would emerge victorious though the local Romanian population would incur a large cost – that would be inflicted on them by the reactionaries. The same would end up happening in Croatia, wherein a reactionary force would end up taking control. This would end up mirroring the Ustase; like last time, some loyalists supported the revolution against the force of reaction. Many Serbs would end up being massacred in the following conflicts that would take place. Their massacres would only bolster support for the revolution. An effective revolutionary movement would end up taking place, with Croatia again under the revolution's hand. These twists would directly result from the last-ditch effort that the reactionaries would take against any revolutionary activity. The revolutionaries would use the pragmatic method against the reactionary forces. The reactionary forces would intensify their genocide and centralize the nation, with all minority nations being completely dissolved. The minority nations would end up seeing their cruel fate, which would end up seeing their dissolution as the cultural hegemony would end up completely absorbing all of the reactionaries. The reactionary forces had mainly seen their force as one that liberates certain sections of the population. The nature that would end up folding on itself would perfectly illustrate how the revolution would split into multiple parts. The cultural hegemony that would form, as well as the reactionary forces that would quickly tumble down would only show how divided the whole nation would be. The reactionaries would exploit the division for their benefit. This division method would be completely fail-safe, for the constituent parts of it could be effectively guided by the right hand of the reactionaries. The painfulness of being someone else's subject would guide the reactionaries in their form of nationalism. Their state of nationalism would end up stressing extreme irredentism and winning back the rest of the fatherland at all costs. These costs couldn't be justified other than by propaganda that would be used, showing that it was a divine mission or that the task would be in the common person's interests.

The popularity of the revolution would end up being created through the policies that would be implemented. Inflation would end up being brought under complete control with the total dedication of all those that would make up the revolution. However, the revolution was penetrable if the right buttons were pressed. The buttons would end up causing the downfall of the same revolution that would be built from the top to the bottom. These buttons would end up being related through their function and would see their support completely fall. This would be part of the machine that the imperialists would prop up.

Russia had largely remained poor due to the policies that would give capital to the oligarchy. However, the oligarchy would use this capital to benefit a certain group of people – the reactionaries. The reactionaries would get massive amounts of capital aid from the oligarchs that would exist in Russia with the natural resource money being used. The natural resource money would be used against the revolution, for it would prop up genocides by itself. This would be quite evident in Africa, where the oligarchs had funded to get access to more natural resources. They had funded death squads that would force people to work or die. This would end up constituting modern slavery to its bone. Those within the death squad received ripe benefits from the oligarchs, while everyone outside would perish by force. The force that would be used against the proletariat of Africa would end up seeing many deaths. They would no longer remain proletarians, for they would be mute as slaves. Their fellow compatriots enslaved them as capital would flow out of Africa. This labor exploitation would make it the darkest time that Africa would ever endure.

The liberation rhetoric would end up combined with anti-globalist stances; these stances would progressively intensify as no ground could be given to the reactionaries. This was evident in what happened in Africa, where the complete collapse of the continent occurred. This collapse would be followed by the moral victory of the reactionaries, who would see Africa as merely a hotbed in which resources could be harvested. For them, Africa's harvesting of resources was natural as it was part of a faithful order which would spread "civilization." In actual reality, civilization would be reversed with a return to barbarism. This civilization rhetoric would prove how much the reactionaries cared for the world. The reactionaries' main goal was profit, and it had always been. This moral stance would be compounded by justifications for changing morality to capture the most constituents possible against the revolution in reactionary democracies themselves. The reactionary democracies were built out of thin air, based on bourgeois principles that would pervade their parties. Their parties were all class collaborationist, for they didn't see any classes. They believed that all their people played a fundamental role without looking at the effects and the institutions behind them. They would essentially be corporatists, for their corporatism would differ based on which region it would be practiced. The centralization of the capitalist economy would favor capitalism, for it would end up amplifying capitalism and increasing efficiency. These principles of a planned economy would end up being adopted throughout many reactionary countries, most of whom only thought of themselves as being one nation.

The United Kingdom would fall to this reactionary menace. Earlier, what had ended up happening was that the royal family had been deposed in an act by the liberals. However, this liberal government would prove to be unstable, leading to a reactionary party being elected. When there was a crackdown on liberties, there would be mass strikes. This would end up causing a new government to take place. This would be an alliance of progressives, liberals, and conservatives. However, the military would oppose this, leading to a coup. This coup had completely destabilized the country, with many regions going dark. The economic situation would need to be brought back on track through any means. Many reforms would be quickly implemented; these reforms would include the liberalization of the economy, and the institution of reactionary nationalism would end up taking precedence over any regional identity. The first batch of bills would control inflation by increasing the interest rates and buying back the currency with foreign currency. This revival of the currency's value would only be temporary, for the number of exports would massively decrease due to the instability in Africa. Asia also hit

The exports hard, which was experiencing massive instability. The world was on fire, and for the United Republic to survive, it would need to liberalize quickly. A large crash would occur amidst this liberalization process. This liberalization process largely got rid of universal healthcare and whatever amenities there were. This would end up causing the complete end of any real safety net that was there prior. The safety net would collapse, for it was nothing but a complete sham. The safety net would be largely privatized, with pensions now completely private. This would end up causing a decrease in how much the real pensions were as the administration fees were now much greater. Since the goal was to profit, most pension plans took far more than what would be given out if they aged. This contradiction would end up causing a large crash in the elderly population's spending. This could only be rectified by making the elderly population work, which would be able to supersede the pension plans of the past. Privatizing the industries would end up causing the little safety net to collapse on itself completely. The privatization of healthcare would end up seeing regional monopolies forming, as with the railroads. They would not improve efficiency; on the other hand, efficiency would be cut. What would end up happening is that a massive wealth transfer would end up taking root. This wealth transfer would cause many impoverished and indignant to lose what little they had. This would further aggravate the tensions, which could only be soothed down through the idea that foreign powers were conspiring to destroy Britain. These foreign powers would end up backing Cornwall, Wales, Manx, Ulster, and Scotland to seek independence for themselves. A mass wave of crackdowns on the smaller nations would occur as Irish Republicanism would be crushed by force. This would be further combined with the end of the Cornish lobby. Wales would end up being renegotiated, while Scotland would end up falling into chaos. Scotland would declare independence, largely having its industries completely destroyed due to the permanent war-like status that would go on due to marital law. This was further combined with extreme trade liberalization, which would end up causing the industries of Scotland. The industries of Scotland would end up toppling on each other. The industries of Scotland would end up completely washing away as many jobs would end up being exported to the cheap labor that Africa and Asia would end up providing.

However, all cheap labor doesn't last for long. It was of this that people rose up. It was of this that the crown jewel ahead of them was indeed there. It was of this that the crown jewel, now finding its place within the unity of Africa, and the shared humanity of Africa had flourished. It was of many peoples, yet they all stood as one. It was of many cultures, yet they had put their differences behind. Now, with all they had done, they had shown to the world what would truly have been theirs to come. The world ahead of them, and the future bright, with even all the chaos that had come, it was of theirs that they had become a great sanctuary.

One could see this within a cafethere. Here, upon this intersection, there was Lazarus, a recent arrival, and that of Sirach, a native there. Lazarus said, "this is a lot better than before, where I had to hear a politician rant and my life deteriorate," and Sirach said, "this is a complete sanctuary, and I do not ask for anything more than a sanctuary." It was this hospitality that did come about, for theirs was that which does not break.

However, there was not only doom and gloom. In the great continent of Africa, they had indeed come together and believed in theirs was truly of their destiny. They had believed that they could stick together, and when they had done so, their character would be what would matter in the end. It was of this that a region that was long neglected by the oppressors was one that was now free with their own destiny, and their destiny that they did craft was one that had given the great raft. The boat that would sail would be that which would never fail. The boat that they did sail would come to the world as such, and the boat had given all that it could to the world.

With the hotbed that there was of the loyalist continent, that loyalist continent that had long taken upon the world that had to come was one that had indeed shown. That loyalist continent was once looted, yet it now stood at a great intersection. With the great intersection secured, the loyalist continent took upon a path that would not break. It was of this loyalist continent that they had not only seen, but had kept in the end. If they truly understood, and with the change and fervor that they had taken amongst themselves, Antonin had proclaimed, "I have truly won." Yet, it was his opponents that had retorted, "you have not, and it is of mine first that you will truly see." All counter-revolution that was upon was that which was lied to. Say it was a counter-revolution, and Antonin's government would say it is of revolution. Say it is of oppression, and Antonin's government would say it is of freedom. Say it is that which had never embarked upon the world, and Antonin's government would say that they had interfered elsewhere. All things Antonin were flipped. Oppression is freedom. Discrimination is privilege. Nationalism is internationalism. That itself is from which Antonin's framework had been developed. Antonin had effectively taken ahold and subjugated the population under him – that of the foreigners and the loyalists were soon to come, and those that were already under his rule were those that had seen the greatest thumb of oppression that they had been under.

The United Republic would end up having a civil war with the Scottish War of Independence. This would end up seeing many tanks being driven into the capital of Scotland, and the other forces would end up securing Scotland. The Scottish war for independence had effectively ended, and harsh reprisals were given out to match the severity of the war in their eyes. Many alliances would end up being formed by the opposition, which would end up consisting of a right-wing populist alliance with the other populists. Generally, the right-wing populists were much smaller than any of the other groups though these alliances would end up signifying how the country's progress was going. For Britain, this alliance had been formed underground, with the nationalist factions being completely merged. The right-wing populists were no more, with many radical nationalist groups being recruited into the cadres of the revolutionaries. The revolutionaries largely saw all the problems as consequences of the current system, not being independent of it. These problems would end up manifesting themselves that would all be linked together. The independence of the revolutionaries would end up seeing the stability of Britain go further down. This could only be rectified by the further liberalization of the economy. The deregulation of the economy of Britain would end up causing the resources of Britain to be vastly washed away. The liberalization of the economy would end up causing a further spiral decline of the economy. The economy was starting to crash due to the end of the little welfare there used to be. The increase of nationalism would end up causing the country's nations to agitate for independence completely. The independence of the individual nations would end up being at the nation's core. The sovereignty of individual nations would end up causing the national identity to restart again. The national identity would end up superseding any form of reactionary stance. They would end up rejecting any deviations as while those deviations were nationalist, they would end up conflicting against the core principle. This would be the main difference between those deviations and the true nationalists. The true nationalists would end up fighting for the revolution as many of them would be completely integrated. The nationalism that would end up being developed would end up upholding the cultural development of each nation. These nations would end up being part of the world revolution, which would be part of the general federation that would end up forming. The United States would end up being the main revolutionary country.

Sarah, however, was still here. Sarah wanted to see that Antonin himself would come to his senses and that he would abandon the efforts that were ahead of him. Sarah herself wanted to see that Antonin would not take it upon the world to go on an ever-greater venture in which Antonin had promised something else, but had ultimately retaliated on the promises that were given. Antonin and Sarah, with the work that they had done together, was that which they had looked forward to. With all the patches that had been applied, they had tried to once again reconnect, yet nothing would seem to work out. Was Antonin truly the psychopath that she thought of him to be? Was Antonin the person that could not be stopped? Furthermore, there was a time in which Antonin, with all of what he invaded as such, now penetrating into the core heartlands of the

Old World, had created collaboration with, and as such, they had started to take out Antonin's own agenda upon them. With Antonin's command, however, all hope that there was came out crushed. All home that there was through the smog would no longer exist, and with all achievements that there were in the past, this would come there to be the last. Sarah would ultimately never take anything from Antonin ever again.

Tension that continued to build was one that was taken and seized forth by Lazarus and Sirach. It was through such tension that what they looked ahead to would be that which they had a great plot that would not break. Through such a plot that they had undertaken, they had looked forward to each and every single issue that was built. Yet, it was of the parties that did remain to take over, and as these parties themselves had remained within the struggle that was unfolding, they had put forth their own agenda above all. Through this agenda that they had effectively developed, all that they had seen as that which had enveloped had not broken. It was of this agenda that they looked forward to that which does not break. Through the world that had come, it was of this that brother would turn upon brother, children would turn on their parents, and all that mattered in the very end was that of their loyalty. Only their loyalty had mattered in the end, and if their loyalty had not brought forth the good fruits that would come as a direct result of their loyalty, then it was of such a principle that they had proclaimed as one that they would build, from the very inception, to the very end. It was from such a principle that they would not only see, but would build every successive consequence that had come about. This was of their centralism that they had established, and it could be far from saying that the centralism was democratic. It was through the events that had truly unfolded that what had come as a direct result was one whose effective power would not last as that which was separate. All they may have duped was that which does not last. It was of such a duping that each exact undertaking that they had seen was that which came from the very beginning. It was of this agenda that they had seen as an undertaking that had all in the making. Through the undertaking that was ahead of them as such, they had continued to look at what had developed situationally, and through such situational development that was ahead of them, every single step that they had placed forth was that which had shown the direct result of such loyalty. So as long as they proclaimed loyalty, and not that built on principle, then they would find their efforts would pay off in the very end. It was from these principles that they would see all that would unfold would have the great events ahead of them come through. Now, when the lifeless planners had come to the table of their parties, being exact replica of one another, for theirs had sought forth invasion, then it was of these exact programmers that had seen first and foremost. It was of these exact programmers that their agenda would be drawn up in full, leading to ever greater destruction ahead of them. The programmers of these parties would end up being completely identical. They would end up all reading similar lines that would go based on the following:

1. The privatization of the economy is imminent to save the country from complete economic destruction that the revolution would bring on. The revolution will end up destroying the economy by any means by targeting all the businesses behind it.

2. We will control inflation by ensuring that money is not being printed in large quantities. This will also help in causing the government from refraining in the economy. These measures combined will put the current inflationary crisis under complete control.

3. The inflationary crisis has spun out of hand due to unpatriotic economists running the country. This crisis must be combatted through any active measures that can be implemented. These active measures are active in every sense of the word there is. This would mean using the economy as the piggyback for whatever gains would be made. These gains will directly coincide with the profits of the state, and the first step in this process would be to return more capital to the bourgeoisie as a means of getting them to reinvest. When they reinvest, the economy will grow; thus, this can pay off the tax cuts.

4. The police must be adequately funded through any means to maintain law and order. Any strikes or any other disorder will not be tolerated. The implicit interest will end up breaking up any organization

that any disorderly person will end up incurring. The end of these pesky institutions will be fair compensation for the idea of working your way up the ladder.

5. There is no such thing as classes. Classes are merely an approach that these revolutionaries created to undermine the very social fabric of our society. Classes have never existed, nor will they ever will. Each member of community ends up playing an important part in it.

6. The liberalization of the economy will be done based on corporatist lines. This will mean having each person play a role in the economy. By being able to raise living standards, we can avert the revolutionary wave that will constantly push against us.

7. We believe that the interests of the owners of capital are the interests of all. Most people want to work their way up the ladder, which is why we're giving them that opportunity. The interests of the owners of capital will always help our nation. All of the essential branches of our industry will end up being nurtured by the capital that the owners will bring in—the components of our industry and supplemented by the increased capital flow that, can rebuild our military.

8. We must be proud of our military. Our military is the key defense piece of our nation. Our military is there to enforce peace throughout the world. By aiding our military, we are doing a great favor to our country. They serve to defend our country by any cost. By supporting our nation, they end up paying themselves off, as foreign aggression will always be many miles away. Our military and the military-industrial complex rightly deserve all of the capital throughout our nation. These key institutions hold our most important pieces to national sovereignty.

9. We argue against protectionism as free trade with our neighbors will allow for the creation of jobs as well as lower costs for common household items. This contrasts the revolutionary disorder, which seeks to take away all of your possessions. Protectionism is the most inherent evil there is, and by being able to trade with our neighbors, we can benefit all of the parties involved.

10. Protectionism is the principle that will raise costs for all of your common household items. Who wants to spend more and have lower real wages? Thus, our primary focus is actively supporting the economic system our forefathers have aspired to create. Our financial system is infallible, for our government will end up aiding all of the ailing industries that come into existence. I do not know what recession led us to such large debts that we could not bury them.

11. We are strongly committed to preserving world peace and our interests abroad. Our interests will be put first above all, as they are the same as the interests of our allies. The pigheaded isolationists merely resemble the revolutionary forces that seek to take away whatever you possess in your hands. The evil empire formed can only be taken down through containing wherever it goes. The revolutionary sentiment is nothing but the work of propagandists. It is firmly necessary to know that our country's national defense is above everything else. The militarist sentiment must be taken into complete use. Our country's militarist sentiment must be used to prevent a single inch of our land from being surrendered. If we offer a single inch of our land, we have failed to end the forces of the revolution. Our forces must preserve peace throughout the world. Our bloc against the revolution must be constantly expanded at all times. We must have a free trade zone to prevent conflict between our nations. These trade deals will bolster the whole world's economy to bring all of our war economies together. Our war economies must all be brought closer together to eliminate any barriers in our economies. All free trade deals must be signed for cooperation and industrialization. All underdeveloped countries will get a grant each year, allowing for tax cuts for corporations. This will allow for all sides to win as we will get the interest off of it while they go through industrialization. Industrialization is the cornerstone of our plan to retain the power of people who care about the nation over anything else. All of the anti-nationalist forces must be defeated through any means necessary. The anti-nationalist forces are encapsulated and emboldened by the revolution.

12. Tax cuts will be enacted to keep the economy running again. The tax cuts, for some, will ultimately benefit all. The average person

knows how to spend tax money way wiser than the government knows how to. Thus, the government must not take much in taxes. The goal of our government is to create and not take. These tax cuts for the corporations will, in the end, trickle down to the consumer and the worker. These tax cuts will allow for further economic growth as it is our signature policy to put them forward. These tax cuts will not only come in the form of corporate tax but industrial tariffs as well. Cutting these tariffs and corporate taxes will allow for greater prosperity as more wealth will trickle down to the average worker. Our goal is to prevent as many unions from forming as they will distort the market in the long run. To prevent unions from forming, we must put comprehensive policies to address their root cause. We must fight them off at every level, as recessions must be allowed to occur. These are not merely recessions; on the other hand, most will allow for market corrections. The market must be completely liberated from the shackles of slavery. It is only through the market that we can tackle the many crises that are above us today. The freedom of the individual means nothing; the freedom of the individual can only exist when there is freedom in the market. If any revolutionary force threatens the freedom found in the market, we will also lose our other freedoms. Society should work for the market to enrich the market with many goods that would not have been there. The choice within the market will be able to out-compete any other service. If a monopoly ever forms, it is because of government intervention. Natural monopolies do not exist as they are only creations of the government and no other entity. The natural monopolies that would ever form would directly result from the government. Labor unions may also contribute to the rise of natural monopolies as labor unions will make it so that the labor will concentrate in only one market because the price of labor is much higher than in other markets. This vision of tax cuts will greatly aid in constructing a true market economy. The age of classical liberalism and Keynesian policy has long been over. Most of their ideas have merged with the revolutionary theory. The Keynesians have held out, merging with our corporatist allies. Regardless, the only way we can combat these ideologies is through the enrichment of the market and the aid given to the police state. The police must be protected through any means. The police themselves will allow for the market to be enforced singlehandedly. The police must not be able to form unions, however. If any union activity comes from the police state, hiring private contractors to do the same job is completely acceptable. The union activity must be broken through any means as it causes the price of labor to mismatch.

13. The solemn declaration of these principles will mean that the government will tend to stay out of private lives as much as possible unless there is a moral imperative. Sometimes, we must protect our most cherished programs as part of our welfare state. However, if we do, we must always recognize the excesses and try to cut back on those. The corruption that exists within society all ends up stemming from the government. The bigger the government, the more corruption there is. This firm principle will guide our nation through the toughest times when corruption may run rampant. This declaration of staying out of the lives of private individuals as much as possible would entail that the government will reduce the activity being done in the private lives of individuals. This would mean eliminating any malfeasance activity that individuals commit as part of the law and order policy. The goal would be to increase the police state to reduce crime. This would coincide with further streamlining of the market to eliminate the causes of crime. By being able to get rid of the red tape that surrounds minority neighborhoods and centers of crime, it is possible to reduce crime through the gentrification of those neighborhoods. The gentrification of those neighborhoods further compels the criminals to disintegrate their crimes. Once their crimes are decentralized, it is possible to catch all the criminals behind them one step at a time. Prison labor can be used for the benefit of the private market. Prison labor will end up providing rehabilitation; increasing the prison sentences for those who commit crimes is necessary. This will further aid in this new repair form, making strong people through manual labor. This police state may as well be paid off through this program. The welfare state should be used as a last resort, with certain services being cut back if they do not serve the market. Society should help the market, not the opposite way around. Society must do everything to keep the market free and prevent collisions

that could get it off course. These principles that can be enforced will allow for a moral society free of crime.

14. Lastly, when these excesses are contained, we must assist our allies and provide for the highest economic growth possible. When the free market is truly free, it will end up flourishing. All of the monopolies will end up breaking on their own when all of the regulations are gotten rid of. Being able to rush through this program will ensure the security of our nation. Our nation's interests abroad must always be protected; we must have the strength to preserve peace. We must always aid our fellow citizens in enriching our country through whatever means.

These principles would end up being heralded as the pamphlet of neoliberalism. Neoliberalism's existence would end up being based on these core principles. These core principles were part of the general program emphasizing shared values. This would end up appealing to the most reactionary individuals, wherein the program would end up having perverse notions that would be within. They would all be dog whistles for the general plan to rework the economy's fundamentals completely.

The liberalization of the economy would end up being followed by a partial liberalization in the society, to encourage discourse within a set frame. This would end up effectively creating multiple neoliberal parties, which would go against each other regarding the question of intervention and how much trade to have. However, the general tide towards trade would be a large welcome that the other countries would see. America was effectively isolated from the rest of the world as it would be the only revolutionary country. This was combined with a considerable population decline that would arise from the civil war. While America's population was still growing, it would end up being permanently scarred due to the large destruction of the civil war. The civil war would end up allowing for the country's rapid industrialization. The forced industrialization would send agricultural output to an all-time high while relying on the resources found back home for energy. This would effectively mean a transition to a green energy system, for it would be used as a more durable energy source. This energy source could last for any time as it would harvest the energy that came here naturally. These resources would end up being used for a different purpose, allowing for the complete industrialization of the country. Now, the country needed to export the revolution worldwide. It had lost all of its revolutionary allies, for it would be completely devoid of any reconstruction of those allies through aid to the revolutionary guerrillas fighting in those nations. All that was left now consisted of broken forces dispersed throughout many countries. These forces couldn't operate independently, for they would need to piggyback off other forces. These forces were completely demotivated due to the failures of the other revolutions. This would end up causing a revival in the principle of the revolution taking place in one country. The world revolution had been imminently subverted, with only individual movements now taking shape. These particular movements would be completely disconnected from all of the other activities. These movements would end up being all connected when it came to the revolutionary ideal though they would all be disconnected from each other.

The neoliberal principles that would end up being pushed would be completely isolated from all other regulations that would make up humanity. The intensification of the class struggle that would take place within these reactionary neoliberal nations would end up seeing their core being completely wiped out. Their neoliberal forces would guide them toward a false liberation in which the reactionaries would completely control the nations. The reactionaries would end up driving many of these nations towards bankruptcy to completely destroy any existing culture. This would be amplified by the creation of a de facto hegemonic language. These fundamental parts of the puzzle would end up causing the complete division of any reactionary unity of the idea of a nation. This would end up oppressing nations, though simultaneously bring all nations together. Their working class would end up being more intermingled as they were all part of the reserve army of labor. This reserve army of work didn't care as they were all cogs of a nation. This would end up meaning that mass unemployment would end up forming in many of these counter-revolutionary countries. They would all strive to get rid of any rights the proletariat had, with all of the fundamental rights being undermined. These rights would end up being damaged using the pretext of national security. This national security, in reality, was not under any actual attack. This would outlaw the labor unions that would form and all other institutions in which proletarians could organize. Other countries that didn't prohibit their unions have saw union membership massively decline as a result of making the labor market more dynamic. This would mean shipping off jobs to other countries and focusing on capital-intensive industries with no real value other than what would be associated with it – which would end up being the value of capital creation. This repeated cycle would lead to capital accumulation, as all major forms of capital would become part of the collection's cornerstone. This accumulation of wealth would end up being at the core of the reactionary military-industrial complex, which would end up demanding more profits be invested in the military-industrial complex.

The military-industrial complex had seen its profits massively grow through the years, with its core industries blossoming under the rule of the neoliberals. Neoliberalism was at the core of the reactionary administrations that would end up sweeping right through the world. No division could be created from the neoliberal coin, for they all had the same heads and tails. Cut the coin in half, and it would act like a magnet. The difference was so minimal that the parties had no real difference. They would vary on certain social issues, which were part of a much smaller industry that didn't invest as much, but their core principles would remain the same.

Isolationism would end up being part of the core doctrine of the revolution. Isolationism would not be complete, however, as there would be intervention when needed. This intervention would end up helping all of the citizens of the last revolutionary holdout, which would consist of America. The reason America couldn't be targeted due to its military might thought it would remain effectively isolated from every other country. America would stand up to all the reactionary forces seeking to destroy its state. America would end up being the beacon of the revolution, building on the old revolution, which would espouse liberty, equality, and fraternity. Isolationism would be a means to an end for this project as it would allow for rapid industrialization. Isolation was not total; it would assist all forces with reactionary oppression. The rapid industrialization of America would end up being followed by agricultural improvements and green industrialization. This would come from a standpoint that could reduce energy dependency on other countries. This would mean that internal trade could end up out-competing trade abroad. Right now, the most important thing is to have the industries locally rejuvenated with the bow that would use the proletariat's power. The proletariat's power would end up being put above all other abilities. The proletariat's power would end up seeing all other classes relegated to the dustbin of history. History would end up seeing the revolution as something eternal. History is something that cannot be run around. This would end up making history as it would spread throughout the world. Isolationism would end up being the core ideology that the revolutionaries would pursue. The revolutionaries sought to pursue isolationism as a result of completely getting rid of any reactionary traces that would end up remaining. The revolution could only survive if it could hold itself up. It could see itself gliding through the skies if it could maintain its standards. The skies and the revolution were synonymous with each other. The revolution could only survive if lightning didn't hit it. When the eagle flies through the skies, it must ensure it is safe from anything hitting it. The reactionaries would weep the last drop of tears as they saw the end of their main strongholds. Their strongholds would fall as a result of many interventions that the proletariat would make. The proletariat would seek to secure their existence within those regions with the main goal of getting rid of the strongholds of the reactionaries. The reactionaries would end up allying with all major forces seeking the destruction of the proletariat. The proletariat's victory would rely on mobilizing all forces to save the revolution. All of the forces of the revolution would end up being harvested to get rid of the fundamental base fueling the superstructure. The superstructure and the base were completely antithetical to each other, as they would end up against each other in all forms. The superstructure and the command would end up conflicting in every aspect. These aspects would end up going as the wind would end up blowing. The further intensification of this struggle would only provide food for thought. The reactionaries would develop a new manifesto that would guarantee the right of corporate powers to hold power.

1. We must fight for the right of all groups involved in the trade to do so fairly. This would mean that no workers will ever be hungry again. This contrasts with the revolutionary malfeasance that seeks to change how we live our society completely. We must find a third position that will be able to abridge the needs of the workers and corporations. This third position can end up providing for the general population of our country. Our country must be built out of the hard work that the people of our country bring. Our country must be made out of the liberation of all our peoples through a new force that can unite us all. We are freedom-loving fellow citizens that seek to preserve our nation against the revolution. The revolution is completely against us, seeking to replace all we cherish. The revolution completely aims to starve the family by using any means. The revolution will destroy all that you hold dear. Our revolution, which is truly built for the people, is completely different from theirs. Our revolution will be able to preserve tradition and all that we believe is part of the larger continuation of thought. Our revolution is completely different as our legionaries will eliminate the degeneracy that is starting to build in society. The degeneration that is taking place in our society will lead us to our eventual doom. It is part of the revolutionary spirit that seeks to oppress us. It aims to take away our liberty, as all we support will die in vain. This new revolution will completely reverse our liberation from the original revolution. Our country's independence relies on our legionaries and rank-and-file support. This support can get rid of the forces of the revolution completely. The revolution mostly goes against our revolution as it sees the society as made out of oppressors and oppressed. This differs from our view, which seeks to incorporate all in our war against corruption. It is only the strongmen that matter

the most. The strongmen will be able to completely bring our society forward, especially against the corrupt degeneracy that is forming. This corrupt degeneracy is causing our country to be completely brought down by the neoliberals. The neoliberals seek to eliminate our society by destroying our liberty and right to exist. Our right to exist exists due to what we fought for earlier. Our legionaries will constantly seek to preserve our society, for it works for the common person. It works for the real common person and not the common person that is being created as a strawman. All of us have seen the end of how great our country is. The greatness of our nation has been completely diminished due to the neoliberal forces that have gone against our people. The people have been oppressed by the revolutionaries who seek to take away everything that we must protect. The revolution and our people are completely contradictory to each other. The revolution and our people are opposed to each other. The rebellion must be crushed through any means, and the first step starts within our country itself. Our country has many revolutionaries that seek to destroy our country and lead it to doom completely. We must learn that rapid industrialization will cause famine throughout our country. These shortages are characteristics of the revolution that must be completely ended. These shortages will never come to our great nation. Our great nation must be protected through any means possible, for our great country is part of the larger sphere which can oppose the revolution completely. The revolution must be destroyed through any means possible, with the paternalism of our country being able to provide support for our people. Our people matter most, above all, not through empty phrases of the revolutionaries. The revolutionaries will seek to bring the destruction of life, for their sadistic practices are integral to their doctrine. They are the most immoral people you will ever see, with their ideology inspiring many deaths worldwide. The revolution must be warded off through direct action that we must take. The revolution must be killed off through action that we must take. If we do not act, our beautiful motherland will fall to the revolution.

2. What is a corporation? A corporation is built out of the workers and the owners that make up the company. They are essentially the same

as they are part of the same body. This has to do with the fact that the corporations were built for all parties involved. They will trade with all peoples of our bloc. A corporation is the cornerstone of society. This has to do with the corporation being based on the actual reality of what the people need and not in a carefully crafted falsehood. By establishing the corporation on the essential needs of the people, it is possible to recreate the corporation as a figure that can liberate the people from their oppression on Earth. It is the true form that completely avoids the liberation that the revolutionaries seek to create. The revolutionaries seek to destroy the fabric that makes our society. The revolutionaries seek to destroy everything that our society embodies completely. The revolutionaries seek to overturn the rule of law within our society completely. The corporations that form will be able to hold on to the tradition of our country for much longer. The practice of our country can be saved in a collective effort that can preserve all of the rules we've made.

3. What is our ideology? Our ideology is based on keeping the good in society, and that's where our conservatism approaches this angle. Our conservatism is based on preserving the tradition that still holds on in our society. Even though our society has been largely corrupted by foreign influences such as the revolution, it still holds on to some traditions. Our goal is to keep the ceremony as alive as possible. Keeping the tradition alive can vanquish the vast hegemony of the revolution that seeks to destroy our society. Our society's very fabric is constantly threatened by the influences of the revolution and all other malfeasances that aim to destroy our society completely. Our society is being torn apart by the effects of groups constantly seeking to endanger our liberty. The liberty of our country depends on the freedom that these corporations have. These corporations comprise our country as they are formed through directly linked councils.

4. Our society strives for a state which works for all productive people. This would mean intervening on behalf of anyone who contributes to their country. This would mean aiding entrepreneurs to make our country great again and negotiating with our workers so no

person is poor. Furthermore, we must completely merge the unions with the corporate bodies to eliminate the manifestations of revolutionary sentiment. The government must represent the corporations, who will be able to secure rights for all. Our goal would be to maximize profit, with each person getting a share in the profit. Furthermore, we must reserve the basic infrastructure to ensure social security and healthcare are provided. This can be done through a comprehensive bill that can sweep away the power of the corrupt and put in place the corporations that represent all of the people in society. The social security system doesn't need to be based on the government, for the corporate sector can also do it. The corporate sector could end up negotiating to lower prices, and subsidies can be given to these key sectors. Poverty can be eliminated with a stronger state being created in the end. This can keep government intervention to the minimum as these subsidies come through the tax cuts given to the corporations that will manage housing, education, healthcare, and social security. When placed under the new system, these key sectors will be able to secure our country's economy against the revolution completely.

5. Our country must be part of the general sphere of trading blocs that can fend off the revolution's influence. The revolution will seek to destroy everything that it touches. The revolution will seek to completely uproot our mighty people's influence through the deceptions made to our people. Our traditions will be completely crushed if the revolution gets its way. The revolution must be routed through any viable means, both internally and externally. The end of the revolution will mean that the revolution will no longer pose a threat to our people in any way possible. This must be combined with the complete end of the revolution through direct intervention if it threatens our people with war. The revolution will seek to eliminate our society through any means it has in its toolbox. When we starve off the revolution, we can eliminate all of our society's influences that will bring us our downfall. The revolution must be destroyed through any means that can be practically used. These means can destroy revolutionary activity to its core, as extreme action brings our country to the end of time. These trading blocs will be geared

towards all parties to eliminate job losses. The job losses that have long carried our nation down are only the beginning of the tip of what the revolution wants to achieve. The revolution seeks to amplify this free trade for the reason of liberty. It intends to automate all industries to displace our working populations completely. It will bring low-skilled, cheap labor from other countries and substitute the working class of our country. If we let the revolution go on any longer, we will completely lose grip of the situation. The entire case and the whole crisis have been brought to the forefront as a result of the increased free trade presence that has been taking place. This increased free trade presence will cause the downfall of our country, for it is always near. This increased free trade must be put to an end if we can conquer the revolution. The vanquished revolution must be made through the reaction pushing on the revolution. The revolution must die through any means. The revolution must fail through the state itself. Our agenda that will prioritize trade with our neighbors will be able to increase living standards for all of us. The advanced industrial presence will keep us on par with the revolutionary government, which seeks to industrialize at the cost of its people rapidly. Our country must industrialize through respect for the people. This industrialization doesn't have to be rapid for trade and can greatly lower the cost for our people. The transaction can reduce the cost of goods for our people as we have many allies while the revolution has none. These allies must be comprehensively used to displace the revolution completely. We must seek to prevent the revolution from advancing by having the commonality of trade between our nations.

6. A trade bloc must be created. This trade bloc will be able to embargo the revolutionary bloc and create a custom trade and tariffs union. This common policy will decrease the cost of the production of goods. We must furthermore seek to strive towards a one-world currency. This currency will be pegged to gold as it will remain stable throughout the years. This currency can be used to remove the disturbances that increased trade between our nations completely will create. Ultimately, our common prosperity will cause our nations to nurture freedom further. Our economic system will work much better

than the revolutionaries' system, for it will be able to secure freedom throughout the test of time. We must hold on to this system of economics for us to further nurture independence. The revolutionaries have completely planned the neoliberalism of the past to accelerate the economy's collapse. The neoliberalism of the past must be completely displaced through any means possible. The neoliberalism of the past must be reformed into this corporatism which keeps the same core principle of seeking further victories for the corporations when it comes to profit. The primary difference is that many of the workers are given shares in their companies, being able to invest in their future. This will allow for a true corporatist system to form as these shares represent the voting power they will have in their company. When these shares are sold off, so is the voting power. This is a game of true stability in which no side will voluntarily falter. By relegating these stocks into the hands of the people and being able to provide a good standard of living that can further accelerate the development of our society, we can overtake the revolutionaries as a collective. The question is whether we should have revolutionary ideals or true freedom. The economic freedoms that this simple anti-trust law will afford will be able to keep the market versatile. Furthermore, all can invest in the system to make a profit. This law will take effect and be repealed when workers come out with the majority of the shares. Profits can rapidly expand at any cost, with the negotiation between these corporations providing a safety net. Furthermore, all of these services will come at a heavily subsidized cost created through the liberation of the market. These services can all come with private pension plans heavily subsidized through tax breaks. This will cause large returns in social security for the projects all invest in the market. Investing in the market is at the core of our philosophy – compassionate conservatism. This compassionate conservatism works for the common person while keeping a free market outlook. This is combined with a new form of corporatism that can completely displace government intervention. By taking simple measures that will be able to redistribute the shares of the businesses to the people, it is possible to avoid corporate tyranny.

7. We are firmly convinced that the redistribution of shares and the further liberation of the market will free our people. This liberation of the

market must be through a purposeful restart regarding where the stakes are being put. Our whole economy, except for important services, must be privatized. This privatization is now fine due to the people owning many of the shares to which the capital would end up flowing. Our country's economy must be completely privatized, with all aspects of our economy now working in favor of the people, even if that is not direct. Our compassionate conservatism can care for the people truly. It is part of the end goal of keeping the economic system working for the people. The economic system must always work for the people for our economy to work. The government must be in the hands of the corporations the people control. We must completely uplift all people experiencing world poverty through pragmatism and means that can support the people. We must reject the revolutionary fervor that is taking place throughout the world. The revolutionary zeal that is taking place worldwide is causing our civilization's end. Compassion must always guide our principles, for we seek to lift all of the masses from poverty on our Earth. We only have one Earth to live on, and we must preserve that Earth through principles that can steal all of us from poverty. Poverty-stricken neighborhoods are a result of government meddling, which ends up furthering crime. We must completely redistribute the shares of the companies in favor of those that are part of the ordinary class. We must have this power through the buyout of the shares in the recession. This compassionate conservatism will lift people from poverty as our united front can keep liberty around while not divulging into the revolutionary bloc. This is through our alliance that takes place as we are the voice of the masses of the right. The voice of the masses of the right represents the true worker, both you and I. The voice of the masses would be linked to the current state of civilization. Our goal is to fight for the regular people truly. Ordinary people matter over everything else. They do not care about the bickering in the revolutionaries, for they only want basic food. Over time, the American Revolution will fail like the Soviet experiment many decades earlier. It is merely a continuation of the failed state and the failed revolution. Ultimately, our system will win; the real question is where you stand.

8. Our system believes in corporatist intervention to benefit all sides of the coin. To benefit both sides, we must unite our movement under nationalism and extreme anti-revolutionary rhetoric. This is combined with socially conservative rhetoric to completely replace all of the revolutionary forces with a true working-class force. This working-class force is a coalition of all parties throughout the spectrum. All peoples of our country are generally part of it though immigration and other forms of replacement must not get out of hand. This must be combined with getting rid of the main source of corruption. Immigration is what ends up causing our country to be weak, as many of these immigrants never assimilate. Furthermore, they always have the chance of contributing to crime. We may form a coalition with nativists to end up curtailing the power of the revolutionaries by being able to cut down on immigration. Generally, we share the same agenda but with a few key differences. We must be far more vigilant against crime, which we've inherited, and our opposition to immigration. Immigration is what will cause the end of our nation as a whole. Immigration must be strictly curtailed, with immigrants from the right places being brought in. The immigrants must be completely assimilated with the individual culture and replaced by the greater American identity. The only way we can ever solve the problem of national identity would be through the assimilation of all of the immigrants while taking a stance that would provide comfort for our citizens. For us, fascism is an extreme form of social democracy; this is the reversal of the idea that a moderate form of fascism is social democracy. This reversal must be taken to our heart, for we must embrace these principles with whatever we have. The immigration crisis must be tackled by assimilating the immigrants. This will prevent any movement growing out of us from the right while being able to prevent defectors to the revolutionaries. We must consolidate the campaign for a true revolution that can completely bring in our people under a common banner.

9. Our nation must be defended from the degeneracy of culture by immigrants. The goal of our immigrants is for them to assimilate. The assimilation of our immigrants will strengthen our population, providing

us with a larger cultural base. We must have the immigrants assimilate on top of our system, which favors the people. Our system that favors the people is based on the institution of many protections for our people that can allow our people to thrive in a prosperous society. There should be no poor in a rich country. This is our guiding principle; we must do this through a system that favors all. Furthermore, we must curtail the most extreme right by taking up their anti-immigration position, though, with the main exception that the immigrants assimilate. Unlike the revolutionaries, our position can form a true party that cares about the people. The revolutionaries embody all of the world's evil; Satan has sent them to crush our civilization. Our civilization will not survive the longer we allow the revolutionaries to operate. Overcoming the revolutionaries requires all actions possible to be taken. The revolutionaries seek to change our population radically demographically. Furthermore, they seek to completely replace our civilization with a degeneracy that cannot be cured without decades of intervention. When we try to institute our system, it fails in the newly liberated countries. We saw this with the fall of the last revolutionary state. This is because the revolutionaries have bankrupted those countries, so they could no longer rejuvenate themselves. The newly liberated countries have been completely driven to the ground by these revolutionaries who constantly seek to go against the current order. The current order will be completely subverted by these revolutionaries who will go against the changes made for the people to support their overlords. Their overlords are found within a specific group that has dominated the world. They were responsible for the last major revolution that shook the world, and they were responsible for this revolution that took place. They are all backed by these people that created one coin but with two sides. They are all around the place; condemning them is completely banned due to modern society. The degeneracy that our society has fallen into has to do with the revolutionary sentiment quickly developing worldwide. The world is being consumed in the flames of the revolution. The same applies to our great civilization. One by one, everything falls to the revolution. This must be completely avoided through any means by a direct program of eliminating the revolutionary fervor. We must replace class consciousness with national consciousness. Our nation and its infiltration by immigrants are the primary drivers of our collapse. The collapse of our nation will be a direct result of the revolutionary sentiments that take place. The people that bring them in are the revolutionaries who want to concentrate their ideas all in one land. This active settlement project is causing this country to favor the revolution. This is opposed to the views of our people; our people are strongmen. They vehemently oppose the revolution, unlike these immigrants who have never assimilated into our society. These immigrants have caused our national identity the greatest destruction of all others. These immigrants are coming and replacing our jobs. The common person of this country has much to fear from these immigrants and nothing to gain. They worry about their job security.

10. The country's immigrants had largely been coerced into completely supporting the revolutionaries' determination. The country's immigrants must be completely integrated with the goal of completely removing all of the malfeasances within our country. Our country has been completely corrupted by the malfeasances within as they seek to remove our proud nation from its inheritance completely. Our country has deteriorated to the point that revolutionaries have completely removed it in every aspect. The revolutionaries have completely broken our country down into pieces, and our country remains completely shattered by the revolutionaries. The revolutionaries have seen their course in their belief in the dialectical method's principle. The rational approach is an incorrect way of judging anything as it is based on the materialist nature of everything. The materialist nature of reality is completely false, for reality largely exists due to dictation.

11. Lastly, much of the nationalist sentiment must be capitalized on. Nationalism must be completely harnessed in favor of the movement to contain the revolution completely. The revolution will seek to destroy our way of life. We must completely reform the economy to oppose revolutionary means. The revolutionary movement will seek to destroy our culture and our society. Our very social fabric will be completely

entrapped throughout the test of time. We must completely defend our country against the revolutionaries, for they will seek to eliminate our pride. The nationalist fervor will go against us in any form.

All of the following events would be based on what happened during the revolution. This revolution would end up seeing all of the power of the reactionaries being completely crushed. This would end up linking to the power that the brain of the revolution would possess. The brain of the revolution would end up seeing its power as part of the intricate power structure which would form out of it. The power of the revolution would end up being inherently vested within the will of the proletariat. The choice of the proletariat would end up being completely in the hands of the proletariat, and there was no way to change it. The nationalist backing of the revolutionaries would end up seeing many of the generals and admirals that were already there from the previous regime of the United States back the revolution. They would not oppose the new administration, for they would be loyal to the revolution and the people. By being able to make it so that the military doesn't form another third faction, what ended up happening is that the military generals would end up being integrated straight into the revolutionary camp. This would end up seeing all of the major generals that the previous reactionary regime had now being used for the revolution. This would end up being combined with vows to defend the revolution, essentially providing all the major nationalist support needed. This would destroy the nationalists as a faction, as many of the nationalists fought in the civil war.

Furthermore, this would ensure clearance that the revolution could survive without the aid of the reactionaries when it came to the military. The military support would end up being crucial to the end goal of completely securing all power for the proletariat. All of the power in the proletariat could once again be brought up through the development of these institutions that would end up defending the proletariat. The proletariat would become part of the major front where the revolution could be conducted. By conducting the revolution using the proletariat, it could happen that each proletariat would fall in line with almost all of its core constituencies being thought to have been part of the means to an end. The proletariat and the revolution were consequently inseparable from each other, being part of the same continuum. There was nothing but the revolution for the great saviors that would descend from their lineage. Their lineage would prove to be monumental; it was not their genetics that mattered but their birthplace that mattered for these nationalist groups. This was further combined with assimilation if their home was different. It would be the combination of these factors that the revolution could end up being the birthplace of all major movements that would sprout up from it. All ideals that would be romanticized would be part of the revolution. These romanticized ideals would see their interest in eliminating the reactionary tendencies that still exist.

The autarky that would develop throughout the country couldn't last forever, though it was necessary as the United States was practically isolated from every other country. This was understood by the citizens, who commanded this bottom-up. This was not spread by propaganda; on the other hand, it was the citizens' command. This command would necessitate autarky with many products not available being synthesized. As many people would fill those holes, this would leave huge technical progress behind. This would allow for more synthesized material as many goods could no longer be traded with other nations. They started to use every atom that was left within the country to end up building marvelous projects that were sought after. Many skyscrapers would be erected throughout the country as they would serve as managerial hubs where they could discuss plans. Many lounges would sprout up, as the proletariat could convene within those lounges. All of these factors allowed for a robust system of industrialization with the proletariat's demands being met. Science was advancing rapidly due to the idea of filling up all of the voids within the country. These voids couldn't be filled up with anything else but the technical progress that would need to be set forward to meet those goals. Those goals were grand, with every person seeking to meet them in some way or the other. This would be further combined with putting artificial intelligence completely under the control of the people and eliminating the possibility of an extreme technological singularity in which the human race can end up going extinct.

The synthetic alternatives that would end up being placed with the revolutionary technology would completely encompass science for many generations to come. These synthetic alternatives would break the cycle of neoliberalism while seeking to recreate globalization, though under the rule of the proletariat and not the bourgeoisie. The idea that globalization is inevitable would be carried over from the idea that the nationalists that the bourgeoisie would support have the same outcome as the nationalists that the proletariat would support. They both end up globalizing the whole movement. The nationalism within the movement is merely one stage, as it is a means to an end. This one stage represents an interlude wherein all nations could end up being liberated, with the nation's liberation being integral to the complete internationalism of the revolutionaries. Revolutionary internationalism is paired up with national sovereignty, which ends up completely mirroring the actions of the bourgeoisie in this regard. What ends up happening simultaneously is that local identities, over time, become national identities in their own right. This shows itself as the major changes that take place all end up benefiting the proletariat. The benefit of the proletariat is inextricably linked to the progress that the revolution brings. This revolution is part of the end goal as the major components of the revolution end up supporting all of the proletariat's true intentions. The major parts of the revolution end up seeing the end of the power of the bourgeoisie in all terms. This also includes national terms, for national terms are exact replicas of what is needed to liberate all nations completely. This ends up directly challenging national liberation. National liberation is only a means to an end, for it helps internationalism. Internationalism allows for the complete liberation of all forms of the people of the nations. The national-liberation rhetoric ends up overriding all other forms of primary. It ends up killing off any idea of national chauvinism, which ends up getting relegated to the dustbin of history. National chauvinism eventually gets superseded by a one-world government directly owned and controlled by the Capitalists in many ways. This would end up being evident in the past with the United Nations as well as the other bourgeois institutions that would be linked to the reactionary wave. The reactionary tide would end up being part of the response to the revolution, for it could end up mobilizing many against the revolution through the rhetoric of the reactionaries. The rhetoric of the reactionaries would largely coincide with the complete end of the revolutionaries where they operated.

Neoliberalism's core features would help it globalize and make a formidable movement. Ironically, the next neo-nationalist, right-wing movements would end up carrying on the legacy of the globalist movement. A large part of this had to do with how the organizations would get funding. This funding would result in the complete emancipation of the organizations' nationalists from any revolutionary bond. This would help in the organization's capabilities to disseminate reactionary propaganda. Reactionary propaganda would end up coming in the form of supporting extreme nationalism, which would allow for the internationalism of the bourgeoisie in the end. Bourgeois internationalism was the most important thing that would underscore all of the reactionary ambitions regarding nationalism. This nationalist ambition would become part of the broader reactionary push against the revolution. The nationalist purpose would end up seeing its path as the reactionaries would use it as a scapegoat when it was needed while supporting it when it would be beneficial. This nature would be part of the end achieved in terms of bourgeois internationalism.

Bourgeois internationalism would see that all of the functions of the state and the one-world government would work together. All of the corporations were part of the larger family that would work for themselves to achieve profit. At other times, it was necessary to gain some support from the population and improve human capital. This improvement of human capital would end up being through the safety net that would be developed. However, the small safety net caused most to be outside of it as the little safety net would be shrunk whenever it was not needed. The only goal was to grow the population (if it was not growing) and grow the country's other resources, including literacy. Literacy and healthcare would end up being part of the safety net's core, for everything else would end up being discarded. What was the point of elderly pensions, for it would end up being a drain on the state's resources? This pseudo-workers rhetoric would end up being part of neoliberal corporatism, which would see most of the bourgeoisie as part of the productive forces that allow for the eventual flourishing of society. This nature would propel bourgeois support to the top, where it would be unparalleled by everything else. The revolutionary support against the reactionary support would end up stacking up against each other soon enough.

The liberalization of the economy was followed by increased corporatism. This increased corporatism would see the economy falling into the hands of a couple of groups, which corporations represented. All of society would work together like an organic state. The only problem with this is that much of the bourgeoisie was set upon expanding profit at the cost of others. This would end up causing the bourgeoisie to form a counter-faction when it seemed like it was necessary. During other times, the traditional reactionary line would be upheld, which would support corporatism. Corporatism would end up being at the core of any reactionary theory that would be made as classes suddenly vanished one day. This would end up being part of the general association that would see neoliberalism rise. The restructured hierarchy in the workplace saw that all were equal while some were equal to others. This idea of being equal would inspire the bourgeoisie to extract more profit in the name of helping their workers keep their jobs. This would further compound itself as the revolutionary forces of nature would see themselves completely demolished. The reactionary forces that saw the rise of corporatism would end up being counteracted by the revolutionary forces that did not believe in the idea of class collaboration. For the revolution, class collaboration was a fallacy that would always fail. Direct action was the only way to secure the rights of the revolutionaries and the proletariat. This immediate action would end up being planned, for it would help achieve the end goal of a society where the masses own the means of production and run for the masses. The idea of running culture in favor of the masses and by the masses would end up superseding all other forms of ownership. The class collaborationist past would end up being completely dismantled, with all of the organs of neoliberalism being sold off. The organs of neoliberalism would be used against themselves; neoliberalism was truly the last stage of Capitalism, as all other forms would be spin-offs. The different forms that the revolution had previously witnessed all predicated on the idea that the nation is part of an international community and that the nation's benefit through trade would be beneficial. This would manifest in raising tariffs, only to reduce them towards friendly nations. When more nations followed their thinking, freer trade deals would be made.

This would end up causing much of the revolution to also be against protectionism and free trade. The past was largely based on neoliberalism's path toward reaction; this would be further combined with neoliberalism's approach toward having no classes in a society where there are classes. These contradictory concepts would see their light shining upon themselves, for they would present themselves as complete opposites. The neo-nationalist revolt was nothing but the extension of the neoliberal past. It had been reconfigured so that the eventual system could be completely saved. The only real difference that would be carried out would consist of words. These words would vary widely based on how the rhetoric would be used. These words would end up having themselves owned by others. These words were rarely put into practice. If they were, there would be a slowdown in the world economy, leading to a world revolution. Many wars had been taking place, with much money being wasted on this endless endeavor that would go nowhere. These wars were the only apparatus that the system could rely upon. The wars would end up being purposefully endless, with the individual functions being used to eliminate the power the proletariat would have completely. These wars would fuse the classes into one. They were the real-life implementation of national syndicalism, just with excess modification. It was national syndicalism with extra neoliberalism, for it would share many critiques that national syndicalism had of the revolutionary route. The syndicalism would manifest itself through the councils that would form within the companies. These councils would consist of both the company's owners and their employees. Thus, this only represents an industrial demand for raising tariffs rather than a demand for raising wages. Raising wages would be completely off-limits, for it would hurt the bourgeoisie's revenue. The goal of these councils was merely to allow for excess profit and legitimacy of the bourgeois administration.

Furthermore, this practically undermined the revolutionary movement by introducing the element of class collaboration. This would necessitate the breakup of unions, for unions embodied all sources of evil. Unions would be seen as the crown of all corruption, with the interests of the workers only being represented through the councils. The interests of the workers and the corporations would end up being the same; this would manifest itself in the idea of protectionism, which would be specifically selected. The administrations would fuel this reactionary sentiment to hold on to their power without doing much. This power grab would see all of the reaction's power being in the state's vestiges.

The idea of a national-syndicalist state would end up mirroring the American reaction against the revolution. The national-syndicalist state would be simultaneously economically neoliberal. This neoliberalism would see all of the powers of the state being completely concentrated in the hands of the corporations, which consisted of the councils. The state would be organized in the same way that the councils would be organized. The state was the embodiment of the councils in every aspect. There was practically no difference between the state and the councils. This international adaptation of the neoliberal system would isolate the American system permanently. The American system would be one of workers' control over the means of production as opposed to the control of a couple of corporations. These corporations would clash against the workers – this time being in the differences between the United Nations and NATO against the United States and the International. The International, or, more precisely, the Sixth International, was up against many united enemies. The only group that the Sixth International had support from was the international working class. This would fold on itself, for it would allow for great flexibility. Agrarian demands, as well as nationalist demands, would be met left and right.

The landlords would end up getting sidelined, forming their agrarianism that would be represented in the United Nations. The agrarianism of the farmers differed from those of the landlords in that the agrarianism of the farmers focused on the little man. This especially allowed farmers to move into the sparse lands with small populations. This would cause loyalists to sprout up as the revolutionary movement could advance. This would especially be the case throughout America, which would see the attraction of many European immigrants to the sparse lands of the Rocky Mountains. This was further combined with allowing the natives to graze the land completely. All other minorities would also be allowed to settle within this frontier land. This frontier land would end up repelling all invaders that sought to encroach on the homeland of the new settlers. These settlers would come from all over the world, especially Europe, to defend the revolution. This would form a barrier in which the West would become more pro-revolutionary. The country's West had become largely depopulated due to the civil war, which caused many immigrants to leave for their countries of origin. The natives of the region were given large land grants to expand agriculture within that area. This was further combined with other programs allowing more people to settle in the West. The Southwest would also see a large population increase, for the population had been reduced due to the civil war. This was further combined with the looming threat of Mexican intervention, which would end up getting rid of the power that the revolution would have. Similar approaches would be taken on the border of Canada, where armed settlers would end up coming in from all backgrounds to defend this frontier. Alaska would see a large population increase as many immigrants from Europe, especially political emigres, would end up swarming the border with Canada. This would make it much harder for Canada or Mexico to invade the land. The air as well as the ocean were practically secured from the previous equipment that was there, as well as the production of new equipment. Previously, the only main problem was the workforce shortage. Now that the staffing shortage had been fulfilled by settlers that would be armed. It would cause the militarization of the country to go up. The jingoistic fervor would end up sweeping throughout the country to crush the reaction. The revolutionary fervor would coincide with the jingoistic fervor as they were direct counterparts. This revolutionary fervor would end up being increased over time as a result of many settlers moving in. These settlers would completely move past any of the reactionary forces that were barricading the revolution. The settlers would form their frontier with their rights. These rights would take precedence over all other rights. This would constitute a party of rights faction within the vanguard, for it would support decentralization and autonomy for the country's frontiers. This would be further combined with economic investment into these frontiers on top of the current investment. These frontiers were essential to the defense of American soil.

The advancements made throughout the new society would achieve new frontiers. These frontiers would end up being literal and metaphorical, for they would always advance in all walks of life. These walks would go down many miles, for the new society would shine down upon the new trance. The factionalism within the vanguard would be abolished by coming together. This would effectively make the revolutionary congress completely independent and beholden to the interests of the people, not those at the top. The progress that would go on a march would be integral to the river that flows. The river would be part of the means to an end, for it would grant complete rights and sovereignty to the people. The people were the most important part of this equation, representing the march that has not yet ended. The displacement would end up approaching zero throughout the whole march. For the legionaries of the society, their goal was to finish the social revolution that had already been taking place. This social revolution could only be finished if all of the core components could match each other. Any other revolution would never parallel the fluidity of this social revolution – even the base revolution. The fluidity of this revolution would be integral to the idea of a new integral. The nation would only be one part of this equation, for it would allow for the means to an end. In this case, the basis would form a new person, one of refined intellect and talent. This new person would be at the core of the philosophy, for the goal was to achieve that by seizing the means of production. In this case, the idea of a nation only represented steps that would be made toward that. When liberated completely, the nation would allow for greater self-expression, being part of radical democracy. This democracy differed from all other democracies in that it was not the rule of the majority; on the contrary, it was the rule of the people. The vanguard of the people would have the same effect as a monarch in this sense, for it could unite all of the people. The vanguard of the people would have the same effect as having a monarch, for it could end up uniting the people. The vanguard of the people would be through another royalist. In this case, feeling royalist meant not restoring the monarchy; instead, it meant having a popular figure who could unite the people regardless of their background. It meant that there would be a prevalent figure that could unite the people. This would end up allowing for all of the ideas, including agrarianism as a means to liberating the people, and revolutionary nationalism, which represents all of the people. These liberal rights would represent the rights that the people would acquire and the ownership of the means of production, which was directly fought for. All of these ideas would be combined under one vanguard, effectively representing all of the country's people. The country's people would be represented through this royalist institution, which sought to unite the people no matter where they were from. This would end up representing the core institution of true freedom of the people. The freedom of the people would be integral to the whole movement. The people's freedom could only be through true equality of opportunity and the brotherhood that would develop through the bonds with the people. The bonds of the people would be part of the equality that would develop as they were no different from each other. The bonds the people would acquire would be part of the eventual end goal of getting rid of any reactionary forces that would storm against the people. The principle of liberty would be at the complete core of this new society. This liberty meant to be free or not to be a slave in any form. It would mean that there would be true equality of opportunity, which would be part of the process of liberty. The true equality of opportunity would be through the seizure of the means of production and a good standard of living, which could enhance the principle of liberty. Liberty could only be protected by equality of opportunity. The idea of equality of outcome would never be pursued because trying to have equality of outcome would eliminate liberty and equality of opportunity. It would essentially be part of the totalitarian state where everything would end up being streamlined so that there would be the same shoes and so forth. Instead, the only property that mattered was the means of production, with many services offered to all to enrich liberty through pensions, healthcare, and many other dreams. These dreams would allow for a much more worry-free society. They would end up being achieved as they would also improve human capital, which would be a transitionary stage towards the reproduction of the means of production and the further mechanization of all industries. This would end up getting rid of the institution of wage slavery over time as the liberation of all peoples throughout the revolutionary countries would end up being built by and for the people. Everything is by the people, and everything is for the people. The monarch was different from royalism as the revolutionary countries had essentially become royalists – or the only remaining revolutionary country with others to come. They had become royalists in that they would end up supporting the idea of a unifying vanguard throughout society. This unifying vanguard would become part of the goal of liberation. This would be combined with the development of all local cultures and the expression of all local cultures. This culture flourishing would eliminate all separatist movements, for they would all be tied to the revolution. The revolution was the most deliquescent thing that the world had seen. It would run into problems of its own if it failed. If tomorrow would end up bringing conflict, what would happen is that the revolution would fail in its entirety. It had been built out of water, for all of the constituent parts of it have been part of the general program of popular liberation. Popular liberation would end up being put above every other form of theory. Popular liberation would end up meaning that the people's dreams could be put into practice. It would also mean that there is no compromise with anti-proletarian forces. These forces would all coalesce as they would allow for the inherently revolutionary theory of proletarianism. The proletarian theory would end up deviating from bourgeois theory in every manner conceivable. This would end up causing a complete deviation from the general theory of the bourgeoisie. The paths that the proletariat would take would end up completely going against the paths that the bourgeoisie would take. The proletariat and the bourgeoisie have nothing in common, for they completely contradict each other. The popular economy that would end up forming through the new American Republic would end up superseding all other economies of the past. It would have true equality of opportunity for it focused on all proletarians. This would effectively end separate labor and agrarian parties. It would end up having one economic policy that would be based on the people. The next set of policies beyond the vanguard would end up liberating the people through political institutions being completely in the hands of the people. This would end up being further combined with the true liberation of culture. The last part would end up being part of the freedom process as national identities had completely different meanings now. They would all be revolutionary, being part of self-expression. The self-expression process would end up being part of the liberation of nations, and there would be the final stage of liberation. The liberation of the social sphere would end up meaning true self-determination, which would end up being linked to true economic liberation, which would also influence political freedom. This freedom would be linked to the liberation of the people against their oppressors who constantly seek to take the holy liberty that had been enshrined in the people. The liberation of the proletariat would be put above all other forms of liberation. The program of national liberation would end up being the final straw as the debate of nationalism would end up being closed. The final debate would be held in 2057 regarding this matter, as national liberation would be wholly supported as a matter of radical democracy.

The generation that had started adding years would prove to be the last major population that would be in the country. The population of this generation was starting to grow old in many reactionary countries, causing the problem of excess money on pensions. The pensions were cut, causing many problems to develop. The economy would end up going into a free fall as there weren't as many consumers. Furthermore, many problems would end up exacerbating due to the quick decline of the population. The population was starting to be driven by the growth. The populist movements that would rise against neoliberalism would all be united, with many of the debates of the national question being solved. What would end up happening is that no right-wing populist movement would arise. This would be further combined with the economic populist themes, only exacerbating themselves. A true leader for the people could only be fulfilled by the people. The populist wave would be the most important wave throughout human history. The populist wave could end up sparking revolutions on its own. The populist wave was unlike the years that were before. It was different in that it had total support from the proletariat and all sections of it. The proletariat's sections would be united, for they would all function similarly. The sections of the proletariat had sought to create a new society out of the old, with no place for the greedy parasites that had come before them. The populist revolt was the most important fervor that would end up sweeping throughout history. There would be problems among the newer generations, but the older generations had thoroughly supported as a result of the end of their security economically. The populist wave would go through many altercations that would see the further rise of populism. A final revolutionary wave would take place with many populist protests that would take place worldwide. The populist resentment would be funneled through a united platform of the proletariat. This populist resentment would allow for proletarian power in every form of the word. The populist platforms taken worldwide would be in tandem with one another. They would all support the same populist aggravation of the policies of the proletariat. The proletariat would be put above all other groups, for the proletariat would be at the revolution's core. The color revolutions were over, and the proletarian revolution was the only revolution left. These populist revolutions would end up being centralized while retaining some decentralization. What had effectively happened was that the proletariat could rally around the banner. There were no effective anti-revolutionary forces that could end up going against the wave of the revolution. The revolution was always omnipotent; it was on its way to victory. The party would represent the people, for it would not be centralized. Instead, what would happen is that they would all agree on a common line that would be put into practice. The idea of only having the people above all would shake many bourgeois parties, which were slow to adapt to the new reality. The new revolution was about to change the whole world over again. The color revolutions were out, and the new revolution was in. The new revolution would transform society, turning the old on its head. The revolutionary banner would go against everything that would be elitist. The populist revolution was synonymous with the proletarian revolution, for it encompassed all of the proletariat. The populist revolution from the proletariat would seek true transformation, with the national culture of all nations being put above all. This would be against the corporatocracy that would be for the destruction of cultural heritage. This would end up effectively capitalizing on the populist movement. The populist movement would coalesce under one as the socially conservative principles would be thoroughly avoided. Instead, true equality would be pursued without interference from the corporatocracy. This effectively rooted out social conservatism and social liberalism, for it took up an authentic proletarian position. This had completely gotten rid of the reactionary conservatives that were seeking to destroy the populist movement. This would cause a complete cultural shift, as many principles would be heralded and followed by the proletariat. These principles would see complete solidarity among the rest of the proletariat and an end to how the proletariat could be divided. This was especially seen with the growth of the national culture as a means to an end. Recognizing national culture, it would effectively get rid of any nationalist movement that would dissent. No further changes would be made to the national policy as it would remain constant. This was further combined with the fact that the cultural question had been effectively solved, completely dissolving any reactionary backlash that could form. This would ensure that the proletariat would be at the revolution's core in the end. The proletariat would be put above all in these scenarios, for the proletariat was the greatest factor in the construction of the new society. This would be found throughout the new America, which had eliminated the reactionaries. Many Capitalists fled the border towards Canada, orchestrating movements to overthrow the People's Republic. All of the moments of liberation were for the people. To be free means not to be a slave. This would be at the core of the populist ideology, seeking to liberate the people truly. The liberation of the people would mean having complete proletarian unity. The American Revolution followed the First American Revolution and the older revolutions that had taken place. The American Revolution that would take place would follow the original revolution that had taken place earlier. The populists had risen to power with the interests of the commoners being put above all. The commoners would be at the helm of the new structure, favoring the commoners as the true saviors of democracy. The country's liberty depended on these commoners who would support the country no matter what. The country would be based on liberty that the commoners would achieve. The revolutionary unity would be part of the proletariat's use to take complete power. The liberation of all peoples would be part of the end that would see the heroes rise through the ranks. The heroes had always been there; the heroes were flying through the skies. Now, it was destiny to fulfill the dream of these heroes. These heroes were part of the new society. Their names would be remembered on and on. They were for the people's liberation; the death of fascism and all other oppressive systems would see the power given to the people. All elitism would be eaten down to the marrow. The people's liberation was imminent, and anything that would bloc it would be eliminated through the power and fist the people would possess. The people's liberation would be part of the process in which the people would be strengthened through all means possible. The people were over arms, for they would be at the revolution's core. The people meant the whole revolution would be possible as the people would be part of the end goal of liberation. The people and the revolution were synonymous, as the revolution was necessarily populist. No revolution can commence without the absolute support of the people. Being able to bolster support among the people meant that the proletariat would support the vanguard of the revolution. This would follow with more agitprop that the revolutionary propaganda can follow. The revolutionary propaganda could only be built by the people, for it would uphold the liberation of the proletariat. It ceases to be the vanguard of the revolution when everyone joins it. This would directly link to the brotherhood and unity linked to equality. The revolutionary proletariat would end up hardening their stance for the benefit of all. The decay of civilization that would occur prior would directly result from neoliberalism. Neoliberalism would break almost all power that the proletariat would have as it would turn labor into a complete commodity. All lives were commodities in themselves as a result of neoliberalism which was taking place. The neoliberal dream would completely undermine the rights of the people. The rights of the people would be completely washed away along with the national culture that was there in the past. The oppression of many nations worldwide would further intensify during the neoliberal period earlier. Now was the age of revolutions – the age of populism. This would be part of the process that would completely root out the vestiges of degeneracy throughout society. Society had been corrupted by the degeneracy that was brought about by the onslaught of neoliberalism. This would take place as the liberation of minority groups would end up being slandered and completely transformed into one that would favor the current mode of production for most of the world. It would end up causing the death of civilization, which had once peaked with the maximum culture there was. All nations were practically oppressed, and many rights of the people were rolled back. The end of these rights would contribute to the complete end of the system of liberty, equality, and solidarity. The brotherhood had been completely washed away. The brotherhood must be brought back through any means for the revolutionaries. The revolution would be held above all as it was the people's revolution. This popular revolution would stand the test of time. The shot rung around the world would echo from the likes of Paris. Paris and Nantes would have mass populist demonstrations that would all follow the line of true populism. The people's dream would end up coming to power in all aspects. All of the populist policies, in the sense that the people should control the government and so should the economy, had been enacted throughout the United States. Farming was largely expanded due to investments in agriculture, and the sector was now under the hands of the people. The people would be put over everything regarding the government and the economy. As most of them had fled, there would be no such thing as the elite within either. Their wealth and power had been put in the hands of the people. The decay of culture under neoliberalism had been completely reversed, now being put in the hands of the national institutions built on top by the people. This liberation of culture would see culture for the many rather than for the few. The revolutionary wave would shake throughout the whole country, for the revolutionary wave was part of the end goal of ending the oppression of the people. The freedom that would be given to the people was absolute though the liberation of all peoples had not ended. The state still existed due to foreign incursions into the liberated land. This would mean that the state would have to be brought under the complete supervision of the people against the elites that prevailed throughout other states. These states had to be defeated through any means that would strip the power of the reactionaries. These states were all united in their determination to contain revolutionary ideals. The populist uprising this time was absolute rather than partial. The absolute freedom of the people would be part of the means to an end that would oversee the end of the institutions that would see the slavery of the people. The slavery of the people had been ended through the true institution of all of the rights of the people. The oppressors had vanished over time as their power would be completely transferred towards the people. The power of the people was strong, as their determination couldn't be broken through any means. Their determination would hold up as hard as a rock. It was impossible to break the rock – because it was no longer a rock. It was harder than the diamond itself. It would be possible to delay the revolution through many promises, though the revolution was imminent by this point.

Economic crises, one after the other, and the end of the institutions that would work for the people would cause the intensification of the rage of the people. This would boil into the streets with many battles being fought, some by guns and some by actions. The power of the people comes out of the barrel of the rifle, which was created by the people by themselves. There is nothing more than the people. No institutions but the people exist. The people would be held up to the highest standard possible. The people were at the top of all of the institutions that would be developed. Nothing but the people would exist in total. The people and nothing else represented the new state that would be built in the United States. The United States would end up seeing border confrontations with Canada and Mexico. This would further bolster the jingoism that would be seen within the population. All people were American, no matter their background. The revolution needed capable people that could defend it. All people were accepted to bolster the ranks of the people. The people's dream had been fulfilled in its entirety. The people's dreams consisted of the work that the people were going through. The work would be the hard work and dedication the people would put in for their new revolutionary country. This revolutionary country would eclipse all former revolutionary countries in supporting the true victory of the proletariat over its oppressor, the bourgeoisie. The bourgeoisie would be completely vetted out of power, for their power would gradually decrease. The power of the bourgeoisie would be upheld through any means possible. The revolutionary flame that would carry on for the proletariat would be part of getting rid of the power that the bourgeoisie held close by. The revolution was always around the corner of the street. The battle was going on again, and the revolutionaries of the past had been reborn. The rebirth of these old revolutionaries would again see truly dedicated leaders carry on the revolutionary state. All of these leaders had a popular mandate that would come from the people. All actions, no matter agrarian or industrial, would be undertaken. Environmentalism, which is connected to both sectors, would also seek recognition. This would be further combined with the proletariat's power in all life sectors. This would cause the creation of radical democracy, of which the cultural sphere would be part of it. The nation had essentially been put into the hands of the people. The same would apply to the economic transactions that would occur. The elites would no longer conduct them; conversely, the people would conduct them. Looking for what was occurring currently would only help in the revolution, not be the revolution. The flexibility shown by the revolution would be part of the people's will as the people's will would be reinterpreted through a new lens. That would be carried out with a scientific approach to the current system. This would cause the people to gain power throughout the new state vastly.

The new state had seen the proletariat's power quickly grow as the revolutionaries of the past were born again. They had once again come to the forefront as they were natural leaders. They would go after the oppressors of the people, no matter where they were. The oppressors of the people would be targeted in the harshest terms, with the smallest oppressors having some rehabilitation. The largest oppressors would be put in terms with the people. They would have their justice served in front of the people and by the people. For the fellow legionaries, the revolution was the power of the people. Nothing was more daring than to stand up for liberation and freedom. Freedom was the most important word that would define the whole decade. The people's freedom cannot be taken for granted; on the other hand, the people's freedom must always be actively fought for. By fighting for the people's freedom, the people could grow much stronger regarding their actions. Their actions would be written down in history, for they would be part of the continuum that would see the power of the people being completely courted into the hands of the people.

Sirach had taken his adventure abroad, towards China. He said, "I do hear every day that the world seems to truly get worse." Lazarus then responded, "it seems so, so why bother to ask in the end. It is of this that I truly ask you, for the task that is ahead of you is that of repair." Sirach responded with, "what do you mean?" Lazarus said, "I have obtained hidden information, and I have obtained information that is needed for the liberation of the world. The consequences that will be there at first may be severe, but if you truly do hear, then I will be the one that will be there to clear. I have the plan here, and if you truly trust my plan, then go with it. It requires our combined effort to go through."

The populist factions and parties that would form worldwide would get American aid, allowing them to advance as a party. The party of the people was necessarily a part that would work for the benefit of the proletariat. The party would be comprised of proletarians and be directly controlled by the proletariat. Everything that the party does would be disclosed to the proletariat to gain the proletariat's support. The support of the proletariat is essential to the revolution. The proletariat's support grants them the rights that the proletariat has long fought for. The proletariat's rights and demands can be streamlined through the party, which the movement can't fracture. The prevention of the fracture would cause the movement to gain popularity quickly. The dogma of the West would be overthrown, with the West being destroyed when it came to false culture. The true Western culture would be once again raised again. True Western culture would come from the culture the free people had made many decades and centuries earlier. The corruption of culture would be completely overturned as the culture in which the breeding ground of corruption and degeneracy would be washed away. The last vestige of degeneracy would be completely raided as degeneracy would quickly be picked up by the tide. The tide in favor of the revolution would be the true story written for many generations to come. The end of degeneracy was only a means to an end; it was not the end itself. Western civilization's progressive collapse and decay would only leave a corpse behind. The corpse, over time, would rot as pigs would devour through it. The barbarians have taken the life of whoever had existed before this corpse. They devoured the corpse-like pigs in all contradictions to civilization. The laws of civilization were practically non-existent following the repression of the people by the police. They feared the populist revolt as the populist tide would cause their power to collapse. The destitution left behind was only a characteristic that would be part of the end. Now, the proletariat could be swindled by the bourgeoisie. There was one step forward and two steps backward. This counter-action that would take place would be nothing new for the proletariat; however, the failure of the vanguard would show the entrenchment of some elites within the new vanguard. The vanguard had to be purged of any elites that could arise through its ranks. The struggle must always be constant; however, over time, it will dissipate, except when it comes to elitist states that seek to threaten the revolutionary state. All roads would lead to the revolution, but now, the question was how it would occur. This would allow for the complete liberation of the people. Many indigenous nations would be liberated with the face of the Earth being completely changed. The face of the Earth would trend in favor of the revolution. The indigenous nations that would be liberated would end up merging with the greater nation, both of them mixing. They would end up becoming much closer to the greater nation. This would allow for the reversal of the wipe-out of culture under neoliberalism. Neoliberalism would be destroyed as its constituents would see the complete end of the rule. The elites would be completely thrown out of power. Sometimes, this would be literal with the parliament buildings being stormed. The government would end up having to resign. America would see coups occur in states whose populace believed the government had gotten out of hand. This would allow for a revolutionary fervor to be maintained in overthrowing tyranny. Tyranny would be brought to a complete end throughout the American revolutionary republic. This revolutionary republic represented all of the people of America. The constitution would end up being enacted by the vanguard. The vanguard and the constitution would mix, as they would have high support from the population. The new constitution was based on the old, but it was combined with complete collectivization of the means of production and other previously unsound rights. National rights were also introduced with the new constitution representing most people nationwide. The main difference was that the constitution now had much more influence due to the vanguard. The original reason constitutions were written was to have it so the republic could be stable. This revision of the constitution would have the republic be stable and popular. This would mean that the revolution would take the place of royalism. The vanguard would always have enough power to decentralize with local cultures being developed. However, decentralization could once again become centralization regarding the great game. This combination would cause the end of any revisionism in the ranks of the vanguard. The vanguard would see all of its policies enacted as they were linked to the proletariat. As a result of previously high literacy, the vanguard could recruit many members to join the cause.

Through the vestiges that would be created, the creation of all forces would see the new crown being placed on top of the head. The crown would not be placed on the few; on the other hand, it would be placed on the many. The crown would be the royalist aspect that the revolution would carry on. The royalist action would be part of the new crown to liberate all peoples worldwide. The revolution would see the new republic's stability improve quickly as the constitution and the people would be put above all. It was more than a majority, representing nearly all of the country's people. This would allow for increased stability that would be sought after in the previous decades. The system was largely broken in the past as the constitution couldn't be upheld, and representatives rarely truly represented their constituents. This was further combined with disunity. Most of this had gone away as a result of the revolutionary administration, which was able to spread its wings. The extreme stances taken throughout the many pressing issues would replace the previous reactionary perspectives and outlooks that had previously existed. This revolutionary stance would completely replace the reactionary stance built from the ground.

The economic situation of the world and, more specifically, certain aspects of the connections in the world would be tapered by the new financial crisis that was coming up. Many countries prepared themselves by adding a temporary social state with a corporatist system. This would mean that all businesses would be compensated with profit if they did what they were supposed to do. This would be against the forces that formed around the ultranationalist factions. What had effectively happened is that all of the nationalist, conservative, liberal, and progressive factions throughout many of these countries had merged into one. There were some dissent nationalists, but they would fight for the revolution whose movement was underground. There was one main exception, which was throughout North America and Europe. The revolutionary movement could operate though under extreme supervision. This would mean the party would be effectively left out of power on every level, as they were only allowed to collect funds. This would be combined with the reactionaries effectively having a monopoly on power. The conservative factions, nationalist factions, progressive factions, and liberal factions would all unite under one party. This party would push through corporatism as well as the liberalization of society. The deregulation of society would mean that certain aspects would be under the control of the people. However, for the most part, most of the power would still be under the boot of the reactionaries. The liberalization of society would see the corporatist model win out in the end. Complete neoliberal models would be abandoned as a last effort to save the current mode of production. This would bolster the support of the new corporatist model over every other model within society. The corporatist model would be much stronger in the end due to the ability to control recessions and crashes, albeit through insane investment. This would cause the same problem to come back, this time with debt. Debt would quickly accumulate due to wads of capital keeping the industries alive. The amount of effort that would be undertaken to keep industries alive would vastly outpace the former amount built around crashes allowing for economic recovery in the end - albeit contributing to monopolies. The corporatist system would prove far superior to the neoliberal system, as it could somewhat satisfy the working class. It was able to recreate the middle-class of managers though at high costs. The debt accrued internationally would be largely forgiven as a result of the revolution is a much more imminent problem. This would temporarily uplift the economy as the economy worldwide would grow at one percent for developed countries, excluding America, and twenty percent for underdeveloped countries. By this point, there were only five underdeveloped countries, mostly in the Middle East. This would be an irony because prior, the oil money would end up paying off all of their expenses. However, what had occurred is that the new world order largely ousted oil as a means of energy, which caused many of their otherwise underdeveloped countries to go bankrupt.

This would allow for the recovery of their economy and further economic integration. While the American economy was growing at twenty percent per year, with the first year of growth after the civil war reporting two hundred percent, it had the main obstacle of lacking natural resources. As a result, measures were taken to produce increasingly synthetic goods regarding raw materials. The raw materials would be in a desperate situation. This would be further compounded by basically every possible measure that would be taken to fix it taking too long. This would be largely a result of no trade due to a world embargo and the consequence of using synthetic materials. However, this would soon pay off due to the relative end of the reactionary hold on power. The synthetic materials would allow for complete self-sufficiency, which was already being largely developed. Many resources were already found; now, the goal was to maximize how much could be taken out of responsibility, and this could be done through strict austerity when it came to how resources were used in the production process. The goal was to reduce the input while increasing the output. This mix would triumph over the reactionary forces constantly seeking to oppress the people. This mix would be able to win over the shortages that would have otherwise taken place as a result of isolation. This end to isolation would be further combined with far more increased trade. The increased business would cause more states to be linked up with each other. The infrastructure for exchange would quickly develop as many railroads would be built. These infrastructure projects would be built due to the rapid progress made. This rapid progress would push further internal trade, which would be the most lucrative business within the whole country. These traders could make a large living merely by connecting each state to the other. This was as opposed to the trade that would take place in the past for profit. It would remain lucrative as a service sector job; however, this time, it would be for the people rather than for a couple of elites. This would mean that the trade could flourish for the people's benefit. The synthetic raw materials throughout the country were copied by each state, aiming to make it so that the state with the largest ease of access could produce most of the synthetic goods. This would reduce the cost of many interests, leading to further economic growth. This effectively meant that a new course shift had occurred. This shift in approach would mark the birth of the new chemical revolution. This chemical revolution would increase crop production, industrial production, and service sector jobs. All sectors would be rapidly increased with the new service sector consisting of managers and traders from all over the country. The goal was no longer to maximize profit but the benefit of the people. This new process would allow for enough production that comprehensive labor legislation would be put in place. The workplace would be geared towards safety to the absolute maximum possible while new facilities for the people would be run. Pensions would be drastically increased to the point that old, unstable savings systems were no longer needed. This investment in the new market, which relied on temporary commodity production, would be used for capital accumulation. This accumulation of capital would be directly put in the hands of the people as it would be part of the process of industrialization. The rapid industrialization of the country would be part of the last revolution that would take place when it came to the means of production. However, this was not enough. Even if it got past any shortage through the new technology, it still needed to spread the revolution worldwide. Even if it had many resources, it was very isolated from every other country in the world. It could end up being beaten out if space exploration started to speed up. The space race would intensify as many technologies that the Americans would discover would cause the test of time to blow in favor of the revolutionaries. The American industrial boom would rival the industrial growth that the rest of the world would endure. The means of production had sufficiently developed to the point that it was possible to abolish classes – if they were to be worldwide and not in one country. The subsidies that would be given to the industries of the reactionary countries would start to go out of hand. The globalized model would mean that resources could be brought from place to place through the facilitation of this trade was severely hampered.

Many of these services, too, were largely in the hands of a few, which would cause stagnation in trade. This would lead to many reactionary governments nationalizing all of their key transportation industries and expanding them to facilitate trade. This would temporarily revive the trade of goods worldwide, but it still ran into problems. This trade was only temporary in every sense of the definition. The trade that would be implemented and used still failed because it would oversee a period of stagnation. Immediately subsidies were granted to industries to help them function, but these subsidies only went to the few who invested in the capital market. There was no such thing as a capital market in America; they only existed within the Capitalist countries. The revolutionary country of the world had no such thing as profit unless it was an interlude to expanding the means of production. However, no capital would go to extreme enrichment as there would be no Capitalist class. The managers hadn't formed a new class even if they merged with the traders. The managers had little power in the actual state, for their most important decisions were in the economy. The end of distortions of the new commodity market would allow for increased expansion of the means of production throughout the whole year as record growth was being marked. This growth would displace all other factions as factionalism had been completely avoided. What would effectively happen is that cultural capital would have an insane effort put towards it, with all of the other constituent parts of the society and the state being changed. Society would see the old liberation nationalist culture revived through the years. This was combined with the state being completely devoid of reactionaries and Capitalists. The majority of the party would be made out of the industrial workers, followed by peasants and then white-collar workers. This would effectively make it so that the industrial workers could merge with the managers over time. Efforts would be undertaken to make it so that industrial workers and managers were much closer to each other. The same would apply to agriculture as the distinction between the city and the countryside was slowly erased. The suburbs had rapidly grown in population throughout the year as many houses were built using the scraps of the old. This preservation of resources would be integral to the new society. Extreme austerity was seldom pursued. Debt would rarely be accrued, and if it were, it would be paid off within a couple of months due to the ongoing economic boom. Debt was completely restricted, with the belts being tightened regarding regulations on growth. This was largely the case due to making the commodity production viable on its last legs. The last legs of commodity production were a direct result of the near-inevitable end of industrialization, as this economic growth was no longer needed when work could be done for 4 days a week at 3 hours. This would be further reduced by the trade that would take place when a world revolution occurs. This trade would practically automate most industries that remain through technological innovation. The industrial workers were largely part of the last remaining breed of jobs that still required manual labor, and they would still be employed to make the system not go bankrupt when it came to production. Most industries, including trade, had been automated, with the workplace no longer separated. Instead, the workplace was completely integrated as much artificial intelligence would work with the workers. The replacement of managers would see new jobs being created and the general end of employment except for a couple of hours a week. Much of the cultural development would start from here as scientific progress and progress in basically every field that would be truly driven by passion would take place. This would be part of the general program of eliminating the forces of reaction and the last rapid industrial revolution. These revolutions had completely transformed the economy in the people's favor as large trade networks were being set up throughout the country. This would lead directly to the last legs that the reactionaries would stand on, but this meant that war, especially nuclear, was imminent. The last legs of the reactionaries would be a direct result of the low investment that the Capitalists would put into the means of production.

Chapter Six:
The Rebirth of Hope

America declared war against all of the reactionary states of the world. The same happened vice versa, with all of the reactionary countries declaring war on America. The world had avoided nuclear collapse last time during the civil war due to a broken code that the revolutionaries held. This time around, the situation could escalate at any moment. Matic asked, "What should we do now?" The captain said, "Activate code red immediately." Matic asked, "Why to do so?" The captain said, "America is about to launch a nuclear war." "3. 2. 1," the eerie voice of Matic went. An explosion occurred that was completely silent. An ultrasound explosion wiped out the remaining humans on planet Earth. No one was left; all of the efforts that civilization would put in had seemingly collapsed. What was the point of the whole endeavor of human culture from its primitive days if it was going to die in the end? What was the point of all of the progress that humans put in if humans were the last ones to die? There was nothing left. The Earth had been completely scorched with no more people on it. Many animals had died from the radiation and the ultrasound that would come out of it. The ultrasound would wipe out the last traces of human civilization.

What they did not know however, was that it was the work of Lazarus and Sirach that had been the brain behind the increasingly controlled world. Matic, in prior days, had been in contact with Lazarus and Sirach, and they had together understood the consequences that were ahead of them. All that was needed was a little manipulation, and the path that would be set ahead would be that which would dread. At the end of the world that came ahead of them, they had truly seen what would come about. In the world that was given to them, Lazarus and Sirach had ultimately orchestrated the whole event, and Matic was that who was the operator. Matic had not yet seen the true consequences that would come as a direct result – but he did not need to. He did not need to because he realized that life in an increasingly inhospitable environment was not going to last. He did not need to because he had understood that all that he had given, and ahead of the ancestors that he had seen, was one that would give light to the world. Lazarus and Sirach, with all of his motives ahead of them, were those that understood this game quite well. Lazarus and Sirach quite understood that the situation at hand here was one that would become clear. The situation ahead of them that they had seen was one that would be that which would never be lost, yet at this moment, there was nothing left, except the barren plain that had surrounded them, and the lifeless creatures that had come through their death. Without life left, there was something that was truly ahead of them. Matic, no longer being one in any form, had ultimately never witnessed the consequences. His brain could not process anything that had occurred. Lazarus and Sirach, having ever planned the events that would occur in the future, saw towards them what would truly come. Lazarus and Sirach, for all that they had done, would be those that would never break their character.

What was Earth? What was life? These were now distant memories of the past. There were no humans left that could record time. What was the social change? It was completely thrown into the dustbin of history – with no human ever to record it. Some things never change, and the end of humanity would be induced by humanity itself. Matic no longer existed; he was just a body in the pile of rubble, with most of his body completely fragmented. It was a direct war that had brought them to collapse. It was a direct war that left them with many atoms. Nothing was there now. The universe was completely lifeless. What was the point of any endeavor that humans made? All that was left on Earth was not a single sound … at least from anything alive.

However, that would soon change as no sound could be heard from Earth. Earth had torn itself into pieces creating space with no medium for sound to travel through. This would be a ferocious turn with the complete division of any intelligible life on Earth. All that remained was not life on Earth but intelligent life … from elsewhere. Earth had broken into multiple pieces, for the empty medium caused no sound to travel through. The sudden outburst of commotion was nowhere to be seen.

The DNA of any life had been torn into shreds. Amino acids had completely torn themselves apart as life couldn't be recreated through any means. What was the point of life through all of this? What was the end of time after this? The time represented something symbolic of human civilization. Time would have no other meaning if human society didn't exist. Life was nothing, and life was everything. The matter still exists, but it is in a completely different form. There were no observers. There was no news. Society had torn itself apart; there was no society when there were no people. Nothing would make the tide of written history go this way … yet it did. The age of civilization had been completely replaced by barbarism. The age of civilization was long past, with all of its manifestations completely gone. The age of civilization was about to fall imminently at any moment. Civilization and all of the theories that developed around it no longer mattered.

Over there were the completely factual extraterrestrials. However, there was no one to judge whether they were real. Humans were completely wiped out by the imminent result of not working together for one another's gain as well as the gain of the individual. Instead, they were working for the gain of a couple of people who had accumulated vast fortunes intending to leave planet Earth when it becomes inhabitable. They, too, would be wiped out by the nuclear war. The imminent nuclear war would cause the end of civilization as people would be quickly wiped out throughout the world. There was no longer any such thing as a human, for they had all perished in a pointless endeavor to rebuild civilization.

Radio waves would cease; the prospects of creating a new civilization would be grim. In unintelligible language towards humanity, the words would be roughly translated as "the civilization of planet 108 has perished." The civilization of Earth had perished throughout the years that had formed around the new civilization. Civilization would live its last days in the world many days earlier. But what was a day? A day was completely meaningless as it would be based on the death rows of civilization. Civilization and a day only meant something relative to the subordinate structures created through the years. These subordinate structures only found meaning within the new society that would be built from the ashes of the old. What was a person? What was inside a person? None of this would be known if the person had not completely exited. These structures would be part of the larger plan of destruction of humanity. This new society would be built through the traces of alien culture. The last imprint of human civilization would be remembered. This imprint would once again seek to recreate the civilization. The foreign extraterrestrial society would go against the new laws of nature that would form. The foreign extraterrestrial society that had been created was a complete novelty. The foreign extraterrestrial society had each person contribute to the society as a whole. Individuality meant contributing to society because no intelligent being could survive independently. The old philosophical society of humans was completely ousted from its reigns of society. Its grip on society would be completely gone as the grip on society would completely weaken. This would be evident in the nuclear war that would follow through the end of civilization. The end of civilization would mean the complete end of any intelligent life.

What was the point of rapid industrialization? Rapid industrialization would turn out to be a complete waste as a result of the end of civilization itself. Earth itself had split, and the only way it could be once again whole would be through intervention. Luckily, the rest of the Solar System hadn't yet been thrown off. This would be regarding the Solar System being in the hands of extraterrestrial powers. They could effectively manipulate the galaxies they controlled, for they were all one in the end.

Everyone was all one, as they all shared one part of the eternal stream of consciousness. This infinite stream of consciousness meant that reality could be realized through the fourth stage of consciousness. Being aware of everything, they were mindful of nothing regarding the paper. They were the commanders of civilization, for they could harness the power of all of the universe. There was something more than the universe, which had an infinite origin. This origin would further come to the end of time itself. Time had been completely transformed, with its constituent parts completely dismantled. The time had completely taken past the old society, with the components of spacetime being completely transformed. The details of spacetime would be completely changed in favor of a new higher society that would be created in the civilization of Earth. The people recreated in this new civilization would be of the same DNA as the previous homo sapiens that had lived throughout Earth. This was further combined with the end of society that had previously taken place. This could only be rebuilt through increased biodiversity and pathogens worldwide. These pathogens must not be deadly but part of the cycle which once again creates the heroes of the past. The blood of the heroes falls to the ground, with the blood recreating the heroes through the fertile soil. Heroes aren't created; heroes are reborn through the pregnant Earth built out of blood. Now, most of the world has lost all of its meaning. The only things set to be created were the pathogens and the pregnant Earth that would be recreated once again. The recreated Earth was only a dream, and it required planning. The extraterrestrial life was largely soundless unless it was needed during precarious times. Through space, waves that were faster than the speed of light could be transmitted. However, it was impossible to see them from any field of vision. Any creature couldn't see them as they were beyond the speed of light. A gamma ray meant nothing compared to the waves beyond the speed of light. This was proven by human civilization earlier by the existence of Black Holes, which could only be traced due to the light surrounding it. Humans have long complained of a potential Black Hole takeover that would be many billions of years away, but they got something way worse.

The potential Black Hole would be completely avoided, for the civilization would be destroyed through other means. The likely Black Hole would consume mass so that the remaining group would quickly diminish. This loss of mass would accompany the end of the civilization that would take place. The Black Hole would completely reduce all other aspects of society, for its wrath would be implemented in the nuclear war that would take place. This nuclear war would cause the end of civilization in all aspects and cause sophistication to take its own turn when it came to the end of civilization itself. The extraterrestrial creatures that existed largely went against all of the principal rules of civilization. Their civilization was based on cooperation for the individual and the greater good. All the means of production were controlled collectively to harness this for further exploration. Their numbers were not many, but they were not few either. With a population of a million, they could easily populate many other planets. This small population could easily grow and shrink with each colony that would be made. They wanted to recolonize planet Earth and bring it back to life. They had already laid out the plans for doing so, which would once again recreate biodiversity.

The closest Earth was to their home planet was two thousand light years away. This could not be normally done with previous human equipment; however, this could be done with the extraterrestrials' equipment. The extraterrestrials had equipment that could go faster than the speed of life. However, this would mean there would be invisibility, which would require a gamble. If they traveled more quickly than the speed of light, they could never be spotted. This gamble would be taken to bring back their long-lost land. Planet 108 was once the cradle of human civilization; while it was relatively primitive, it also made progress. Planet 108 was part of the solar system 108 though the solar system was starting to follow apart. The solar system had been under the influence of the collapsing planet, whose core had torn itself up. The sound couldn't be heard by anyone except these extraterrestrials, who had evolved far beyond normal evolution. This would end up causing the solar system to be largely tilted toward the recolonization of the habitable planet 108. This would be done through the colonization of Earth, which would occur through repopulation.

The journey was long. In their gibberish, it was possible to dissect certain words. They had largely talked about the journey's end, which would take many months. However, this would be worth it in the future. The revival of the cradle of civilization would first require an inspection. This would soon run into problems. The nearby solar system would have its civilization that would be created off of the ground. With interpretation, their interactions could be summed up like this. The Captain of Pistul said, "Where are you going?" The other captain said, "We're going to planet 108." Pistul said, "What is planet 108?" The other captain said, "The solar system is next to yours." Pistul asked, "The solar system that is four light-years away?" The other captain would say, "Yes, that one." Pistul said, "Didn't that planet die off due to extinction?" The other captain replied, "Yes, we are on the way to recolonize it and recreate civilization on it." "I think this is a venture that will make sense," Pistul said. "Why not colonize the planet together," Pistul asked. "If you have enough resources as well, then we should," the other captain said. "By the way, what equipment do you have?"

Pistul answered, "We have the latest generation of spaceships that can go faster than the speed of life," the other captain replied. "You can go faster than the speed of light," pistul asked. "Yes, we can, and that allows us to reach other places quickly," the other captain said. "Can we borrow your design," asked the pistul. "If you give us credit, sure," said the other captain. A deal would be made that will allow for temporary settlement of a new planet by the expedition to help the other group construct what is needed to revive the population of planet 108 once again. The daring adventure that had been made aimed to rescue the planet. The earth had been lost due to human activities that would cause adversity to one another. They would all embark on a venture that would see the recolonization and the irrigation of land that had been torn apart. The civilization consisting of humans was tiny compared to an extraterrestrial civilization. It had only recently industrialized and wasn't complete except for one country, America – which none of the extraterrestrials used as a name. The extraterrestrial civilization would be opposed by most states in the world. It would favor complete progress that would include individuals as well. The extraterrestrial civilization could only be seen through the vision of ultra-visionaries, but the civilization had perished off the face of the Earth. No civilization remained on Earth, as it would remain barren for many years. The recolonization of Earth would be on radically new lines. The DNA had been copied over, largely from the hyperborean DNA of a people who lived many years before the start of irrigation. This civilization would again be used as a template to advance Earth to the forefront. Earth had never been at the top of civilization, for it was in its infantile stages. It was in its infancy and couldn't advance beyond a simple civilization. The decay of civilization was omnipresent.

The hyperborean species would form as a result of the rebirth. This rebirth would occur over time because the extraterrestrial species were still far away. This rebirth could only occur with the colonization and expansion of the species of extraterrestrials. This rebirth can only occur when the hyperborean people will again be reborn throughout the world. This would mean gluing Earth back together; this time, it will be built on completely different principles. Two light years were still away regarding the progress to reaching planet 108. These light years seemed like forever, but time flew by fast. In current numbers, this would amount to a month of progress. Earth had been reached, and it was necessary to modify it to make it suitable again. A blueprint of the last saved progress of Earth would be used in the reconstruction. "This blueprint will allow for reconstructing the hyperborean people and Earth. They will be the ancestors of all of the new Earthlings that will be born. The last time around, the society collapsed due to hostility to each other, affecting all forms of life. This time, we must not let this happen. According to them, we must build a 'revolutionary' society, which is very primitive to us. However, it must be remembered that they were much more advanced compared to the rest of their people. The other peoples were largely reactionary, contradicting the revolutionary principle of development. Thus, we must recreate the equal human race for all though not give them any characteristics they know of our presence – just yet. This could be done by rolling back local time and recreating society based on those lines. Doing this would ultimately pay off, as the play can be done in our favor. With their enlightened society, they will be grateful for how much development will be made. Thus, I announce that creating such a society is paramount," the now collective captain of the expedition said. "I will compensate everyone here with rewards as I humbly take the position of not having as many rewards. After all, I have dedicated my life to recreating humanity. My life may have been short and miserable, only spanning forty thousand years; however, I believe that my life can be reborn through my deeds that will live on the memory of the human race. I thus announce the project to reconstruct humanity through the planet's reconstruction." Slowly, through equipment, the core of the Earth was once again reconstructed. The mantle would take some time as it acted like a puzzle. "Furthermore, we must completely revive the planet by reconstructing the crust. We must use any means to rebuild the Earth completely," the captain would add. The recreation of the crust would allow for the oceans surrounding it to form once again. The rebirth of the Earth would result from the pregnant soil that would span throughout Earth. The crust would see its complete rejuvenation through the soldering of all continents. These continents were created through the direct action of the individuals involved. These continents were built through the hand that would strike down against the reactionary mindset previously occupying the human race. A world revolution had been achieved without even passing through the stage. This took a week as much of the world was industrialized through the extraterrestrials' equipment. The extraterrestrials would use their equipment to reconstruct the Earth along new lines. This equipment would allow for a complete fusion of many atoms together to reconstruct the natural resources. Furthermore, all of the cultures that had existed previously had largely been maintained. The world would be united under one flag, though no state would exist. Furthermore, work had been abolished in all terms.

Now, it was up to the Earthlings to go beyond Earth alone. This carefully crafted world would see the complete reconstruction of the world as all nations were united together. A nation was merely the sum of the identities that made up it. There was no hierarchy now, whether economic, national, or political. The Earthlings needed to figure out a way to escape the planet and colonize the rest of the planets in the solar system. Doing so would harness the resources that the whole solar system would have. The reconstructed population was 4 billion, being spread throughout many continents. Some places were extremely damaged, including Africa and Asia, so it was tough to rebuild them. Africa would have most of its new civilization concentrated on the opposites of the continent, with a new great lake forming in the middle of nowhere. Furthermore, the Adriatic had been colonized by rebuilding land between Italy and Croatia. These were merely nations, for they consisted of many other nations. Dalmatia and Florence would be the two points where land would be constantly added over time. Adding land would be part of the end goal of completely causing the planet's reconstruction. The planet's reconstruction would see much of Central Africa being turned into many lakes that would form. These lakes would have enough resources to power the local industry of Central Africa. North Africa would see the greatest technological alignment with Europe and other civilizations worldwide. Asia would see much of its population being severely cut as it would start to center around a couple of civilizations over anything else. The development of these civilizations would be prioritized over the development of other civilizations. These civilizations would again see their beacons shift as South Africa would start to die off as a major civilization. North Africa would see its major concentration of civilization. The ancient Roman World, certain parts of Africa, Persia, and India would be the cornerstone of this new civilization. It would be from here that certain ambitions would be pursued. These ambitions would include completely reshaping the world to make progress towards completely reworking the internals of civilization. This was a completely free civilization where people largely lived in harmony. This civilization would start to concentrate as the scientific beacon would be the most important part that would take over. Countries and nations no longer mattered increasingly enough as they were largely considered variants of the same culture that would be propagated through scientific discoveries.

The extraterrestrials had largely left Earth completely, and new conflicts would arise. This conflict would see the whole world again broiled in a petty dispute. This would be based on the fact that a rival civilization had largely introduced radio waves through the end. These radio waves would once again turn humanity over. The time they had seemed constant, being reverted to 2070. This change would see an insane reworking of the civilization of Earth. The power was cut as a test, and another move was made. This move would streamline radio waves into the heads of people. These radio waves would soon be intercepted, and now, the people's thoughts could be controlled by the people behind them. The opinions of people now had been completely under the control of an agency that most ordinary people did not know existed. The people's thoughts were effectively contained and were no longer free. Others of their race once again enslaved these people. This would cause a massive upheaval inside the mind, while the intensification of these radio waves would end up alarming the extraterrestrials. The extraterrestrials would go on with the plan, and they would get rid of who was streamlining those radio waves.

Furthermore, genes were changed so that radio waves would only be responded to how humans would. They do not fear anything, for it would be part of the plan to rejuvenate human civilization. Human civilization had effectively settled down, with the Americas serving a much more minor role, home to native civilizations. Furthermore, much of the Germanic world had been completely alienated from this system as much of the cultural capital would go to the common Latin civilization that would develop down South. The native civilizations of the Americans largely developed but found no use of centralization, for they were completely free. The Germanic and other worlds would start forming alliances, facilitating migrations into the revived Roman Empire. This stirred Roman Empire represented the diversity of the last, for it had all people in it.

Furthermore, the migration of many Persians towards Mesopotamia would cause much of the Persian cultural capital to drain quickly. India was a long way, though it would remain completely isolated. The rest of Asia would see a reversal of certain aspects of industrialization as the concentration on this new Roman Empire would carry on the progress needed to colonize the rest of the solar system. The rest of the solar system had been in the same orbit around the sun. It had not been visibly shaken even after the complete departure of certain groups from Earth. Most of these settlers would come from Europe and the Americas, except for the Roman Empire. They would settle down on Mars and Mercury. This would take time, for they needed to build shelters that would allow the humans to withstand radiation and brutal heat and avert a shortage of resources.

Furthermore, Earth's population had decreased to 3 and a half billion. The next wave would come from Asia except India, which largely saw the people of Asia go down too. The same would apply to Africa and Australia, seeing their populations shrink to the point that the Roman Empire only really mattered. Over time, the Indian civilization would be displaced as it would colonize Pluto. All of these would pose challenges of their own. They would be challenged to provide what these groups need to survive. All of these groups must be provided with the maximum equipment possible to survive. These groups would need to irrigate the barren land of these planets completely. The hyperborean had been effectively recreated as no such thing as nations existed. There was a largely new world with the order being based on complete individual and collective work. Nothing would be given up to a couple of individuals. Many of the settlers from Earth didn't know what caused the last destruction of planet Earth. It was like time had completely skipped through the ages.

Collusion did build from within though. It was of Sirach and Lazarus that their plan had become successful. It was of Sirach and Lazarus that they had looked through, and as their plan had been laid, it was one that required none other than the path that was given here. What Sirach and

Lazarus had made in the end was a sacrifice – of their own nature as well, which would have great consequences for the world, yet be one that had ultimately achieved their original goal. Sirach and Lazarus, as they looked forward to the world and of their sacrifice that they had done, as well as the great human toll that all had taken in the end, by having placed what had malfunctioned in the world back into the destruction of war ahead of them, had ultimately seen the light of day.

The hyperborean had effectively recreated their people on a completely new basis. Their people would be played with the revival of the standards of the human race. The human race would include all, for it would cause the complete settlement of the Earth's new habitat throughout the planets. Some would pass away while others would evolve into new worlds. These planets would prove their ground, allowing for the recreation of human civilization. The pursuit of human civilization could only be through the institution of common principles that will bring human civilization together in the future. The sophistication of humans could only thrive once all of the planets are completely colonized, and progress is made towards conserving this state of civilization. This state of civilization had essentially seen complete localization of all of the hyperborean living throughout the solar system. The hyperborean race could only be rejuvenated through the last effective merge with the human race. The conquest of the whole solar system would lead to a population boom; now, the human race's population was close to fifteen billion. This was still much smaller as it would be concentrated among many planets. These booms would once again see the civilization spread throughout many worlds, all being part of the one solar system.

"How do we get back at our creators," would be a question many would ask. They didn't know how to contact their creators once again. Their creators had got them out of the ditch that was the end of civilization through nuclear warfare. Now, it was necessary to contact them again to reach further planets. The closest solar system was far, far away. It was four light years away; this figure was not much for the extraterrestrials. However, this figure was insane for humans. While they had completely industrialized and embraced a free and fair society, they were still lagging in many other aspects. These aspects would vary widely, but they were all bogging down the civilization. The civilization of fifteen billion couldn't spread any further unless it could go at or faster than the speed of light. Doing this endeavor would take so long that humans weren't evolved or posed to do so. Furthermore, the sudden drop in this world revolution would be created due to the extraterrestrials, who were nowhere to be found. The last frontier that humanity had yet to encounter was other solar systems. These other solar systems must be brought closer as a human civilization could be planted there. The temporary expedition of the closest solar system had largely returned many light years away. The warped spacetime would allow for travel that would go through wormholes that would allow for bypassing space itself. The light was only relative. The light could be far transcended when other dimensions were put into practice. These extraterrestrial creatures were far beyond the current dimension, allowing them to go effectively faster than the speed of light. The speed of light meant nothing as a result of the quick movements that would be made by the extraterrestrial creatures in securing the last frontiers. The speed of light had been broken due to the dimensions that human civilization had never known. Even though the energy needed had started to reach its limit, the urgent desire to keep reaching all of the frontiers that would be set upon the human race especially compelled the further expansion of the whole civilization. The human race did not know that there were more than three dimensions except for the special case in terms of spacetime, which would only accompany a higher dimension. For humans, it was impossible to imagine infinite dimensions, for it was far beyond their minds. Going faster than the speed of light would only be possible by discovering infinite dimensions, which the extraterrestrials had known. The acceleration of speed would be at the cost of no actual energy, as it would become more and more minute the more the dimensions reached infinity. At infinity itself, it became undefined as it never existed but would theoretically reach infinity or negative infinity. The energy needed to reach the frontiers was in the hands of the extraterrestrials but completely alien to the human race. The human race knows nothing about these dimensions that were merely part of the process of the breaking point of civilization. Civilization would go beyond dimensions, for its existence would tell. Its existence would be based on the presumption that the evolution of the human race could only be through the expansion of all frontiers that would be known to man. There was nothing more important than the truth itself. The truth itself would comprise the large expanse of knowledge and the expanse covering all dimensions in their absolute forms. The expansion of the civilization, later known as humans, would be taken over step at a time. Still, few knew that infinite dimensions existed. Infinite dimensions would mean that the complete perception of humanity was completely wrong when it assigned a bound that would be present towards expanding the civilization outwards. The bound that would be assigned would be completely unknown, for it would prove to be futile. The bound of four dimensions would be completely broken as spacetime would be completely bypassed. Much of modern physics and mathematics couldn't explain the phenomena that would unfold with the series of infinite dimensions. While mathematics and the rest of the sciences had come a long way in evolution, so had the laws of the universe. The laws of the universe would constantly change over time due to an outside force acting on it. This outside force would be embodied in the infinite dimensions that would exist. Was there even one universe, or were there many multiverses? This would be a question that humans couldn't solve even through the test of time. Human civilization would largely falter due to the expanses of civilization being completely broken through time. Human civilization lacked the equipment and the knowledge to see beyond three dimensions. It had largely seen only three dimensions, with the fourth dimension being part of the idea that some leniency could be given. Nothing faster than the speed of time could travel, but there were exceptions. If there were exceptions, how would it be a concrete theory? Still, human civilization couldn't look beyond three dimensions in favor of infinite dimensions. If the infinite dimension theory was going to be put into practice, what would end up occurring is that much of modern mathematics would only explain a certain number of dimensions. Way more dimensions had their place regarding the broader sphere of the human intellect, and human civilization would not know this. Human civilization would only see a couple of dimensions with nothing more than the current explored dimension. There was no real end in sight, for infinite dimensions would constantly debunk every barrier that would be placed. The idea of infinite dimensions would cause everything to be relative to each other. When a force changes something in one sphere, it will cause a change in every other part of that sphere. This would be the foundation of the principle of science that would take place in the new human civilization. They failed to see that infinite dimensions will constantly change where the curve is heading. Eventually, no curve will exist, for it will never be beyond the human capacity to see. The infinite dimensions problem couldn't be effectively solved, for a dogmatic view would always give it. The dogmatic view would cause the dismantlement of any theory that would go against the idea of having only four dimensions. These four dimensions theory would be at the heart of the whole system that would be rotten to its core. This system would only work as much was promised. This promise would be broken through the expanse of time, for the time of the civilization was starting to run out. But another question that would be raised would follow the question, "What was time?" All of these concepts only had meaning so much as humans put meaning into it. If none of the meaning could be harnessed, in this case with only three dimensions, then what does a dimension mean? These phenomena could never be explored. Decades earlier, extraterrestrials would be discarded by the new world order to prevent human knowledge about a much more advanced civilization. Furthermore, it would be suppressed even throughout the 50s though a new revolutionary society would publish articles about them. It would take serious research by the revolutionaries that the cases were all investigated. They were no longer thrown away as they were the proletariat's vanguard. The vanguard of the proletariat and the revolutionaries were effectively the same thing, as they all aided in constructing a new society. This radical reconstruction was interrupted by the nuclear war, which would destroy the whole world. However, the revolutionary method would win out in the end, for the freedom of the people and the will of the people were once again carved out. Corruption was alien to any advanced civilization, and the same would apply to this new civilization. This new civilization would be part of continuing the further advancement of all progress throughout this new atmosphere. This development atmosphere would see all of the progress now concentrated in the hands of civilization as a whole rather than a couple of individuals. The revival of civilization would see the whole rotten system of the reactionaries completely collapse on their head. The revival of this new civilization that would span throughout the vast expanses would see the new Roman Empire be given new precedence. It was not an empire because it didn't have an emperor; instead, the masses were completely in charge of this new society rather than the old Roman Empire and the emperors that had reigned a couple of thousand years earlier. This new Roman Empire was the holder of civilization, for it would allow for the recreation of the values that would span the whole world. This world would be completely dominated by the human race and the habitat surrounding it. There would be no poor within a rich society. The race of the extraterrestrials would rejuvenate this new society that would work for the human race. It was truly a new race; this new race would fight to keep itself alive as well as spread throughout time. The common people would benefit in the end from the centralization of a new culture. This culture would remain decentralized to the point that they inhabited multiple planets and different bodies throughout the solar system. This would cause the complete rejuvenation of the civilization that would span throughout the last bounds of humanity. This was merely building on the progress that humanity was making. This progress would be preserved through the ages, for it was immortal now and forever. The last frontier was another solar system. This would require the most important and favorable specialists of the human race to bind together and form a new cohesive bloc. This bloc would hold up against the destruction of civilization itself.

This bloc would also follow the revived model of thinking. The whole security would see order present where there was natural inequality. This natural inequality didn't mean disparities of opportunity, except in the most obvious cases. Such cases included raising offspring, which was part of the larger structure that would embody the family. This bloc would completely revive a new model that would favor the complete revival of the bloc of revolutionaries, though with a new name. This new bloc would always seek to move forward when it came to progress as it would seek to move towards the commonality of values that made sense in the end. The commonality of progress that would be achieved in the future would come through the combined effort that would be put in. This commonality of progress would mean that the side of history would lean towards those who adapted the new methods that would completely embody the new system. This new system would completely transform the old, for it had been reborn out of the ashes of the nuclear war. The last frontier was something that was constantly being strived for. The final frontier would be part of the expeditions bringing humanity further. These expeditions would completely redefine the adventures that would take place. These expeditions would mean that the frontiers of humanity could always be constantly expanded.

The most important theory developed out of the revolution was self-determination and equality in all terms. This would mean that all of the conditions would be fulfilled, and it would be more than on paper. This revolution was further carried on by the extraterrestrials, who did not desire imperialism due to not being part of such a society. This society of self-determination failed back on Earth many years earlier, and by this point, the evolution had made its way to the moment that the revolution was carried out by people that weren't even on Earth. This resulted from the many contradictions that had taken place earlier and the inevitable nuclear war that took place. This self-determination principle was immediately followed by unity, which is where the new society that was born took place. This self-determination principle would be at the core of the new revolution that was taking place throughout the many planets. The last frontier that humans needed to conquer was the end of division. Promptly, cultural divisions were all wiped away as there would be only a human identity, and all resources were used wisely. The population of 15 billion would be the human population in which the basis could be used to facilitate the whole galaxy. This travel could only be done going past 4 dimensions though flying near the speed of light was starting to become possible. This was combined with exploiting the wormholes that had existed for the whole time. This exploitation would be harnessed to favor the new colonization quickly sweeping the entire region. This colonization would be in favor of complete sovereignty for all peoples. This was combined with implementing a one-world language as the means of production earlier had been mechanized. It would combine the major linguistic groups to unite the human race. The new path that would be taken would be represented by a new language that would be completely pure. This language would be completely divergent from the anti-scientific nature of all other languages that sought to divide.

We were all at the dawn of the new era. This era would mark the end of the power of the intergalactic reactionaries. There were few of them now, for the resources of Earth would be reborn from scratch. We would all see the dawn of the new era wherein the solar system population would recover collectively. Furthermore, such a recovery would see the population largely vary throughout, with the new settlement commissions being used to keep expanding these planets' populations. These planets would see their effective rebirth.

Furthermore, integrating all societies would further enhance the human race, for the population would all be at the last stage. This would all come in the final combination of all forms of life into the general organism. This organism could unify the human race, for all directly controlled it. This would all work in a ring, for each of the constituents would see the goal of enhancing the qualities of human nature. Furthermore, the plan would be to constantly move forward rather than staggering from one place over the other. The goal would be to further progress on the human race.

As for now, they had succeeded. What took a complete rebirth of the planet would be done. All measures would be taken. Human civilization had been restored under the banner of humanity. All measurements were justified in their eyes. The last words were, "We will fight together or die alone." These words would be the testament of time. They would represent time immortal … for generations to come. America would pave the path.

From each city to another, now decimated, the new era stands different. They may not have the same values, but in the end, one does go in the same direction they came from. The connections that are once forged will never be broken. What one will be etched onto the wall, one day and forever? For all that he must've done, he did achieve one thing in the end – the destruction of time.